# The Best Cadet

By Lucas Kinkaid

Copyright © 2023 Lucas Kinkaid

All rights reserved.

ISBN:  979-8-9893896-0-5 (eBook)
       979-8-9893896-1-2 (Paperback)
       979-8-9893896-2-9 (Hardback)

# Dedication

This book is dedicated to the memory of Paul J. Wilding II. A good guy and a great friend.

# Other Books by Lucas Kinkaid

*My Canvas Bag*

*"Be careful because you never know what lies beneath the surface of every person."*

\- Unknown

# Table of Contents

# Chapter 1

## *Academic Achievement*

Paul Wildman hates bullies. Most people don't realize he has dedicated his life to defeating them. He is small in stature but extremely intelligent and possesses a well-developed sarcastic wit. The type of wit that has been both a blessing and a curse to him. Paul considers these attributes to be his superpowers. He skillfully uses them to defeat bullies and get what he wants from the world. Paul is not physically strong enough to stop anybody from doing anything. His lack of physical strength has caused him to develop a unique ability to get those who oppose him to destroy themselves. This only happens because he views life differently from other people. Paul knows all members of society have been conditioned to think in certain ways. He regularly puts this to his advantage. Paul refuses to conform to society's expectations. He believes when his intelligence and sarcastic wit are combined with his family's wealth, he has a distinct advantage over anyone he encounters.

It is common for people to view institutions of higher learning as places to obtain an education that will provide them with a successful career in the real world. Some view this as an opportunity to have a good time and meet family requirements until they are forced to become part of the real world. Paul Wildman has a rather unique attitude concerning institutions of higher learning. In his mind, they are places he has been forced to attend against his will. His goal is to be dismissed from them in a memorable fashion. This is his father and grandfather's punishment for bullying him into attending college when he does not want to go. Paul's father and grandfather are the only bullies in his life that he has never been able to defeat.

Paul is aware that being thrown out of universities is upsetting to his family. It causes them extreme anger and frustration. This is an aspect of being forced from a university that Paul likes the most. His father and grandfather realize their control over him is not as strong as the two of them believe. They think Paul owes them for the privileged existence he has been provided. Paul sees things differently. He thinks he should be permitted to live his life as he wants.

As an embodiment of hurt and anger toward authority figures, Paul is a master at hiding his feelings. His father and grandfather have always had their way in his life. Since he was young, Paul was expected to do what they told him without complaint. He was mercilessly mocked and taunted by his father and grandfather for the slightest mistake.

Before graduating high school Paul tried to tell them what he wanted to do with his life. When Paul mentioned he'd like to start a company making action movies as well as be a book publisher. This suggestion was seriously mocked. Upon hearing this, Paul's father and grandfather could not stop laughing. They did not care how much Paul disliked their plans for him. In their minds, he would do what they asked of him or be forced into compliance.

The expectations of his father and grandfather are for Paul to one day take over the family business. They have dreams of Paul successfully running the corporation. This is what has always been most important to them. To accomplish it; they insist Paul have a college degree in business. This is part of the important family image his father and grandfather want to maintain. Paul's father has often told him he would get a college education whether he liked it or not. It was not a request. Since then, Paul has always been willing to sacrifice any possibility of academic success to punish his father and grandfather.

Paul views the current situation with family as an undeclared war. He enjoys upsetting them. In Paul's mind, he is defeating some of the biggest bullies in the world. His father and grandfather have bullied everybody and everything from employees to small corporations and more to get what they want. He has watched them play dirty and stop at nothing to get what they want. Paul considers these lessons more valuable than anything he could learn at a university.

* * * * * * * *

It is the spring of 1983. Finals week is taking place at the most recent college where Paul is a student. Many of the other college students have spent hours during the previous weeks studying and preparing for their final exams. They want to get the best grades possible. These students feel this is a stressful time.

Paul has always taken his own unique approach to preparing for finals week. He doesn't worry about it and simply has fun. The jealousy of Paul's cavalier attitude toward finals has always given way to some of the most fascinating rumors being spread about him on college campuses. They are usually created by jealous college students and believed by those who are susceptible to believing such things.

The most current rumor states that right before the final exams, Paul got busy with a waitress he met at a local restaurant. She is said to be an innocent girl who has trouble with immigration and is going to be deported in a week. The waitress is allegedly from some South American country Paul can't remember. He promised to give her a great last week in the United States. According to the rumor, Paul believes this is the perfect way to spend the time before finals week. He has no intention of seeing her again after she is gone.

When Paul learns about this, he finds the rumor extraordinary. He believes it is one of the best ones that has ever been spread about him. Paul prefers this one over the old rumors about him spending time in a mental institution or having a drug problem and being in rehab.

He actively participates in furthering the spread of the waitress rumor. Paul hopes it lasts for a significant amount of time. The detailed version of this particular rumor also states that Paul takes great pleasure in using his father's credit card to pay for everything during the time he spends with the girl from South America. This includes hotel rooms, going to expensive nightclubs, restaurants, and more. The rumor concludes this situation has provided Paul with someone to be with since all his friends are busy studying and being serious students.

Paul is aware his father and grandfather will be upset when they hear this latest in a long series of rumors about him. They have had people in every college Paul has attended to inform them of his activities. Paul knows he will never face any serious consequences. He is his grandmother's favorite grandchild and this gives him quite a special standing in the family.

If questioned about the rumor, Paul intends to tell his father he was simply trying to help a beautiful struggling female from South America have a better life. Paul has always realized the desire of his father and grandfather to protect their family image gives him leverage over them. They will have people come and investigate the rumor and do whatever is necessary to stop it. Paul considers most things, such as a college education, to have a different type of importance to him and his family. To Paul, it is another battleground in his ongoing war against the biggest bullies in his life. His family seems to consider it another situation involving Paul they must control to maintain the family image.

* * * * * * * *

On the last day of final exams, Paul decides he will attend one of his classes. The professors in his other classes simply ignore Paul when he tries to disrupt things. He considers them boring. Professor Kleef is different. Paul likes him because this professor tries to be strict. Professor Kleef often gets very angry at Paul and threatens to have him kicked out of the university. He will call Paul all sorts of nasty names during class when he becomes upset with him. Paul considers Professor Kleef to be one of the most enjoyable professors he's had during the years he's been getting thrown out of universities. He is considering sending the professor a Christmas card.

Paul can spot a person who successfully hides their bad deeds behind an impressive image. It is the sort of behavior his family has mastered over the years. He knows Professor Kleef's secret bad behavior could qualify him to be an honorary member of Paul's family.

Walking into the building where his class is being held, Paul notices the hallways are quiet as students in the classrooms are focused on taking their exams. His class started fifteen minutes earlier. Paul is a strong believer in never being on time for a class and feels now is not the time to break his tradition. He is wearing dress pants, a name-brand shirt, a rather expensive sports coat, and dress shoes. They are intended to make people ignore the fact he is a short person with blonde hair, blue eyes, and a rather prominent nose in the center of his face. Unlike other students who carry their books to class; he uses an expensive leather briefcase he always has with him.

Paul starts whistling and likes the sound of it traveling down the empty hallway. It goes well with the sound of his dress shoes hitting the polished floor. When he comes to the room where his class is being held, Paul looks at all the students inside through the glass in the door. Paul doubts many of the students or the university's faculty know about the secret life of Professor Kleef. A man who can impress students and peers with his resume and conversational skills. Few of them could handle the truth behind the illusion. Paul feels nothing but contempt for Professor Kleef. He knows the real Professor Kleef is a clandestine bully who secretly takes unfair advantage of students who want to succeed in his class. Paul does not like him. He stops whistling and goes inside the classroom.

Inside are approximately fifty students focused on writing in their notebooks. They are watching Professor Kleef write things on a chalkboard located at the front of the classroom. All the students are quiet except for Paul who is excusing himself to other students as he makes his way to a seat in the auditorium.

Professor Kleef is a stocky older man wearing a dress shirt and pants. He has a mustache and a balding head of hair. Some students say he was a Ranger in the Army at one time. Without turning around, he begins to speak.

"I see Mr. Wildman has graced us with his presence. I suggest you sit down and be quiet. You should be thankful I'm in a generous mood today. I will permit you to sit for my final exam. Now, copy down the questions I've put on the chalkboard. They are part of the test."

"Ah, that doesn't work for me."

Professor Kleef slowly turns around and says, "What?"

"I'm sure there are some others in the class who are like me and don't understand why we should be made to copy down questions. After all the tuition paid to this university, and especially the generous donations made by my family and others, I think it is only fair for all of us to correctly assume questions on a final would be written out on paper for us."

Professor Kleef smiles after hearing Paul's statement in an attempt to hide his anger.

"Mr. Wildman, I'm sure you are aware the university has a problem with students illegally obtaining test questions on finals. When I write questions on the board, it is to make certain nobody has the questions from the final before I give it. Do you understand?"

"I understand this is giving an unfair advantage to those students who have nothing better to do with their time than study. There are those of us who do important things and illegally obtaining test questions for finals may be the only way we can succeed. Why do you want to punish those of us who have important things to do in life?"

"Mr. Wildman, either you copy down the questions I've written on the blackboard for the final exam or leave and take a zero for the class. What is your choice?"

"I think there is a bigger picture here you aren't seeing."

"What bigger picture?"

"As you've taught us in your business organization class, employees are paid a wage by their company. I can't emphasize enough how your wages are a result of me as well as the other students in this class paying tuition in addition to generous contributions made to this university. According to what you've taught us, that would make us your employer. We may need to discuss your forcing us to write down test questions. I think we should all get together with you to address your negative attitude of yours."

A few students are struggling to not laugh but a few laughing sounds can be heard.

"Get out," screams Professor Kleef.

"See, it is that demeanor of yours and showing a total lack of respect for authority. I hope you realize this could damage your teaching career here at the university. Maybe you don't realize that unlike the other students here who have been simply studying for this final exam, I've been applying what you taught us in the real world. Isn't that the true goal of a professor to have your students apply what they've learned in the real world?"

"What are you talking about?"

"I've started my own successful business and have organized it based on what you've taught us in class."

"Really?"

"Yes, it is a monthly magazine I call *Dickhead Illustrated.* After my experiences in your class, I believe you are worthy of a cover story. So, when can we arrange for an interview and pictures?"

Professor Kleef screams, "Get out of my classroom right now you pompous, arrogant, asshole."

"Okay, okay, okay, no reason to be upset. I'm sure a person of your advanced age must be concerned with high blood pressure, heart disease, and all sorts of ailments that go with living to your advanced age."

"Get out of here now," yells Professor Kleef.

Paul slowly moves toward the door, then stops and turns around.

"With your behavior today, I believe you are a strong contender for Dickhead of the Year. It is a highly coveted award and one I think will win you the admiration and respect of all your fellow dickheads. You'll be considered a dickhead among dickheads."

Some students are not able to hide their laughter.

"Out."

"I'm sure you realize; I won't be able to give you a good recommendation for your next employer. You seem to have a desire to punish your best students for no reason at all."

As Paul goes out and closes the door, he thinks he hears the sound of chalk hitting the door. Professor Kleef is considered one of the most respected and influential teachers at the university. Paul knows it is only a matter of time before Professor Kleef goes through the proper channels to have him removed from the university. He also knows there will be some surprises during this process that Professor Kleef doesn't anticipate. The uncomfortable truth about this professor and his bullying of students is going to be revealed. Paul considers being kicked out of his class during the final exam one of his greatest academic achievements. It is one more time when a plan of his would result in the defeat of a major bully in the world.

# Chapter 2

---

## *Nothing Work*

Inside a very impressive and expensive home are two well-dressed gentlemen sitting in silence and avoiding eye contact. Neither one has the desire to begin the uncomfortable conversation that is about to occur. Both are experienced at ignoring unpleasant things until they can no longer be avoided. Each is enjoying the last few seconds of quiet before the inevitable discussion takes place.

They are in the kind of large house people notice when they drive past. It is an object of envy for many and a source of jealousy for others. Like all huge homes with only two residents, its purpose is to feed the immense egos of its owners. This house says to the world that they are wealthy and successful. Look at them in all of their splendor. Very few people know the privileged lifestyle the home's residents enjoy has been made possible by past generations of successful people in their families. Without their inheritance, the residents of this stately dwelling would not impress anybody.

The suits worn by the two gentlemen happen to be some of the most expensive available. One of the men is fifty-year-old Walter Wildman.

Sitting across from him is a distinguished-looking man in his seventies named James Wildman. These are Paul's father and grandfather.

A woman wearing a formal maid's uniform walks into the room holding a polished silver tray containing the best possible coffee and freshly made pastries. The woman places the tray on a table between the two men. James Wildman thanks her and tells her this is all he needs for now.

Both men are quiet as they get their coffee and place a fresh pastry on a plate. They are meeting to discuss the problem with Paul. Neither of them likes having to address any type of personal problem directly, but they know there is no other way this time. They're used to having other people handle things for them. James and Walter firmly believe there isn't any problem that can't be resolved with money. This is something they have always had in abundance during their lives. It is how they view the world. They don't understand why it isn't working with Pau.

The only sound in the room is the ticking of an antique grandfather clock located in a corner of the room. After James takes a sip of his coffee, he carefully places the fine china cup back on the tray. He settles back in his chair and clears his throat.

"Now please tell me, what kind of problem with Paul is of such importance you felt it necessary to make an unannounced visit to my home? You know how I hate to have my day interrupted by unscheduled events," says James.

Walter sighs and runs his fingers through his hair. He looks around and the desperation he is feeling shows.

"Well, I need to do something drastic when it comes to Paul. He is your grandson, and I need your advice on what to do with him. He's gotten himself expelled from three colleges in the past year and a half. He's not even doing so well at the one he's at right now. I got a call from them about an hour ago. They're starting the process of having Paul expelled because of his behavior and attitude," says Walter.

"I wish you would have come to me sooner. With this level of struggle, I wonder why Paul is in college at all."

Walter laughs and says, "Are you kidding me? You know what our world is like. Everyone's child goes to college. The children of our clients are in college. Many of our suppliers have children attending Ivy League universities or have children who graduated from them. If Paul doesn't go to college, it could damage the reputation of the family. People will think less of us. Our competition may seem more attractive to our clients. He has to go to college and that is all there is to it. This is the only way he can be part of the family business."

"All I'm saying is that something is wrong. Paul is obviously not the type of individual who will blossom in an academic environment. Maybe he is just not ready for the challenges associated with obtaining a college degree."

"Let me ask you something. Is anyone ever ready? When I started college, our company couldn't make any major contributions to an academic institution. We had no way to influence the selection process or grades. I had to study and make grades just like all the other regular students. It was tough. I suffered through being put on academic probation before I could scrape enough funds together to pay someone to take my final exams. I was lucky and didn't get caught. I don't think Paul realizes how easy he has it."

"Paul is not like you or me. He is too much of an independent spirit. Paul has always been this way. Based on that, you should have anticipated his behavior before this happened. You've never had much in the way of parenting skills."

"Hey, I'm just like you, I did the best I could. Right?"

"Point well taken, but I bet the multiple affairs you had when you were married to his mother didn't help matters. After divorcing her, you went on to have multiple marriages and divorces. I think we refer to your previous wives as the bimbo, the ice queen, and the gold digger."

"So, I didn't set the best example for my son. I just need you to help me figure out a way to motivate Paul into getting a college degree."

"What have you done so far to address the situation?"

"I did try the heavy-handed approach. It didn't work."

* * * * * * *

It's a warm and sunny day a few months earlier. Paul is sitting in a new sports car convertible with the top down. It is bright cherry red and has a white interior. The recent detailing of it makes the vehicle have an impressive appearance. The sports car is located in the driveway of a rather expensive home where he and his father live. He's wearing a white polo shirt, dark shorts, and tennis shoes. He also has on sunglasses and a tennis hat. Paul's father comes down the driveway and quickly comes up to the driver's side door. He is so angry his face is red. When Walter reaches the car, he takes the keys out of Paul's hand. He stands there looking at Paul and breathing heavily. Paul calmly takes a bottle of Perrier from the car's bottle holder. He takes a drink and puts it back.

Paul smiles at his father and says, "I'm going to go out on a limb here, but I think you are upset with me for some reason. My well-developed ability to anticipate such things is telling me it's probably associated with you not understanding something I've done."

"You are damn right it has to do with something you've done. The college you're attending wants you out. They said you were charging homeless people money to stay in the dormitory basement."

"I'm sorry, but I believe my intentions have been greatly misunderstood. Nobody seems to appreciate my desire to help the homeless. There was an empty basement in the dormitory building, and I merely let people who were down on their luck have a place to stay. I'm shocked that you, as my father, don't take pride in your son's desire to make a difference in the lives of the less fortunate."

"They said you took money from these homeless people who got it from social security as well as selling cans and bottles and even begging in the street just to stay in the basement of that dormitory. They told me some of the homeless people were selling drugs to the students on campus. I was told there was even prostitution happening. These homeless people did all this, so they could pay you to live in the basement of a building you don't even own."

"Isn't a college campus a place for growing and learning? Weren't these people learning how to find ways to meet their financial obligations? I must admit some of their methods could be considered a little unorthodox. I believe they all had good intentions and would have eventually benefited greatly from being around the learning atmosphere of a university. It was probably only a matter of time before they turned into productive members of society. I had a dream to change the world. This university is doing everything possible to crush my hope of a better future for the unfortunate. I thought you'd understand how much this hurts me."

Walter yells, "Oh, I understand alright. I understand you are doing nothing but making my life miserable. If you're not willing to change your attitude about attending college, I want you gone. I want you to leave this house and not come back here. Do you understand me?"

Paul once again takes the bottle of Perrier from the car's bottle holder, calmly takes a drink, and puts it back. He looks at his father and smiles.

"What I understand, oh father of mine, is that the only reason for me being in college is so you can run around to all your clients as well as business associates, tell them your son is in college, and you are a great father. If you make me leave, I have no place to go. I wonder what the news media would do if they discovered your son is living in a homeless shelter. The son of the wealthy Walter Wildman is forced to live in a homeless shelter as the family's business does billions of dollars in business each year. I think I have the press release written in my mind. I know about homeless shelters. You do realize, I've actually owned one."

The expression on Walter's face is one of shock. The color seems to drain from his face. The idea of such a story being on the news horrifies him.

"You wouldn't dare do such a thing."

"We both know I would do such a thing, and I'd take great pleasure in doing it."

The two stare at one another for a few minutes. Paul slowly reaches up and takes the keys from the hand of a motionless Walter Wildman. He starts up the car and waves as he pulls out of the driveway.

* * * * * * * *

Walter and James Wildman are both staring off into space and thinking about the story Walter has just told. Both are trying to decide what would be the best course of action for their progeny, Paul Wildman. Walter and James are trying to think of something to do that would benefit them as well as the family business.

"Have you tried anything else besides the failed heavy-handed approach?"

"Well, I did set Paul up to meet with a therapist. I thought it would help him recognize his problems and deal with them."

"How did it go?"

"It didn't go well."

* * * * * * * *

It's a few weeks earlier and Paul is sitting across from a well-dressed woman named Dr. Robinson. She's sitting at a desk and is busy writing on a notepad. On the wall behind her are many educational degrees in frames. She stops writing and looks at Paul, who is looking down.

She clears her throat to get Paul's attention and says, "I always have a feeling we never make much progress with our sessions. You never seem to want to work with me or participate in our therapy sessions. How can I help you if you won't trust me even a little bit?"

Paul feels about these therapy sessions the same way he feels about the universities he's forced to attend. It is one more instance of being bullied into doing something he doesn't want to do by his father and grandfather. Paul looks up and smiles at Dr. Robinson.

"You have to understand Dr. Robinson. The only reason I am here is to placate my father. I sincerely believe that man should be here instead of me. I also thought it would be an interesting experience to visit a therapist."

"Well, what do you think? Have I met your expectations?"

"To be quite honest, I find this boring. You are ready to climb into my mind and fix things you see as broken. I'm ready to leave and never come back here. I often ask myself what psychological damage has been done to someone, such as yourself, to make them choose a career like this one. I wonder if it could be something really juicy such as being forced to witness sex between horses and people or something like it. Based on your rather rigid demeanor, it could be something even more bizarre. Do you ever have a deeply disturbing emotional response when hearing the song *Camptown Races*?"

Dr. Robinson looks at Paul and then quickly writes on her notepad.

She looks up at Paul and says, "What is something you like to do, Paul?"

"I like to do this."

Paul leans forward and the sound of a zipper being unzipped is heard. The sound of liquid hitting the carpet is then heard. Paul is making a funny face. The sound of stops and a zipper being zipped up is then heard. The expression on Dr. Robinson's face shows she is horrified.

"Did you just urinate on my carpet?" Dr. Robinson yells.

"Relieving myself on a Berber carpet has always been a dream of mine. Now that it's happened, I can honestly say it didn't meet my expectations. Do you have any toilet paper? I feel this is a safe and secure environment. I'd like to play out another dream I have concerning leather chairs. With your professional help, I'm now ready for the experience."

Dr. Robinson is struggling to keep her composure. She's very upset. Dr. Robinson gets up and walks over to the door to her office and opens it.

"I think you need to leave. We may be done with our sessions."

Paul gets up and goes toward the door.

He stops in front of Dr. Robinson and says, "You know, I think there may be something to this therapy stuff. I've experienced quite a bit of relief since we had this talk."

Paul walks into the waiting room and hears the door slam behind him. He pulls out a handheld tape recorder, rewinds it, and plays the sound of the zipper. Paul then takes out a bottle of Perrier from his pocket that is almost empty. He can't stop laughing as he makes his way out of the waiting room and into the hallway.

* * * * * * * *

After the last story, James and Walter sit in silence. They are both in deep contemplation as to what needs to be done concerning Paul. They have dismissed the idea of placing him up for adoption and dropping him off at some unknown place in the Amazon forest to be lost forever. These are tempting options, but their family is too well-known. The press coverage would be extremely negative and could damage the family name.

Suddenly, James smiles, claps his hands, and says, "I think I've got it. Don't you see the real problem here? Neither you nor Paul has ever been made accountable for your behavior. Our family's money has always given the two of you a pass from the responsibilities of life. I just may have an idea about how we are going to solve our problems with Paul."

"At this point, I'll try anything," says Walter.

"I suggest we have Paul attend an academic institution that provides both the accountability and discipline he needs. A place designed to reward good behavior and punish bad behavior."

"You think he should be sent to prison academy?"

"Don't be ridiculous. I think we should send Paul to a military academy. I would like to suggest Saint Michael's Military Academy. It's a private school. I'm serving on its board right now. The place seems to be tough, like the other military academies operated by the government. They wear uniforms and do all sorts of serious military things. I've personally witnessed what happens there. You should see how they salute and refer to you as 'sir' when you go there."

Walter chuckles and says, "He will refuse to go to any military academy. You know he'll talk to his grandmother and try to get out of it. Paul believes he is her favorite grandson."

"You leave that to me. I think we can both agree there is one certain family trait we all share. The money in our trust funds is something that has immense power over us all. I think Paul can be persuaded to attend any military institution if it is in his best financial interests. If I explain to my wife how Paul will benefit from this; I know she'll support such a move."

When Walter looks at James, the two of them smile and then start laughing. They both seem to be struggling to control the joy they are feeling. The idea of Paul experiencing life at a private military academy is something they both find quite enjoyable and funny.

# Chapter 3

*The Nonconformist*

Paul Wildman doesn't understand why so many people around him simply do what they are told without question. He often wonders if there are other people like him who intentionally reject their social conditioning. Paul intentionally says and does what nobody expects and then closely watches how people react. He believes his rejection of conditioned behavior gives him the ability to confuse people and be in control.

He is always searching for those who can see past his show and realize exactly what he's doing. These are special people. Paul feels this is how he will discover independent-thinking individuals. These are the people he plans to make part of his inner circle. Anyone who demonstrates they are destined for a boring life of conformity will always be ignored by Paul. These are the people he enjoys confusing the most.

Being in college has given Paul a desire to capitalize on what he believes is his attitude advantage. While spending time as a student in academia, he has developed ways to test his fellow students. He believes his testing should be made part of the curriculum by all institutions of higher learning. Why should only professors and administrators have all the fun?

On a grassy area near a college campus, Paul Wildman is speaking with a student who is holding several books. The student is a young man from India. His name is Ramesh. On the ground between Ramesh and Paul is something with wheels and a seat that resembles a rickshaw. It is an item Paul saw outside his home during his drive to college. A homeless person took it to Paul as payment for staying in the basement of a dormitory.

Seeing this pile of metal resembling a demolished rickshaw gave Paul an idea for a test. In Paul's mind, a person from India might be excited about being part of a rickshaw company. If anybody gets excited about this they will be categorized as not strong enough for his inner circle. As Paul tries to describe his business idea to Ramesh, he realizes that Ramesh does have some real inner circle potential.

Paul smiles as he looks at Ramesh and says, "I am telling you right now this is the chance of a lifetime. You could be getting in on the ground floor of a unique business opportunity that has the potential for unlimited financial earnings."

Ramesh looks down at the old rusted item that appears to have been a rickshaw and can't hide his disgust. He looks up at Paul and smiles.

"You are most crazy Paul Wildman. I am not going to pull people around in this pile of junk. I don't care how much money you believe I would be making."

Paul appears to be shocked.

"I have no idea why you would refer to this fine piece of machinery as a pile of junk. It was carefully retrieved by a homeless craftsman and given to me to pay off his debt. You don't seem to recognize true earning possibility when you see it."

"If it is so great then why don't you go and pull people around in it yourself and simply keep all the money."

"Me? I think what we have here is an innocent clash of cultures. In my country, I am considered an entrepreneur. I'm the one who takes on all the business risks and provides others with the opportunity to become wealthy off of my ideas. I'm giving you a chance to be my potential business associate. I've always admired you people from Turkey."

Ramesh yells, "I'm not from Turkey. I'm from India."

"Oh, don't get upset. My major is business and not political science."

"Okay, suppose I do this. How much money would I get?"

"Like all business propositions, it will depend on how motivated you are as well as the effort and energy you put into it. The only limit on your earnings is you."

"Let me ask you this. How much money do you make?"

"Why on earth would you worry about how much money I make? I think you could give me a thousand dollars for a franchise fee and then pay me a daily rental fee for the rickshaw. We could then split any money you make from taking people around fifty-fifty. So, you see, I would hardly make any money at all. The only reason I'm doing this is to help a student like yourself from a foreign land achieve his dream of being a wealthy American like the members of my family."

Ramesh yells, "You are crazy."

He then begins to walk away.

Paul begins to yell, "Crazy? You are the kind of person who would have thought Ronald McDonald was insane for selling hamburgers. I thought this would be something that would appeal to you Buddhists."

Ramesh stops, turns back toward Paul, and yells, "I'm not a Buddhist, I'm a Hindu."

As Ramesh continues walking away Paul yells at him again and says, "Oh, be angry with me now because I'm not a seminary student. I bet when Wendy started selling hamburgers, she did it without obsessing over religion. I'm glad you're walking away. Do you know why? It's obvious you have a lot of confused emotions about religion."

Paul is impressed with Ramesh. He makes a mental note that this person has some very impressive attributes he could use in his inner circle. He qualifies for further consideration.

An Asian student walks past Paul.

He quickly walks up to the Asian student, puts his arm around his shoulder, and says, "My friend today could be a day that will change your life forever. I happen to be someone who has dedicated his life to helping people from other countries achieve their maximum financial potential here in the United States. Let me start by saying, I do admire you people from China."

The Asian student looks confused and says, "I'm not from China. I'm from South Korea."

"Close enough. Look, I never tell anyone I'm an expert on people from the Malaysian continent."

"That's the Asian continent."

"Asian, Malaysian, what's the difference? Let's get things straight from the start. I am a business major and no expert in geography or you people who practice the Shinto religion."

"Shinto religion is from Japan."

"Whatever, let's not obsess over trivial details. I think what we need is to discuss the big picture concerning a very lucrative business opportunity I'm offering you."

Paul keeps talking and the Asian student continues to be very confused.

* * * * * * * *

There are certain things in the world Paul does not like. He hates it when physically strong people try to intimidate and bully weaker people.

This is the kind of bully who has athletic ability and will take advantage of everything that goes with it. The free college experience. The mindless girls who make themselves available to such people. The notoriety around college and elsewhere. The idea of such people having egos almost as large as his makes Paul angry. These are the types of bullies Paul has determined need to be taught a special lesson. He considers it an important academic experience for the physically dominating.

Paul's father and grandfather taught him the importance of obtaining information about people. The type of information they don't want to be known. Paul has an impressive ability to skillfully obtain and use such valuable information.

Paul is sitting in his sports car. It's parked in the university's student parking area. He is drinking a Perrier and looking around. A thin young man wearing glasses and holding a lot of books runs up to Paul's car. His name is Chuck. He and Paul have known one another since they were in kindergarten together. They aren't close friends, but two people who have been part of one another's social circle since they were very young.

Chuck says, "I just got done talking to my mom on the pay phone. She said your grandfather told her to tell you to go to his house right away."

Paul smiles and says, "You call your mother every day from college, and you have always lived at home. For some reason, I believe there may be psychologists stalking you right now."

Chuck just stares quietly at Paul for a few seconds and then says, "Why do you always do it?"

"Do what?"

"Screw up on purpose. Everybody is talking about what you did in Professor Kleef's class. You're going to get expelled for this and you don't care. Why do you do these things? You've been doing them ever since we were kids."

Paul takes a drink from his bottle of Perrier and puts it back in the cup holder in his car.

"I don't consider it screwing up. I consider it more like expressing my uniqueness in ways most people just can't appreciate. College may not be for me. I'm a businessman."

Chuck laughs and says, "You call yourself a businessman? You bought packages of women's underwear and sold them to some perverted frat boys after telling them they were the cheerleader's underwear."

"Hey, that's the first rule of business. You find a need, and you fill it."

Chuck just looks at Paul and seems disgusted as he says, "You just don't get what you're doing to yourself. Do you have any idea?"

Paul sighs and says, "Hey, I know you're done with classes for the day. How about you hop in and I'll give you a ride to your house on the way to my grandfather's place."

Chuck gets into the passenger side of Paul's sports car. A rather muscular man wearing only shorts and a T-shirt walks up to Paul and crosses his arms in front of the sports car on the driver's side.

Paul notices the man and says, "Well, it is good to see my friend Hammer. How have you been? I see the exercise program for players on the football team is doing you quite well."

Paul puts out his hand to shake and Hammer knocks it away.

"Cut the bullshit, Wildman. Them pills you sold me weren't no steroids. They was just some damn baby aspirin."

Paul gasps as if he is shocked and says, "They were? I think that is terrible. I will have a serious discussion with my supplier. I feel awful."

"I want my money back."

"Now, I feel really awful. All sales are final. Unfortunately, I have a no-refund policy."

Hammer reaches down and grabs Paul by the shirt collar.

"I'm not asking you for a refund, asshole, I'm telling you to give me one.”

Paul smiles and slowly takes his hand and removes Hammer's hand from holding his shirt.

“I'm afraid what we have here is a lack of communication. See, I know and you know, NCAA rules forbid steroid use by student-athletes. It's a big no-no. Why, if someone was to have made many copies of a note from a particular student-athlete, such as yourself, requesting steroids, and a copy of that note was somehow sent to the head football coach as well as the dean and NCAA officials, I predict they would not look favorably on said student-athlete. Can we agree on that?”

“I'd kill you if you did something like that to me.”

“Oh please, and add murder to your long list of indiscretions? You're not that stupid. If that happened, then everything I know about you would be published in newspapers across the country. I know more than you realize and have connections that would amaze you. This is something I can make happen, alive or dead. Why don't we just agree that copies of such a note or anything else need not be distributed to anyone? You get to play football, and I get to have you out of my life. Most people come to college for an education. Consider this a lesson on how not to be an asshole.”

“Wildman, you're a real mother fucker.”

“Would you be shocked if I told you that you weren't the first person to refer to me in such a way?”

Paul starts his car, smiles at Hammer, and drives away. He looks in the car's rear view mirror to see Hammer giving him the middle finger. As they go down the road, Paul looks at Chuck, smiles, and says, “Ah, another satisfied customer.”

As Paul gets onto the freeway, he puts on sunglasses and starts humming.

Chuck struggles to say something and then yells, “You always do it.

You screw with people, screw up and get away with it. Why don't you just do what you're told like the rest of us and be normal?"

The sports car speeds up and begins to pass other cars at a fast rate.

"I remember growing up how you were always one of those kids who colored within the lines, turned your homework in on time, and came in from recess when the bell rang."

"That's what normal people do. We obey the rules. We don't all spend our time being jerks."

The car speeds up even faster as Paul is weaving around traffic. Chuck notices the speed and begins to get concerned.

"Didn't you ever wonder what would happen if you colored outside the lines? How about if you were late with your homework just once? Being alone on the playground after everyone has gone back inside? Did you ever think about how that would feel?"

"You're going a little fast here. How about you slow down?"

"Did you ever realize all great people in the world refused to conform to what everyone else said was normal? Don't you get it?"

Chuck screams, "I get that if we wreck it won't be good. You've made your point. Now is the time to slow down."

"Benjamin Franklin said kiss my ass; you bastards. I'm flying a kite in a thunderstorm. I'm doing something you don't understand, but that's okay."

"How about you discover how to use the brake pedal?"

"The Wright brothers said hey all you shitheads. Maybe you can't fly in the sky, but we can, and we're going to invent the airplane."

The fear in Chuck's voice is apparent when he says, "I don't need a history lesson. Right now, I just need to get home alive."

"Did you know Steven Spielberg would skip school and sneak onto the movie lots at Universal Studios as a kid to see how movies were made? Not following the rules didn't keep him from his destiny of wealth and success."

Suddenly police cars are behind Paul's sports car. He takes an exit ramp and after making some sharp turns, he goes up a driveway and parks in an empty shed. As the police pass by Paul calmly gets his bottle of Perrier and takes a drink. He then slowly pulls out of the shed and carefully drives to Chuck's house. He pulls up onto the lawn and drives his car to the back of the house. The police cars again go past the front of the house with sirens and flashing lights blaring.

Chuck has his head down and is trying to catch his breath.

"Thank you, God, for letting me live."

"My friend, you need to know the world is a different place outside the lines of conformity. Turning in homework on my terms or being alone on a playground while everyone else has gone inside is where I belong. Do you understand what I'm saying?"

Chuck lifts his head. His hair is disheveled and his glasses are just hanging on his face. He gathers his books and gets out of the car.

Chuck screams, "I understand you're bat shit crazy. What's wrong with you? Couldn't just drive me home, could you? We could've gotten killed. If the police would have caught you, you'd be in jail. But you'd probably just buy your way out of it. Your problem is you are a real asshole."

Chuck slams the car door and starts walking toward his house.

Paul yells, "Yeah, and your problem is you're nothing but a mindless conformist wimp who is too afraid to do anything that isn't socially acceptable. Besides that, you don't own a sports car."

Paul drives off of the lawn and onto the street. He is going to his grandfather's house. He has no idea why he would be asked to visit on such short notice. Paul figures maybe his grandfather is going to tell him about an increase in his trust fund allotment.

# Chapter 4

*Military School Proposition*

Paul is let into his grandfather's home by the maid. He makes his way to the room where his father and grandfather are sitting. They both have intense expressions, and Paul instantly knows there is something wrong. He has seen these expressions all during his life. They are the expressions they gave Paul when they tried to force him to play football in high school. He told them more than once that playing football did not appeal to him. They did not listen. Paul's refusal only made his father and grandfather more determined to force him onto the team. They felt Paul was intentionally robbing them of the recognition and accolades that go with having a child on the high school football team.

To avoid their constant complaining, Paul agreed to join the football team. He decided to do it his way. Paul paid a student to take his place on the football team. He didn't see anything wrong with it. The student loved playing football, the team liked him there, the student got money, and Paul didn't have to engage in physical activity that could cause him to experience pain. He thought it was a perfect situation. These are the same expressions his father and grandfather had when they came into the principal's office to discuss his football player business. He knows all about their intense expressions.

Paul's father and grandfather look at him and then look away. There is an uncomfortable silence in the room.

Paul is the first to speak. He says, "If somebody called you about a shipment of edible female underwear, I can explain."

James simply shakes his head and points to a chair and says, "Please sit down. Your father and I would like to discuss a few things with you."

"Things? What things? You know there are some things that should never be discussed between a man, his father, and his grandfather. I'm sure you don't want to cross that line."

Walter sighs and says, "We need to discuss how you have managed to be expelled by three colleges in less than two years."

"Expelled is such a harsh word. Let's just try to keep my academic experiences in proper perspective. I view it as me simply using my own unique method of eliminating institutions of higher learning that don't quite meet my specialized educational requirements?"

"I call it getting kicked out."

"Yeah, and so did Mom."

Paul and Walter exchange angry stares and a quiet moment passes between them. James clears his throat and gets the attention of Paul and Walter.

He looks directly at Paul and says. "We're worried about you. We feel strongly something is needed to change your bad attitude."

"What bad attitude?"

Walter yells, "The attitude that you can do whatever you want and not be held responsible for it."

Paul calmly responds, "That's not a bad attitude. That is simply an example of my deep aspirations to one day pursue a career in politics."

James looks at Walter and says, "You know, he does have a point there."

Walter screams, "You're not helping."

James puts up his hand and then says, "Yes, you are right. We must remain focused."

"Thank you," says Walter.

"We've noticed some serious flaws in your character," says James.

Paul is shocked and says, "Flaws, what flaws? What character flaws do you believe I could possibly have?"

"How about cheating?" yells Walter.

Paul rolls his eyes and says, "Let's call that a strong desire to get around red tape."

"Greed," says James.

"A strong desire to do well in business," says Paul.

"Lying," yells Walter.

"I view it more as simply altering the truth a little in order to cut down on people's stress levels. I'm sure you realize I'm a giver."

James says, "It appears you are unable to grow and mature in a conventional academic setting. We feel something a bit different would work best for you."

"Something that will teach you discipline," says Walter.

"A place that will help you mature and develop a sense of responsibility for something other than yourself," says James.

Paul looks at his father, then grandfather, and says, "I refuse to work for public television."

"Your grandfather and I have decided it would be best for all of us if you attended a military academy," says Walter.

Paul starts to laugh. He thinks to himself if getting kicked out of a regular university was easy, he may only last a few hours at a military academy. Paul can't believe his father and grandfather would even consider such a thing.

"Sorry to disappoint the two of you. Paul here doesn't do the soldier scene. I don't like wearing green and the idea of bullets piercing my flesh is something I don't find appealing. In case you forgot, I just turned twenty and drive a new sports car. The military school is out. What else do you have?"

Walter and James look at one another and smile.

"Paul," says James.

"Yes, Grandpa," says Paul.

"You know your grandmother and I control your trust fund until you reach the age of twenty-five. I've spoken with your grandmother. She agrees that attending this school will be good for you. If you don't attend the military academy as we request, we'll cut you off from your trust fund immediately."

Paul is taking a drink from a bottle of Perrier when James makes his last statement. The shock causes Paul's throat to close. He spits out some of the Perrier. He then coughs for a few minutes until he can speak again.

"Don't you see how this is the best solution to our problems?" says Walter.

Paul simply gives James and Walter a cold stare.

"You can't do this to me," says Paul.

Walter smiles and says, "I think you know we can, and we will. We may even take pleasure in doing it."

Paul's face shows the rage he is feeling. He calmly says, "Okay, maybe you guys got me this time. But don't forget, I'm going to become quite proficient at killing people."

The anger and rage Paul begins to feel is something profound. He does want freedom from his family but only on his terms. These feelings go deep and trigger a strong desire to get even with his father and grandfather. Paul decides to continue hiding the intense anger he feels toward them. He is now focused on devising one of his special lessons for these bullies. Paul is determined to make it a learning experience they will never forget.

* * * * * * *

Paul is sitting on a bench in a beautiful park with his arm around a very pretty twenty-year-old girl named Monica. She has long silky dark hair and bright blue eyes. Her figure is the envy of other girls her age. Monica has known Paul since they were young. She has always had strong feelings for him. Monica hates not being able to let go of her desire to be with Paul. She remembers how he was so nice and fun when they were in high school. Monica and Paul dated during this time and it was special to her.

They broke up when Paul began to change. This happened when his father remarried more than once after his parents got a divorce. Monica has no other boys in her life at the moment. She is happy to be here in the park with Paul. Monica likes him having his arm around her. She misses the Paul she knew from high school and all the good times they had together.

Monica doesn't realize Paul never liked how she constantly tried to control him with her tears and drama. He considers her an emotional bully. Paul finds it easy to ignore these things since she is absolutely beautiful.

Monica looks at Paul and says, "Are you sure you got drafted by the French Foreign Legion? I thought people just went to France and volunteered to be part of them."

Paul takes a deep breath and appears to be in a state of shock.

"I don't understand it myself. Obviously, there is an important covert war happening somewhere in the world that requires people with my special abilities to participate. It's the least I can do for my country," says Paul.

"But the French Foreign Legion fights for France. Besides that, you have no special abilities."

Paul leans forward and looks directly at Monica.

"Then you need to think of me as a trailblazer. The first American with many unknown special abilities to be drafted into the French Foreign Legion. Hey, I want you to know how much I appreciate you providing some physical comfort for a man about to face war and death. I don't know if I'll come back from this alive, but I'm going in there. I know I will always cherish these special moments with you during the remaining days of my life and through eternity when I'm gone."

Paul runs his hand up Monica's leg. He holds her closer and slowly goes to kiss her. Monica suddenly pulls away, looks at him, and laughs.

Paul is confused and says, "What's wrong?"

"You are so full of it. Why do you always try to bullshit me just like everybody else? I know you."

Paul shrugs his shoulders.

"Because it has always worked so well in the past."

Monica's face shows she is now angry. She stands up to leave, Paul grabs her arm and gets her to slowly sit back down beside him.

Monica says, "You don't have to lie to me. I'm the girl you grew up with who saw you at your best and worst. I hope you don't forget that about me."

"How could I forget? You constantly ask me if I remember things about our high school years. It's like always answering test questions on a never-ending personal history exam."

"You are still really lacking in many boyfriend skills. That's why we're not together right now. It seems like the only time I see you is when your hormones are raging or you're in some kind of trouble."

"Then don't complain we never spend time together."

Monica gets up again like she's going to leave. Paul grabs her arm and again gently pulls her back down to the bench.

"Okay, I'm sorry. Please sit down. I admit I've not treated you too good in the recent past."

"No, you haven't. You come around and we have a great time. We go on trips and do things together for days. Then you're gone, and I don't hear from you. Do you understand how that hurts?"

"I hope you realize hurting you is not where I intend to go, it just seems that's where I always end up."

You're just a pathetic self-absorbed asshole."

"I suppose that is a view of me held by you and others."

Monica slowly moves over and hugs Paul.

Paul smiles and says, "Now that we have that settled; there will be nobody at my father's house for hours since he left on a date. We'll have the entire place to ourselves. You could do your naughty nurse routine. You know how I love it when you perform your special examination."

Monica yells, "Paul."

Paul is confused and says, "What? I just thought it would be easier than using my sports car. We both know that is a bit of a logistics challenge. I think using my father's house would make things much easier. I'm just thinking of you."

Monica moves away from Paul. She is still not looking at him, trying not to cry, and says, "I talked with your mother the other day."

Paul yells, "My mother?"

Monica looks at Paul and remembers the strong emotional response he always has when the topic of his mother is discussed. She knows this is the one thing that always weakens Paul. Monica has seen how Paul's mother has power over him like nobody else in the world. Few people know this about him.

"Yeah, what's wrong with that? I was at a store near the art gallery where she works. I saw her and we talked. She just got a promotion at her job and is going to move into her own apartment this month. She'll be glad to move out of her sister's house. You know how she's lived there for the past few years. I assumed she told you."

Paul runs his hands through his hair, stands up, and starts walking around sighing. He's struggling to control his emotions.

"Well, that's just wonderful. I'm glad to hear it. How great that her only child has no idea what's going on in her life, but my mother takes the time to tell you, a former girlfriend, what's going on with her."

Monica yells, "What's wrong?"

"What could be wrong? I have a mother who can't pick up a stupid phone, dial seven digits, and say 'Hey, my only child, I just got a promotion at my job. and I'm moving into a new apartment.' No, I've got to hear by chance from someone like you."

Monica sits back, folds her arms, and smirks.

"Don't you just hate it when someone you care about unintentionally hurts your feelings all the time?"

Paul's face becomes red and his jaw becomes tight.

"What I really hate is my parent's bullshit, and your non-stop whining about everything I do."

Monica stands up and yells, "Fine, I've had enough. Get out of my life and this time stay out."

Paul composes himself and says very calmly, "I want to clarify one thing. Does this mean we're not going to engage in some type of fornication tonight? I'm sure we can make it something impressive. I'm willing to put forth the effort if you are and besides that, I'd hate to have the free time at my father's house go unused."

"Go screw yourself asshole."

Monica turns and walks away. Paul starts walking in the opposite direction toward his car. He suddenly stops, turns around, looks in Monica's direction, and yells, "If that made me happy, do you think I'd need you? As we say in the French Foreign Legion, baby, arrivederci."

Monica turns around and yells, "That's Italian you idiot."

Paul screams, "Hey, guess what? I've never been a language major."

Paul gets in his sports car and revs the engine before driving down the road at a fast rate of speed. He thinks to himself how Monica is now a strong contender for inclusion into his inner circle.

# Chapter 5

## *First Impressions*

Paul is sitting in the passenger seat of his father's new BMW. They are driving down a rural road toward Saint Michael's Military Academy. He is drinking a bottle of Perrier and humming the tune to the song *The Ballad of the Green Berets*. His father is very annoyed with Paul and continuously rolls his eyes and sighs. He decides it would be better to try to start a conversation than listen to Paul's annoying humming.

Walter says, "You know, we were lucky to get you into this military academy at such a late date. Your grandfather had to pull some serious strings for you to go here. You need to change your attitude. I'm sure you'll benefit from attending this school."

Paul chuckles and says, "You know and I know I'm not going to make it there. You saw how easily I got kicked out of those other schools. With all the rules and regulations at a place like this, I give it two weeks before I'm expelled."

"Then you'll be very poor. We're serious about cutting you off from your trust fund. I was cut off from mine for a while when I was your age and believe me it's not fun. Your grandfather straightened me out rather quickly by doing such a thing."

"So, I'm selling myself out for money just like my father. We have such wonderful family traditions."

Walter yells, "Stop complaining, lots of people would love to have your opportunities."

"You mean like being kept on an emotional leash? Constantly being bullied as well as threatened to be financially neutered by my family members?"

"You just don't understand."

"I understand you hold all the financial cards in my life right now. I wonder what will happen when that changes. What will our relationship be like when you and grandfather no longer have power over me? The two of you may have to spend time at a rehab center for bullies."

"You don't know what you're talking about. I bet one day you'll probably thank me for this."

"What if someday I don't? What if I'm thinking a future lawsuit against my father based on intentional infliction of emotional distress could be in order? The company always likes to get rid of nuisance lawsuits rather quickly."

"I guess we'll just deal with that if it happens. I'm done talking. Let's just be quiet. We're almost there."

As Paul and his father travel down the road they pass stunning scenery. There is a tense silence between the car's occupants. Suddenly, they see the entrance to the military academy. There is a large iron trestle fence. A sign at the top of the trestle reads, "Saint Michael's Military Academy. Where Boys Come To Be Made Men."

As Walter's BMW goes up the road, it stops at a small building on the driver's side at the gate of the military academy. A young man about Paul's age and wearing a very impressive uniform steps out of the small building to greet them. Walter rolls down his driver's side window. He tells the young man his name and says he is here to drop off his son. The young man takes out a clipboard from the small building. He looks at it and tells Walter he needs to go to the main building and explains how to get there.

When they start driving away, Walter says, "That was certainly a well-mannered and impressive-looking young man."

Paul looks back at the boy in uniform still directing other cars coming through the gate. He shrugs his shoulders, and says, "Yeah, I wonder if he does windows."

Walter looks at his son with an expression of disgust and says, "You're impossible."

Paul is feeling very nervous. The only thing making him provide an appearance of calm is the intense anger he feels for his father and grandfather. Dreams of revenge keep him relaxed and focused.

The car pulls up in front of the main building. Walter and Paul get out of the BMW. Walter opens the trunk and starts taking out his son's luggage. Paul looks around and sees boys ranging in age from twelve to twenty-one years old. Some are being yelled at while doing push-ups, others are marching, and some are standing in line wearing camouflage uniforms. Others are standing at attention while a sergeant yells and pours water from a hose on them.

Paul says, "I think we may have made a wrong turn somewhere."

"Why do you say that?"

"This place looks more like some kind of Sadomasochist Academy. I can't stay here. I drive a sports car."

"Quit complaining. There is nothing you can do about it."

"Nothing?"

"Nothing."

"How about if I told you I always felt deep down inside I was really a female from the planet Zernda? A place that doesn't have a military."

Walter yells, "Just stop it."

Walter places three pieces of expensive luggage on the sidewalk. He takes out golf clubs, a suit bag, a briefcase, a six-pack of Perrier and places them next to the expensive luggage.

Paul gets in front of his father and says, "How about if deep down inside I always felt you were a woman from the planet Zernda? You've got to admit that one year when you dressed in drag for a Halloween party, you were way more comfortable than anyone expected."

Walter sighs and puts down the last of Paul's luggage and closes his car's trunk. Paul looks around as he takes another drink from his bottle of Perrier. Suddenly, he tries to grab the car keys from Walter, and the two are struggling and start swearing at one another.

They hear a young female say, "Excuse me, but can I be of assistance with the new cadet?"

When they stop struggling, Walter and Paul are looking at a rather attractive female wearing a cadet uniform. She has deep blue eyes and blonde hair pinned up under the cap she is wearing. The strict uniform she wears can't hide her thin and shapely body. Walter and Paul let one another go. Walter straightens his shirt. He and Paul are looking at the beautiful female cadet with stunned expressions.

Paul says, "Are you the military academy's concierge?"

"The what?" says the female cadet.

Walter steps in front of Paul and says, "Ignore him. I'm sure he's a little nervous about this being his first day at the academy. I bet it's like that with all new military academy cadets."

"I'm Cadet Jane Westin here to take the new inductee, Paul Wildman, to the school Commandant's office."

Walter turns to Paul and says, "Well, I guess this is it. Good luck son."

Walter holds out his hand to shake and Paul just looks at it.

When he tries to hug his son, it is awkward and Paul says, "Please don't try and put on a show for the lady cadet. It's embarrassing."

Paul makes one last attempt to get Walter's car keys but fails.

Walter yells, "Oh, no you don't. Like the sign says at the entrance, it's time for you to become a man."

"Oh yeah? Maybe you should be a cadet here. Don't you think it's time for you to become one?"

Walter gets in his car and starts the engine. He then looks out of the window, smiles, and waves. Paul realizes his father is struggling not to laugh. Paul raises his middle digit in the direction of his father's car as it drives away. When he turns back, cadet Jane Westin is looking at him with a somber expression.

Paul says, "I guess every family has their traditions. Flipping off one another is ours."

Jane says, "Follow me, cadet."

She turns and begins to walk away. Paul looks at all his luggage and then at Jane.

Paul yells, "I don't think I can be a cadet, I'm a Presbyterian. Hey, muscle girl, aren't you going to help me out here with my stuff?"

Jane walks over to Paul in precise military fashion. She puts her hands on her hips and starts speaking in a loud monotone voice.

"Let me explain something to you. I am a senior cadet. As a senior cadet, I am not required to help a first-year do anything. Furthermore, from now on you will address me as senior Cadet Westin. The shortened term is senior cadet. If you don't, you will learn all about the academy's discipline programs for cadets with bad attitudes. Do you understand?"

As Jane Westin continues to deride Paul, he can't stop looking at her and thinking about her beauty. He no longer hears any word she is saying. Paul is lost in a world of imagination involving senior Cadet Westin and him engaging in physical pleasure. Suddenly, she says his name several times. Paul is then forced back into reality and says, "What's up with you?

Why are you so upset? You belong to a union or something?"

Jane looks Paul up and down and lets out a disgusted groan. She turns around and starts walking away.

"Just follow me and be quiet."

Paul puts his golf clubs over his shoulder and picks up his briefcase. On his other shoulder, he puts a travel bag and picks up the six-pack of Perrier. He walks away and leaves some of his luggage.

Walking behind Jane, Paul yells, "If you're the hospitality greater around here, this place is gonna really suck."

Paul stops another cadet who walks near him. He tells the cadet he'll give him some money to bring his other luggage to his room. Cadet Jane Westin tells the cadet to ignore Paul. She then grabs Paul's shoulder and starts pulling him into the main building.

# Chapter 6

## *Introductions*

Inside a large and spacious office located in the academy's main building is a fifty-five-year-old man sitting behind a large wooden desk. He is wearing an impressive academy uniform. His name is General Thomas Loren, and he is the academy's Commandant. He is the top military person at the academy.

On the wall behind him are many military awards he was given during his time in the army. On another wall are pictures of the Commandant getting promotions, medals, and posing on tanks as well as with various Army weapons. There are pictures of previous Commandants of the academy on another wall. A large bookshelf is filled with books on military life. It takes up space toward the back of the office. Another wall has pictures of the academy when it started over six decades earlier, and its changes through the years. Thomas is focused on various papers sitting in front of him on his desk.

He hears a loud knock on his office door, looks up, and yells, "Enter."

The door opens and Cadet Jane Weston walks straight up to the wooden desk in strict military fashion, stands at attention, and says, "Sir,

I've brought the new cadet to your office as requested, sir."

General Thomas Loren says, "Very good cadet."

Paul slowly walks into the office whistling and drinking from his bottle of Perrier. He puts down the things he's carrying and starts looking around the office.

Jane whispers, "I believe this one is going to be trouble, sir."

Paul looks at Jane and says, "I bet if you kiss just the right amount of military butt all this could be yours someday."

Jane tightens her jaws and clenches her fist. General Thomas Loren smiles.

"That will be all for now Cadet Westin. Thank you. You may go."

Jane turns around and walks toward the door in perfect military fashion.

Paul yells at Jane as she leaves, "What were you voted most likely to do in high school? Disarm a landmine?"

Before she reaches the door, Jane turns around quickly. Her face reveals her anger. Paul just smiles.

"As I said, that will be all cadet. I'll handle it from here," says General Thomas Loren.

Jane turns back around and leaves the room.

"I like this military interior decorating. It is quite the army-type office motif you have here. This really makes a statement of I could shoot you or blow you up. It provides a very John Wayne, Green Beret, type of vibe."

General Thomas Loren stands up, points to a chair, and says, "Please sit down Mr. Wildman."

Paul sits down in a chair directly across from General Thomas Loren's desk. General Thomas Loren then removes a folder from a filing cabinet behind him, sits back down at his desk, and opens the file.

Paul says, "I have just one simple question for you."

General Thomas Loren says, "What would that be?"

Paul yells, "How in the hell do I get out of here? Just call my grandfather and tell him this is all just one big mistake. Tell him I've reconsidered and will work for public television if that is what he really wants. Tell him you've tested me, and I'm actually a female from the planet Zernda. Tell him anything you like just work with me to get me out of here."

General Thomas Loren laughs.

"I wish it were that easy."

"Why isn't it?"

"To be completely honest, I didn't want you here either. But it seems we are sort of stuck with one another."

"With that attitude, we're not going to get anywhere on the topic of me being kicked out."

I've spoken to your grandfather, and I know the only reason you're sitting right there is because you want to keep your trust fund and inheritance, right?"

"You got it."

"The only reason I'm letting you sit there is because your grandfather sits on the academy's board of directors and has paid a substantial sum of money for you to attend this school. Do you see how we sort of need each other at the moment?"

"Yeah, we're both money whores."

General Thomas Loren sighs and looks down at the opened file on his desk.

"I've taken the liberty of speaking with some of the professors at your previous colleges, a few of your high school teachers, and your high school principal."

"I'm sure you found that enlightening. You must realize my history is filled with people who didn't appreciate all the things I have to offer the world."

"Strange how your high school principal said you were a good student until your sophomore year and then had many bad things to say about you. Your college professors had even worse things to say about you. Why the start of the bad behavior?"

Paul shrugs his shoulders.

"I don't know. I think it's because my actions have always been so misunderstood. What does my past have to do with anything?"

"We have a pretty intense first year here. If there is something in your personal life that could be causing you trouble, I want to know. Now is your chance to discuss it with me."

Paul sighs and looks away for a second. He seems overcome with emotion.

"No, there's nothing I want to discuss. What happens now?"

"You'll go across the street to the barracks and get set up. Tomorrow morning you'll finish being processed in building fourteen."

"Then what?"

"Then you begin your life here at the academy. You'll be a cadet and wear a uniform while living in a military environment. You're going to learn how to follow orders and respect authority."

"And if I don't?"

General Thomas Loren sits back in his chair, puts his hands together, and smiles.

"We have been doing this for a long time. We have our ways to make our cadets follow the rules, Mr. Wildman. Trust me, when I tell you, we have our ways."

Paul leans forward and starts to talk in a low voice.

"I just want you to know, I'm going to have access to a lot of money in a few years. Whatever my grandfather is paying you to keep me here, I'll double it to get me out. I'm even willing to sign a contract and make it all nice and legal. I would even be open to putting a nice bonus payment in the agreement for one Academy Commandant. What do you say?"

General Thomas Loren closes the file on his desk and laughs.

Keep your money, Mr. Wildman. If money is what I was after, I wouldn't have joined the military. There are things more important than money. Of course, you wouldn't understand that now would you?"

"No, I wouldn't, because I've never seen anything or anybody that didn't have a price. Just think about the offer. That's all I ask."

Paul stands up and says, I'm a little tired. I'd like to go and relax a bit. Just show me to my room. Tomorrow seems like it'll be a real party."

Paul begins to pick up his things and walks toward the door.

General Thomas Loren yells, "Get back here."

Paul turns around and says, "What? What's the problem?"

"As of this moment, you are officially a cadet at Saint Michael's Military Academy. You will ask permission to leave the school Commandant's office like every other cadet."

"Why?"

"Because that is an expectation of every cadet who attends this academy. Now, I want to hear you say it. Say, 'Sir, Cadet Wildman respectfully requests permission to leave the Commandant's office, sir.'

Paul smiles and says, "I guess I can't put it in my own words and say something like 'Later Commandant dude?"

Paul starts laughing but stops when he looks at General Thomas Loren's stern face. General Thomas Loren speaks in a low monotone voice and his anger is obvious.

"Cadet Wildman, I understand you're new but this may be the only warning you get. If you want to challenge the authority here, realize you're in our world. Punishment is on our terms. This can be an easy place to go to school or a place that will be your worst nightmare. You get to decide."

"Just tell me where to deposit my nuts, so we can get it over with."

"Say it," screams General Thomas Loren.

Paul shrugs his shoulders and sighs. He realizes this is a very special moment. It's the time when the academy's power over him is being made clear. The Commandant will not tolerate anything less than conformity at this academy. Paul knows he is out of options. His mind now turns to thoughts of survival. Paul decides to work on getting past this academy experience. It crushes him to give in to this authority, but he is determined to survive.

Paul clears his throat and meekly says, "All right. Sir, Cadet Wildman respectfully requests permission to leave the Commandant's office, sir."

"Now that wasn't so difficult, was it?"

Paul starts to make a sarcastic comment but decides not to and just picks up his things.

"Very good. In time, you'll learn not being a real smartass has its benefits," says General Thomas Loren.

Paul walks out of General Thomas Loren's office. He sees Cadet Westin waiting for him in the hallway. He starts to say something sarcastic to her then stops. She motions for him to follow her. Paul feels completely defeated. His anger and rage have turned into depression. This place appears to be the worst bully experience he may ever have. He is determined to leave this military academy as soon as he figures out a way to do it.

# Chapter 7

*The Military Transition*

There is a very plain bedroom in the academy where Paul Wildman will be staying. It is the first time he has ever lived in a place other than his father's spacious home or a five-star hotel. During his time away at different colleges, he stayed at expensive hotels paid for by his family's business. He knows it will take some time for the accounting department to figure out exactly how Paul made that happen. He isn't worried, because he has done worse.

Paul is accustomed to staying at places with large rooms furnished with luxury items, as well as a refrigerator, a new television, a couch, and more. He is struggling to accept the idea this is not what will be provided for him. The rooms at Saint Michael's Military Academy are quite small and plain. In the room awaiting Paul's arrival is enough space for two single beds, two stand-up lockers, two desks, and two lamps. On the empty mattress of a bed are folded sheets, a pillow case, a pillow, and some blankets. The other bed is made in perfect military fashion. Items on one of the desks are very orderly. The other desk is empty. Paul Wildman is about to experience something he never thought would happen to him during his life; he will not live as a wealthy person.

When the door to the very plain bedroom opens, Paul walks in and puts down his golf clubs, travel bag, briefcase, and a six-pack of Perrier on the unmade bed. He then gets his other luggage and brings it into the room. Paul's first impression of this room is denial. His mind tells him it must be the place where he will store his belongings. Paul believes the accommodations he will be using at the academy will be much better than this. He knows his grandfather has paid a significant amount of money for him to attend this academy. He thinks his grandfather may need to pay a bit more if he expects Paul to be comfortable at this place.

Standing in the middle of the empty room, Paul says, "Oh, I have no idea why they would choose the federal prison look for their servant's quarters."

Paul hears a voice from behind him say, "You must be the new person."

When he turns around, a twenty-year-old Hispanic man wearing an impressive uniform is in front of Paul. His name is Dennis Martinez. He has a friendly smile and puts out his hand to shake.

Paul smiles and shakes his hand. His mind is calculating a business involving Dennis that would make him money. He's thinking maybe some type of sales would be perfect for a person like this who has such a pleasant voice and smile.

"I'm Dennis Martinez. I guess we'll be roommates."

"Hi, I'm Paul. Paul J. Wildman."

"Since you're assigned to this floor, it must be your first year here. At this academy, senior cadets can volunteer to room with a first-year cadet and help them adjust to academy life. I'll be graduating this year. Were you at another academy before you came to Saint Michaels?"

Paul laughs and says, "No, not actually. I'm here due to family discord."

Dennis is confused and says, "I don't understand."

"My father and grandfather have redefined the term assholes in new and never before seen ways. They forced me to come here."

Dennis doesn't know how to respond. In his family, nobody would ever refer to their father or grandfather in such a way. The elders are always respected. He doesn't understand how anyone could be forced into the academy. He simply says, "Oh."

Paul walks around and looks at the room. He touches the bedding on the bed with the folded sheets with his index finger. Paul doesn't understand what needs to be done with it.

"Please tell me this is the servant's quarters. I'm sure we cadets get to stay in much larger individual rooms with refrigerators, couches, and televisions."

Dennis shrugs his shoulders and says, "No, this is it. This is where they assigned you to sleep."

Paul makes a mental note to find a better place. He has previously written down the numbers of his father's credit cards. Paul believes he may be able to use them to stay at an acceptable hotel he noticed on the drive to the academy.

Paul says, "It seems like this fine military establishment has forgotten one simple thing for our sleeping quarters, a bathroom."

"That is down the hall."

"Why would our bathroom be at the end of the hall?"

"So everybody on the floor can have an equal chance to use it, I suppose. It's best to get in there early in the morning. It can get really busy."

Paul's eyes widen, and he seems horrified by what Dennis has just told him. He takes a couple of steps backward and has to steady himself to stop from falling.

"You mean a community bathroom? A bathroom in which many

people with all sorts of various bacteria, and questionable, as well as unknown, hygiene habits can utilize at their discretion?”

“Yeah, I suppose, but it’s no big deal. What’s the problem? Everybody uses it.”

“That's the problem. Everybody uses it. It's unacceptable. I’m going to notify the United Nations and Amnesty International. This has got to be against the terms of the Geneva Convention.”

Denies is laughing when he suddenly notices something out of the corner of his eye. He quickly gets up and stands at attention.

Dennis yells, “Attention on deck.”

A twenty-one-year-old man walks into the room wearing a dress uniform. He is muscular and has very short brown hair. His name is Peter Barnett. He is the top cadet at Saint Michaels.

Peter walks in, looks at Dennis, and says, “At ease cadet.”

Dennis relaxes and puts his hands behind his back but still doesn't move. Paul puts out his hand to shake. With his other hand, Paul is holding a bottle of Perrier. Peter Barnett walks over to Paul and looks him up and down. His face reveals the disgust he is feeling.

Paul says, “I like that attention-on-deck stuff. Looks like lots of fun.”

“So, you’re the new guy. What’s your name?”

“Paul J. Wildman.”

Peter Barnett walks over to Paul’s things. He looks at them and chuckles. Peter turns around and looks at Paul.

“Wildman, since you’ve not even been here a full day and your lack of understanding concerning how we operate is to be expected. However, from now on when you see a senior cadet, or commissioned officer of any rank walk into a room, you are to yell, 'attention on deck,' and then stand at attention like cadet Martinez demonstrated. Is that understood?”

“Do we always have to be so formal? Could I just say something like ‘Stand up cause the big bad super military cadet dude is here?’ You know, sort of put it in my own words."

Dennis smiles and almost laughs. Peter Barnett turns around and Dennis's face quickly becomes serious. Peter smiles and begins walking around in front of Paul.

"You're a smart ass. Good, very good. I love people who think they're too smart or tough to follow rules and regulations."

"Glad I made your day."

Peter Barnett quickly walks over to Paul and puts his hands on his hips and looks at Paul face to face.

"Wildman, I've been here for over three years and have seen guys twice your size cry like babies because they couldn't take it. I've seen female cadets break a tough male cadet like a twig. You're nothing we haven't seen before. Do you understand?"

"That seems to be a common theme around here. I'm sure those experiences have enriched your life beyond words. I still believe it is possible you may not have encountered anything like my uniqueness."

Peter Barnett smiles, turns toward Denies, and says, "Carry on Cadet."

Dennis relaxes and Peter Barnett walks toward the door. He then turns and looks at Paul.

Peter says, "You really need to consider watching what you say. After today, you will be made responsible. Your roommate is one of the finest senior cadets we have ever had at this academy. It would be wise for you to listen to what he has to say about getting along in this institution. This place can be a very pleasant experience or a very unpleasant one. The choice is yours."

"Another common theme. What is it with you people and your shared sayings?"

"My advice is to choose wisely," Peter Barnett then looks at Dennis and says, "Work with this one cadet."

When Peter Barnett leaves the room, Paul lets out a sigh and sits down.

Dennis says, "Don't let it worry you. In a couple of weeks, you'll know the routine and be just like the rest of us. It will be easier."

"When I saw that Barnett guy, I thought to myself this is an example of what happens when someone doesn't get enough hugs and kisses as a child."

Dennis laughs and then sits down at his desk. He opens a book and gets a notebook.

"I'm telling you right now to not mess with that guy."

"He's a real charmer."

"He is the top cadet in the entire academy. Just like his father and brothers."

"That is good justification for genetic research into what causes people to become assholes. It's also good to see nepotism is thriving in this place."

"You got to learn to take it easy. Just study and obey the rules. Then you won't have any problems."

"That's the funny thing about problems. You can either have them or be the cause of them. I guess we all get to choose."

* * * * * * * *

Things get worse for Paul the next day. Early in the morning, he wakes up with his hair disheveled and eyes half open. The sound of a trumpet playing *Reveille* over a loudspeaker is heard throughout the academy. Paul looks over at Dennis, who is dressed in his uniform and looks perfect. He laughs when Paul suggests they purchase soundproofing for their room.

Paul is shocked to discover he is required to make his bed. He tries to pay Dennis to make his bed. Dennis simply laughs. Paul believes he should be compensated in some way for performing such domestic chores and intends to bring this up with his grandfather.

Paul continues to struggle when he realizes he must use the community bathroom. He is nauseated when he sees the rows of toilets and the sinks. Paul tries to control the horror he feels realizing he will have to take a shower in a place with several shower heads in an open area. He thinks about the credit card numbers he has written down from his father's credit cards. Paul intends to use them to purchase a mobile bathroom for himself and pay an attendant to clean it.

Once he gets through his morning bathroom time and making a bed for the first time, Paul is treated to breakfast at a place in the academy they call the mess hall. It is a cafeteria-style operation. During his time at different colleges, Paul would shudder at the thought of being forced to dine in such a place. He usually ordered room service for his meals at the hotels where he was staying.

Once in the mess hall, Paul reluctantly takes a tray and moves it down the line as various breakfast foods are put on it. Paul is given everything from scrambled eggs to sausage and pancakes. When he gets toward the end of the line, Paul asks a fellow cadet serving food where they have the cappuccino and croissants. Everyone around Paul starts laughing. Paul tells himself a mobile bathroom and catering service are going to be necessary for him to stay at the academy for any length of time.

After breakfast, Paul is taken to a building where he is busy filling out forms. It seems every time he completes one form, they give him another. The next stop for Paul is a building where he is outfitted with a series of academy uniforms. Paul tries to negotiate for a uniform that involves sports coats and dress pants, but his attempts only bring laughter. The people give him the uniforms and reject Paul's offer for money to take the uniforms back to his room for him.

With hundreds of cadets attending the academy, there are always many different sounds occurring. No loud, horrified shrieks had ever been heard before at the academy like the sound of Paul getting a military haircut. When he emerges from the building, Paul has short hair and is wearing an academy uniform. Other cadets notice him walking like a zombie into things.

The rest of the day is spent with a cadet sergeant teaching Paul how to salute and march. Paul gets confused and frustrated. He keeps hitting himself in the eye when he tries to salute. The cadet sergeant has never seen a new cadet march so poorly. He rejects Paul's offer of money as well as a promise of access to Paul's future mobile bathroom and catered food. Eventually, Paul learns the basics and seems ready to join the rest of the cadets the next day.

# Chapter 8

---

### *A Mother's Inspiration*

**P**aul is holding a metal tray with food and walking toward a table in the academy's mess hall. His head is down as he puts his tray on a table and simply slumps down onto a chair.

Dennis sees Paul and walks over to him.

He sits down across from Paul, smiles, and says, "So, how has your first couple of days here as an official cadet at Saint Michael's been?"

Paul seems like a broken person. His speech is slow, and he is struggling to lift his head to look at Dennis. He has never felt so defeated in his life.

Paul sighs then looks at Dennis, and says, "Karma is a bitch. It has finally caught up with me. I've been forced to serve a sentence for being found a terminally greedy asshole. I think this place sucks more than an industrial vacuum."

Dennis simply continues to smile and is cheerful when he speaks.

"I know it's tough at first. Don't worry, you'll make it. Everybody who comes here finds a way."

Paul gets angry at what Dennis has said. He shoves his tray of food away from him.

"What if I don't want to make it here? The only reason I'm here at this Gulag Academy is because I don't want to lose access to my money until I'm twenty-five."

Dennis shrugs his shoulders and says, "So make the best of it."

Paul's face reveals the anger and frustration he is feeling.

Suddenly, a voice is heard yelling, "Attention on deck."

All the cadets in the mess hall get up and stand at attention. Paul slowly gets up and stands at attention. Peter Barnett walks in.

Peter says, "Carry on cadets."

All the cadets sit down and resume eating and talking.

Paul says, "You see that? All this, yes sir, no sir, saluting and standing at attention crap just isn't me. I think it's insane."

"I think you're afraid."

Paul sighs and says, "Great, now you hate me too."

"Just stop feeling sorry for yourself. I don't hate you. You just don't see how you're making a big deal about nothing."

"You just don't understand."

"I understand everybody comes here because they want something from this place."

"Is that so?"

Some of us want to be officers in the military someday, others want to be able to show their future employers how they graduated from a military academy. You want money from your family. This school is a ticket for everybody."

"Thanks for the insight, but I've still got to get out of here. I don't think putting up with all this crazy nonsense is worth it."

"I bet you never had to deal with not having things your way. I bet you're the kind of person who doesn't like being made responsible for things do you?"

Paul stands up.

"You may just be right about me. When I got here, the only thing I wanted was to keep my money. Now, the only thing I want is my freedom. Maybe that's what I feel responsible for right now."

Paul walks away. When he leaves the mess hall, Paul is experiencing feelings he's never had before. Paul wants to leave the academy so badly; he no longer cares if he is ever given access to his trust fund. Paul now feels it is not worth his freedom.

As Paul walks out of the mess hall and toward the academy gate. He is feeling intense anger. Paul has reached his limit. He has decided to leave the academy right now. Paul intends to walk out of the gate, go down the road, and figure out what to do next when he gets there. He sees Peter Barnett and walks past him.

Peter Barnett turns toward Paul and yells, "Cadet Wildman, halt. I have something to tell you."

Paul stops and turns around to face Peter Barnett.

"Guess what? I don't care what you say. Do you know why?"

Peter Barnett puts his hands on his hips and in an authoritative tone says, "Wildman, I said I have something to tell you."

Paul yells, "It doesn't matter because I quit. I'm out of here. I've probably had the shortest military career in history, but I don't care."

"Wildman, at this moment you are still a cadet at Saint Michael's Military Academy. I expect you to properly acknowledge your superiors and behave as a cadet. Do you understand?"

Paul laughs and yells, "Superiors? Is that what you said? Oh, how could I have forgotten so quickly people here in this land of military assholes are my superiors. I know I must acknowledge those of you with such vast superiority over me."

"Wildman, you need to stop right now."

Paul hits his fist on his chest and then puts it straight in front of him like a Roman soldier and says, "Hail, Centurion."

Paul then puts his hand behind his head and moves it like he is a member of the Three Stooges and says, "Nyha, Nyha, Nyha."

Paul undoes his shirt and puts his hand under his arms and yells, "How about a twenty-one arm fart salute for you? How's that for acknowledging your superiority, my grand, exultant, academy poohbah?"

Peter Barnett calmly says, "Your mother is waiting to see you at the main building."

Paul puts his arms down. He seems to be in shock and says, "What in the hell is my mother doing here?"

Peter Barnett moves toward Paul and stands face-to-face with him.

"That I don't know. But I do know as of this moment, you have two demerits on your demerit card. One more and you're going to James Hall for a little lesson in proper military respect. Do you understand cadet?"

"Breath mints."

"What?"

"They would definitely be a worthwhile investment for you superior types. Trust me."

"That is your third demerit."

"Yeah, whatever."

Paul turns and walks toward the main building.

* * * * * * *

Paul is overwhelmed with emotion at the sight of his mother. Since his mother didn't tell him about moving into her apartment or getting a job, he refused to tell her about coming to the academy. He did this because he felt she had forgotten him. Now, Paul feels bad because he realizes he did such a mean thing. He misses his mother and is struggling not to act like an emotionally needy little child. Paul is determined to control his emotions.

Mary is Paul's mother. She is standing in the meeting room of the main building. Mary is a little taller than Paul. She is slim with dark hair and green eyes. Mary has on blue jeans, a blouse, and tennis shoes. She seldom dresses in high-end clothes since she left Paul's father. Now, the only time she wears such clothes are for her job at the art gallery.

In a few months, Mary will reach the age of fifty-three. Young men often tell her she's attractive. She knows Paul is upset with her because she hasn't kept in touch with him. Mary doesn't know if Paul will understand what has happened to her. She needed time away from him. Mary had to get her mind and emotions under control after moving out on her own. She didn't want Paul to see her so nervous and afraid. Mary wants Paul to know how important he is to her and that she loves him.

When Paul walks into the room, he and Mary just stare at one another for a few seconds. Mary opens up her arms to hug Paul. He simply takes a deep breath and looks at her.

Paul says, "I'm surprised to see you. It's been a while."

Mary knows her son. He always tries to be so tough when he's afraid of rejection. She walks over to Paul and hugs him. Paul remains motionless for a few seconds then hugs her back, holding her tightly. He puts his head on her shoulders and fights his desire to cry. After a few seconds, Mary lets Paul go, steps back, and looks at him. She's trying to get used to the image of her son having short hair and wearing a uniform. It almost seems funny to Mary, but she refuses to laugh. She feels proud of Paul for being part of the academy.

"I'm sorry. I hope my coming here hasn't upset you," says Mary.

"I'm not upset. I just don't know why you're here."

Mary turns away from Paul and fights back tears. She begins to walk around the room.

"I know I should've gotten in touch with you sooner. My life has just been so crazy lately."

Mary looks at Paul and remembers when she had a bad argument with Walter in their living room. She remembers Paul being twelve years old and standing in the doorway of the room. Mary and Walter were so busy fighting, they didn't notice him. Mary suddenly realizes the terrible things he saw and heard that day. She feels horrible when she thinks about it.

Mary replays in her mind yelling at Walter and saying, "I've had it this time. I will not tolerate another one of your affairs."

Walter shrugs his shoulders and says, "What's the big deal? You know it has happened before. Just go buy yourself something or go on a trip or do something and just forget about it."

"You've treated me like dirt for the last time."

Walter laughs.

"What are you going to do? Leave me? You'd have to make money and pay your own bills. I doubt you're capable of doing such a thing."

"I'm not you. I'm not like you. I've not spent my life being my father's pet as you have."

Walter becomes angry, points at Mary, and yells, "You shut your mouth. You aren't good enough to say anything about anybody in the Wildman family."

Mary becomes composed, smiles, and says, "You're not a son to him. You're just one of his possessions. I bet he'd sell you if he got a better deal on another son."

Walter screams, "Shut up, shut up now you ignorant bitch."

"I would say he's got you by the balls, but I wouldn't be surprised if your father keeps them in a safe at his house."

Mary starts laughing and Walter slaps her. Mary just turns her head quickly and slowly turns back toward Walter. She has a look of rage. Mary slowly wipes blood from the corner of her mouth. Paul runs into the room and consoles his mother. He is so angry; tears are in his eyes.

Paul yells at his father, "You hit my mom. I hate you."

Walter is now composed and adjusts the suit he's wearing. He calmly goes over to a bar in the room and pours himself a drink.

He looks at Mary and says, "If you really want to leave, I'll give you enough money as long as Paul stays here."

Paul yells, "No, I don't want to be here. I want to be with my mother."

Mary goes over to Paul and puts her arms around him. She calmly says, "Don't worry Paul. Everything will be okay."

Walter says, "Listen to your mother. You're a Wildman. You belong here learning about our family business."

Mary turns, walks away, and stops. She turns back and looks at Paul. He has tears running down his cheeks.

Mary says, "Don't worry Paul. We'll be fine. Everything will be fine."

Walter takes a drink from the glass he's holding and says, "Someday, you'll appreciate our family and what we've accomplished. You're the heir to a very profitable corporation. You must learn how that always has to come first."

Paul looks at both his mother and father and runs out of the room.

The memory fades. Mary realizes she is now looking at Paul standing in front of her with short hair and wearing a uniform. She is impressed at how good he looks as an academy cadet.

Paul says, "Why did I have to hear from Monica you got a new job and an apartment? Why couldn't you have called me? That really hurt my feelings."

Mary sighs and sits down on a chair in the room.

"I'm sorry, I should've called, but I thought you'd call me. When you didn't, I thought you didn't want to hear from me."

"You should have just called."

"We've talked before about how calling your father's house is so uncomfortable for me. I don't want to chance him being on the phone. I wouldn't put it past him to have recording devices on all the phones in the house."

Paul sighs and sits down next to his mother.

"You're right, I should've called you."

Mary smiles and pats Paul on the shoulder.

"That's all right. We're talking now. So, how do you like it here?

"It sucks. I'm quitting."

"What's so bad about it?"

"This place seems to be run by rejects from a mental hospital for the criminally insane. They have a routine of daily degradation."

"Is that so?"

Paul stands up and tries to salute.

"I've got to do that just about every time I see anybody. I've almost put my eye out three times. I could be blinded before this is all over."

Mary smiles and says, "Oh yeah?"

"You have no idea."

Mary tugs on Paul's uniform.

Mary says, "Well, at least you look good."

"These things? I think this school got these uniforms from a bankruptcy auction of a mall security firm. They have that mall security guard appeal."

Mary gets up and walks to a window. She then turns back to face Paul.

"I want you to promise me one thing."

"What?"

"You'll stay here until the end of the school year."

Paul is shocked and says, "Why?"

"I spoke with your father before I came here. I didn't know where you were, and I just wanted to see you."

"Okay."

"Your father and grandfather don't think you'll make it here or anywhere."

Paul yells, "I don't care."

Don't you see? You've got to prove them wrong. They've always laughed when I told them there wasn't anything you couldn't do. Do you have any idea how succeeding here would show them they're completely wrong about you?"

"Do you have any idea what you're asking of me?"

Mary walks over to Paul, puts her hands on his shoulders, and looks straight into his face.

"If not for yourself, then do it for me. You need to show your father and grandfather they're wrong about you. Your father needs to know you're a better man than him. It may be the most difficult thing you ever experience in your life, but you'll be so happy to see the looks on their faces when you make it."

"I'm miserable here."

"Please stay and prove to your father and grandfather they are wrong about you."

Paul puts his head down and walks away but then quickly turns back. As he looks at his mother, those deep feelings and desire to please her grow within him. He loves his mother and knows inside he wants to make her proud of him. As the feelings intensify, Paul knows what he must do.

"Okay, I'll stay, but I really don't like it here."

"Neither would you like going back to your father after having failed here. I know you can do it. Make us both proud."

"I hope our medical insurance covers extended psychiatric care. I'm going to need some after spending time in this place."

Mary smiles and tries to hide the tear escaping out of the corner of her eye. She believes she may be the only one who knows her son has true courage when it matters. Mary hugs Paul and can feel his fear and hurt. She is afraid for him but won't tell her son. Paul lets the feeling of love he has for his mother take over him. He remembers her soft touch when he was a child and her singing to him at night. Paul thinks of her holding him after being bullied in school. He saw her at every school event and got her praise for all of his school artwork. Paul thinks about how his mother has always been there for him. Many times she protected him against his father. Paul begins to realize what it must have been like to be married to his father for all those years. He decides to do this for her. For the first time in his life, Paul will sacrifice his happiness for another person. His mother's feelings are now more important to him than his own.

# Chapter 9

## *Criminals and Cadets*

Saint Michael's Military Academy is a private institution that operates like other military schools. It is located near a mid-sized town. The school is considered to be a major contributor to the local economy. Local companies get a substantial amount of income from all the cadets who spend money at their businesses. This is also a situation that attracts bad people who want to take advantage of the academy's cadets.

Most of the town's residents think the cadets are young and not very wise to the ways of the world. There is an honest effort to be nice to them. Saint Michael's Military Academy Cadets are usually treated well by the local population. They appreciate how the cadets spend money in their town. There are many residents who were cadets at one time or had relatives who have been cadets at the academy. Some of the residents don't care about the cadets. Some have anger toward them. This is a common occurrence wherever there is a military school in any area.

The most popular place to eat in town is called Rusty's Dinner. In this busy dinner is an attractive girl named Ruby sitting at a table with two men. She has lovely brown hair and stunning green eyes. Sitting across from her are two very harsh-looking men. One of them is a very muscular young man wearing a t-shirt, blue jeans, and a baseball cap. The logo on the baseball cap is from a local bar in the town where he lives. His name is Seth. He hates every cadet from the academy he sees. Deep down Seth wants to be a cadet, but he knows that will never happen. Not with his criminal history. When he thinks of this, it makes him hate cadets even more. The other man in the booth is a very physically fit older man with a nice shirt, a short haircut, and is wearing a nice gold watch. He has spent years doing petty crimes for many different people. His name is Jake.

Jake says, "It seems the cadets from the academy are going to be permitted to come into town tonight. I understand there will be a newbie among them. Word has it that there is a particular newbie we must get to know. It appears he has money and an ego."

Jake and Seth look at Ruby who is simply looking out of the window next to her.

After a few seconds of silence, she looks back at the two men sitting across from her. She realizes Jake and Seth are staring at her.

Ruby says, "What?"

Jake says, "You know what to do with a rich newbie cadet with an ego, right?"

Ruby sighs and says, "Yeah, yeah, yeah, sounds like my kind of guy. Don't worry about it. I'll handle things."

Jake then looks at Seth and says, "We have to follow orders on this one. You need to remember the newbie is supposed to have an interaction with us. He's to be scared and upset when we're done with him. Take his money and mess him up a little, but we don't hurt him. That's important. This comes straight from Mr. Dean. Do you understand?"

Seth shrugs his shoulders and takes a drink from the glass of iced tea in front of him.

"If Dean pays the going rate, it ain't no problem. If he don't, and I got to make up for my losses, that could be bad news for the newbie. You know what I'm saying?"

Jake yells at Seth, "We do not mess with Mr. Dean under any circumstances. He could make things real bad for all of us. We don't need that kind of trouble. Do you understand? Are we all in agreement?"

Seth shrugs his shoulders as Ruby says, "Yeah, yeah, we agree."

* * * * * * * *

In the evening, the academy bus is going through the town. It is painted with the colors of blue and white. There is the Saint Michael's Military Academy name and emblem on both sides of the bus. Sitting on the bus are male and female cadets wearing Saint Michael's Military Academy Uniforms. Dennis and Paul are sitting next to one another.

Dennis looks over at Paul and says, "A couple of us are going over to a place called The Best Coffee House. There's going to be a band playing there. You interested in going with us?"

Paul seems very sad and isn't paying attention. Dennis nudges him.

Paul says, "Huh? Oh, no thanks. I just want to walk around for a while. I need to think."

"Just be careful. Some people in this town really hate cadets."

Paul ignores what Dennis said to him. He just nods his head, turns, and stares out of the bus window. Paul thinks he may have never been this depressed in his entire life.

The town outside of the academy is known for its nice business district. It is a place with a variety of stores, shops, restaurants, and more. Right outside the business district are many nice homes with well-manicured lawns. When the bus parks, the cadets get out and all go in different directions heading toward places in the business district.

Paul goes into a store and buys a bottle of Perrier. He's walking down a street holding the opened bottle of Perrier. He's whistling and not aware of anything around him.

When Ruby sees Paul, she checks a picture she's holding. After identifying Paul as the man she needs to hustle, Ruby comes out of a doorway and bumps into him. This causes Paul to accidentally hit a lamp post. He staggers back after hitting his head. Ruby grabs Paul to keep him from falling. His uniform is wet from the bottle of Perrier having spilled on it. Ruby takes out a tissue from her purse and starts wiping Paul's uniform and smiling at him.

"Oh, I am so sorry. Your uniform is all wet. Please forgive me," says Ruby.

Paul looks at Ruby and seems to be in a trance. He is overwhelmed by such a pretty female wiping water off his uniform.

"I, ah, thank you very much, I think you got it," says Paul.

Ruby stops, looks at Paul, and continues to smile at him.

"Good. I feel awful. Let me make this up to you. How about you let me get you a coffee at The Best Coffee House? It is a popular place."

"Oh, that's fine. It's not necessary."

Ruby playfully nudges Paul with her elbow.

"Aw come on. I like being with a man in uniform. I never had coffee with one of the cadets from the academy. What is wrong with having a harmless cup of coffee in a public place?"

"I don't know if it's a good idea."

"You won't have to pay. It will be my treat."

"The Best Coffee House here we come."

Ruby laughs and she puts her arm inside Paul's. They start to walk down the street and Paul is very impressed with himself. They pass Seth and Jake who are sitting on a bench near a park in the town's business district. They look at one another and shake their heads. It appears things are going according to plan.

* * * * * * *

The Best Coffee House is a popular destination for cadets. It is known as a place where local bands play the latest musical hits. The audience is always very energetic. It is a destination where the cadets can relax and have fun. There is no alcohol served. This means enterprising cadets must be quite careful in obtaining alcohol and being unnoticed as they put it in their drinks. Doing this is an accepted part of being a cadet at Saint Michael's. Many consider it an academy tradition.

Peter Barnett, Dennis Martinez, and Jane Westin are sitting at a table. A bit of alcohol has been secretly poured into each of their drinks by different cadets. They are all feeling good and enjoying the band playing at the front of the coffee house. Paul comes in and walks past their table arm in arm with Ruby. They all notice the look of pride on Paul's face. He seems to be in a trance and doesn't even look their way. Peter, Dennis, and Jane all notice the girl with Paul.

Peter says, "Looks like our newbie Wildman got himself caught in one of Dean's webs. That is the same type of girl that got me in trouble during my first year at the academy."

"I think we should go and get him. He doesn't know what he's doing with her," says Dennis.

Dennis Martinez starts to stand up when Jane Westin grabs his shirt and gently pulls him back down to his chair.

She says, "Wait a minute. Not so fast."

"Why not? He's a cadet. He's one of us," says Dennis.

Jane shakes her head, chuckles, and says, "You know what Wildman is like. You go over there right now and tell him something bad about that girl he's with, and he'll probably think you're after her or something equally ridiculous. He doesn't trust us. I say let his ego take him wherever it does. We'll keep an eye on him and step in if it becomes necessary. We'll only take action if the situation requires it."

Peter says, "She's right you know."

Dennis shrugs his shoulders and says, "Then what exactly do we do right now? Just let her take advantage of Wildman as members of Dean's crew have done with so many of us cadets in the past?"

"We'll watch how things develop. We're not going to let him get hurt. He's a cadet. I'm sure we can agree, Wildman is not the kind of guy to take advice from us. He seems to be the type who has to learn things by experience," says Peter.

Dennis and Jane nod their heads in agreement.

* * * * * * *

Paul and Ruby are sitting at a table talking as the sound of the band playing is in the background of their conversation. Ruby has a small cup of coffee and Paul has a large deluxe-size coffee in front of him.

Ruby gets close to Paul and says, "Wow, I never met a cadet who spent time working as a spy for the CIA before going to the academy. That's impressive."

Paul smiles and says, "Well, what can I say? I'm a patriot. I just decided to take a break from the old spy game to get a little education. You know when you lead such an intense life of mystery and intrigue; it can burn you out."

Paul pulls out a gold money clip from his pocket. It is filled with several bills of large denominations. He takes out one of the bills and tosses it onto the table. He then carefully puts the money clip with the rest of the bills back into his pocket. Ruby looks at him and her eyes open widely.

"You must be a very successful spy."

"Well, I don't like to toot my own horn, but yes, you are correct. Tell you what. For the next round of drinks, you don't have to treat. We'll each buy our own. How about that?"

Ruby ignores what Paul is saying and can't stop thinking about all the money in his money clip.

"I bet you were one of the top spies in the CIA."

"I guess you could say I was one of the best. Mostly because I'm very proficient in foreign languages. I also drive a sports car."

Ruby leans forward and looks deep into Paul's eyes and speaks in a soft tone.

"You know, you're just the kind of guy a girl could really enjoy being around."

Paul swallows hard, lets out a nervous chuckle, and says, "I know."

* * * * * * * *

When it is dark, Paul and Ruby leave The Best Coffee House. They are walking arm in arm down the street looking at one another and smiling. Ruby guides Paul down an alley. There are small lights from the street showing piles of boxes and trash bins along the sides of the alley. Paul doesn't notice Peter, Dennis, and Jane on the sidewalk across the street. They are following him and Ruby.

Ruby says, "I'm so glad you agreed to come to my place. I'm sure we'll have a lot of fun. My car is parked a few blocks away. If we go down this alley, we'll be there much faster. I hope you realize I feel so very safe with you here next to me."

"No problem. After all the things I've seen, and the people I've had to face, I don't fear anything. Trust me, you don't want to know the gory details. Suffice it to say, you are as safe as humanly possible right now."

Paul is confidently strutting with Ruby down the alley. Jake walks out from behind a pile of boxes.

"Well, well, well. What have we here? A cadet from the academy in an alley with a girl who is way out of his league. What shall we do about this?" says Jake.

Paul's eyes get big, and he takes a deep breath and struggles to control his feeling of being surprised. He lets go of Ruby and puts her behind him to protect her.

"I'll handle this. Don't worry," says Paul.

Ruby moves past Paul. She walks over and stands beside Jake.

"Careful Jake. He worked for the CIA before he went to the academy," says Ruby.

Paul looks at Ruby and is shocked. He starts to slowly take a few steps backward.

Paul says, "How unfortunate for you I'm working undercover. If I give the signal, special forces will be over here in seconds."

Paul turns around.

"Now," yells Paul.

Paul then starts to run toward the street. He runs into Seth who pushes him. Paul falls back against a pile of boxes. He stands up and quickly realizes how much bigger Seth is than himself.

"Guess what asshole? I'm your special forces. Somebody told me you got my money. So, pay up, CIA guy," says Seth.

"I'm afraid you've been misinformed. I suggest you take up compensation issues with the people at the CIA headquarters in Virginia."

Seth laughs, points to Paul, and says, "You believe this guy?"

Seth walks over to Paul and slaps his head.

"Ow, why are you doing this?"

Seth looks at Paul, points to Jake, and says, "Hey, Mr. CIA cadet, I know this guy over here. Believe me when I tell you if you don't give him some money real soon; he'll be upset. When he gets upset, he acts out. Right now, he's focused on you. It could be very bad for a CIA cadet like you."

Paul says, "Forget payroll. I'm sure there's a mental health professional somewhere willing to provide the help all of you require."

Jake goes toward Paul and tries to hit him. Paul moves his head and Jake misses. Seth then grabs Paul from behind and tries to throw him down. Paul breaks free and simply stumbles. He then turns to face Jake. Paul is getting angry. Jake goes to hit him again. Paul then moves and Jake hits a brick wall. Jake becomes furious and goes to hit Paul one more time. Before this can happen Seth grabs Jake's arm and pulls him away from Paul.

"Remember what we're doing here," says Seth.

Jake breaks free from Seth and says, "Okay, Okay, I remember."

Seth looks at Paul, points to Jake, and says, "Do you see what we're dealing with here? This man is an animal. If I were you, I'd give him some money. I don't know if I can get him to stop if he gets going again."

Paul reaches into his pocket and is horrified when he discovers his money and money clip are missing. He looks over at Ruby who is waving his empty money clip at him and smiling.

"Looking for this Mr. CIA Cadet?" says Ruby.

Paul yells, "You bitch."

Paul lunges toward the money clip, but Ruby pulls it out of his reach. Jake grabs Paul and pushes him into a pile of boxes. Paul's face hits the corner of a dumpster. He gets up and there is blood coming from his mouth. Paul staggers a bit.

Seth goes over to Paul and says, "I suggest you not call the tough guy's sister a bitch. Their family does not like such words being used to describe this lovely lady."

Paul wipes some blood from the corner of his mouth and says, "Where is this family from? The psych ward at a local penitentiary?"

He then puts up his fists. He is now ready to fight with Jake. Footsteps are suddenly heard behind them. Dennis, Jane, and Peter are running down the alley. Peter yells, "Hey, stop it. Let him go. Leave him alone."

When they get to Paul, the three of them stand in front of him.

Jake laughs and says, "Look what we have here. The cavalry has arrived."

Seth yells, "Get the hell out of here you cadet assholes. This isn't any of your business."

Dennis and Jane turn toward Paul to see if he's okay.

Paul waves them off and says, "I'm fine, I'm okay, I don't need any help."

Peter stands in front of Paul as he faces Jake, Seth, and Ruby. He says, "Ah, but it is our business. You see this happens to be a cadet from our academy that you've been beating up. You know we can't let that happen."

Paul says, "Attempting to beat up and failing would be more accurate."

"Quiet," yells Jane.

Seth says, "You don't know what you're dealing with here asshole. You need to leave this alone."

Peter turns back toward Paul and says, "Come on cadet. Time to go back to the academy. These lowlifes have had enough fun at your expense for one night."

Paul and Peter start to walk down the alley, but they're stopped by Seth. Seth tries to hit Peter Barnett. Peter easily blocks the punch and hits him a few times before Seth falls back into a pile of boxes. Paul tries again to get the money clip from Ruby but Jake grabs him and spins him around. Paul is about to kick Jake when Dennis Martinez and Jane Westin quickly come over. Jake starts fighting with Dennis Martinez. Peter grabs Jake from behind and throws him to the ground. Ruby tries to attack Jane but is quickly hit and knocked to the ground. None of them realize Paul is feeling upset because there is nobody left for him to fight.

Suddenly a car horn is heard. They all stop and look at the limousine at the end of the alley. A window comes down and an arm comes out and motions toward the limousine. Seth, Jake, and Ruby run down the alley toward the limousine. When they reach it, a door opens, and they get in. The limousine then quickly speeds off.

Paul says, "What in the hell just happened?"

Peter points to the limousine and says, " That was Mr. Dean's cadet welcoming committee."

Paul says, "The leadership members of that committee are obviously not very competent at their jobs. I don't feel at all welcome. There are some serious management issues within that organization. Who is this Mr. Dean?"

"He's one crazy asshole who got kicked out of the academy years ago. Now he hates the academy and every cadet who goes there. He causes a lot of problems for cadets as well as the academy. Mr. Dean has never gotten physical with one of us cadets before," says Dennis.

"Dean managed to become wealthy after he left the academy. He now owns just about everything in this town including the cops. The academy is probably the only thing he doesn't own. He always tries to buy it. See, how it is up to us cadets to take care of our own around here," says Jane.

"We'll sue. I'll contact my family's attorney immediately," says Paul.

All of them start walking toward the end of the alley.

Peter chuckles and says, "Forget it, Wildman. There are something like fifteen lawsuits between Dean and the academy. One more won't make any difference to this guy."

They get to the end of the alley and start walking down the street toward the academy bus. Paul moves ahead of the group and walks backward facing them. He is smiling and seems excited.

"I want to thank all of you for what you did for me tonight. That was something. I'm going to contact my family and make certain each of you is properly compensated for your efforts. How about that?" says Paul.

The others exchange glances. The expressions on their faces reveal how they are disgusted by what Paul has suggested.

Paul notices their somber expressions. He is confused and says, "What? What's wrong?"

"We don't want your money asshole. I know you're new here at the academy, but you don't seem to realize how much you just insulted us," says Dennis.

Paul says, "How did I insult anyone? What you guys did is worthy of compensation. I think it's only fair."

"We're not about money. We don't do things for each other because of money. You're a cadet. You're one of us. We always take care of our own. You need to learn that is how it is among cadets. We yell, scream, and can be mean to one another. It doesn't matter because we are always there for each other when it matters," says Jane.

"Loyalty is the first lesson you learn about being a cadet at the academy," says Peter.

They get to the street and start walking toward the academy bus waiting in the distance.

"I apologize. I didn't mean to insult anyone. Do any of you have an idea how I could go about getting back my money clip? It's gold and was given to me by my grandfather," says Paul.

Dennis says, "Just forget about it. Dean's jerks have it now. Who knows what they'll do with it?"

"Consider it the price of a lesson in trusting females you don't know," says Jane.

Paul says, "Whoever says the cost of an education is out of control has no idea how right they are about it."

"You'll be okay," says Peter.

"Would this be an inappropriate time to suggest we all think about the tremendous business potential this experience has sent our way? Think about it. A cadet security firm. We could get contracts with the families of the cadets attending the academy and offer to provide protection for their kids when they're in town. I think the earning potential is off the charts. What do you say?" Paul says.

Dennis, Peter, and Jane look at one another and start laughing. They reach the academy bus and get on.

"I don't think any of us are thinking beyond finishing our time at the academy," says Jane.

"I'm serious. With your fighting skills and my entrepreneurial abilities, we could go far."

"It's not about making money," says Dennis.

"Well, if there comes a time when it is about the money, you let me know. I think this is a great money-making opportunity for all of us."

After all the cadets are on the bus, it leaves town and heads toward the academy. The cadets are talking to one another as the bus travels down a road. Most are thinking of things they have to get ready for the next day. Paul is wondering who he could get to join his cadet security business. He thinks Dennis, Peter, and Jane are all serious considerations for his inner circle.

# Chapter 10

## *A Big Fish In A Little Pond*

In the days following the incident in the alley, Paul decides to work hard at being a good cadet and conform to life at the academy. He is now marching in step with the other cadets when they go from class to class. Paul is saluting superior officers and using the word 'sir' when addressing them. He now eats the food at the mess hall and no longer complains about the lousy conditions.

The anger caused by the loss of his gold money clip still hasn't left Paul. He is outraged at how it was taken from him. Thinking of ways to get it back is always beneath the surface of his thoughts. Paul is very angry from his face having some bruising after his fall in the alley. He misses driving his sports car and perfecting his method for getting desired responses from people. Paul does everything possible to not dwell on the good times from his past. It only makes his present situation more difficult to endure.

* * * * * * *

It is a nice day as Paul and Dennis are walking on the academy grounds toward the mess hall. When Paul looks back, he notices something shocking at the entrance to the academy. There is a limousine turning onto the academy's driveway. It goes to the front of the academy's main building and stops. He realizes this is the limousine from the alley. Paul can barely control his anger. He starts walking toward it.

Dennis stops him and says, "Don't go over to that limousine. It is owned by Mr. Dean. He takes great pleasure in doing things to cadets. I'm telling you nothing good can come from confronting him right now."

"What is he doing here at the academy? I can't get it out of my mind how Dean had his people attack me, take my money, and money clip. Nobody does that to a Wildman and gets away with it."

Paul tells himself he has no fear of this Mr. Dean person the other cadets talk about so much. He knows the Wildman family has easily crushed such individuals. Paul is going to get his gold money clip back one way or another.

"Don't do this, it's a mistake," says Dennis.

"I'm not afraid of this asshole. All I want to do is discuss how to get my gold money clip back. Besides that, he needs to know his model of limousine is old and has an extremely low resale value as well as a poor safety rating," says Paul.

Paul leaves Dennis and walks toward the limousine. Dennis Martinez shakes his head and slowly follows. The driver of the limousine is not aware Dennis and Paul are approaching. He gets out and goes to the rear door. When he opens it, a fifty-five-year-old man with light brown skin wearing a bright white suit emerges. He has on sunglasses and a wide-brim hat. In one hand, he is holding a white walking stick and in the other, he's holding an unlit cigar that he puts in his mouth. When he notices Paul and Dennis approaching, the man just smiles. He takes off his sunglasses to reveal dark piercing eyes. He removes the cigar from his mouth and smiles.

Dennis whispers, "That is Mr. Dean. You better be careful. He can be a lot of trouble."

"I can also be a lot of trouble," says Paul.

When Paul and Dennis get close, Mr. Dean calmly looks at them.

"Well if it isn't the two delinquents from the alley. Are you here to thank me for keeping the victims of your violence from filing assault charges against you with the local authorities?" says Mr. Dean.

Dennis's face gets tight and his hands form fists as he pushes Paul out of the way, walks up to Mr. Dean, and says, "You need to quit doing things to us cadets. You took something from my friend here, and he just wants it back. Do you understand?"

Mr. Dean laughs and then takes his walking stick and points to the bruise on Paul's face.

"I think that white boys always look better with a few bruises on their faces. Don't you agree?" says Mr. Dean.

Paul goes past Dennis, gets face to face with Mr. Dean, and says, "I want my gold money clip back. I know your bitch Ruby stole it. You can have the money just give me back my money clip."

Mr. Dean looks around and takes out Paul's money clip from his pocket. He closely watches Paul's reaction. Paul tries to take the money clip and Mr. Dean quickly closes his hand and puts the money clip back into his pocket.

"Do you mean a money clip like this one? I don't know how I could have come by it. Alas, I think I may have forgotten. If your money clip is like this one, I will keep an eye out for it."

Paul yells, "That's my money clip you asshole. Why don't you take the money that was in it and get a decent image consultant? This urban pimp look and cigar makes you seem like a pathetic Fidel Castro wannabe."

Mr. Dean's face shows anger, but then he smiles and says, "Unfortunately, this can't possibly be your money clip. I remember now. It was given to me as a present from a very special employee. It has such sentimental value."

Paul leans into Mr. Dean but Dennis holds him back. Paul then starts talking in a low voice.

"Look Dean, you have no idea who you're messing with here. I am Paul J. Wildman. My family's business is the Wildman Holdings Group. I'm sure you've heard about us and if not; you can read all about us in any national business magazine. Do you know what that means?"

Mr. Dean steps back, puts his unlighted cigar in his mouth, lights it, takes a few puffs, and blows smoke toward Paul's face. Paul begins coughing.

"Thank you for telling me about your family's genealogy and business history, but I already know about it. Now, let me introduce myself. I am Julio Antonio Dean. I own this town. I'm the proverbial big fish in this small pond. Unfortunately for you, right now, you're in my pond, and I call the shots," says Mr. Dean.

"Name your price for the money clip," says Paul.

Mr. Dean laughs and says, "This is not about money. How could I put a price on something that has such sentimental value to me?"

Mr. Dean takes out the money clip and watches Paul get angry as he looks at it. Mr. Dean chuckles, then suddenly closes his hand and once again puts it back into his pocket.

Paul says, "I hope you know this doesn't end here."

"I am so sorry I can't help you, but the money clip is not for sale at any price."

"Why don't you just give him back the money clip? It was given to him by his grandfather," says Dennis.

Mr. Dean looks at Dennis Martinez and can't hide his disgust.

"Look at this, a Puerto Rican who actually thinks he says something a fellow human being would want to hear," says Mr. Dean.

"Yeah, well I heard your mother was from Mexico," says Dennis.

Mr. Dean says, "Yes, she was and my father was from the Bahamas. Why don't you just go back to Puerto Rico and become a rum bum like most of your people?"

Dennis starts yelling expletives in Spanish and lunges toward Mr. Dean, but Paul stops him.

Paul speaks in a calm voice to Dennis and says, "Okay, we've brought our grievances to Mr. Dean, and he's rejected our offers for an amicable solution in two languages. You are one the best cadets at this academy, and as such, you should not even consider becoming violent with this worthless piece of crap."

Mr. Dean yells, "You set him straight white boy."

Paul lets go of Dennis. He stands in front of Mr. Dean and says, "I, on the other hand, am nothing more than a rich asshole who cares about nothing but his money, himself, and owns a sports car."

Paul then quickly lunges at Mr. Dean. The driver grabs Paul and struggles to control him. Dennis helps with the struggle to keep Paul away from Mr. Dean. As they keep Paul away, Mr. Dean calmly smokes his cigar and laughs.

hey continue to struggle and Paul yells, "Fuck you, you cigar-chomping, Mexi-Bahamian bastard."

Everything stops when a voice of authority is heard yelling, "At ease cadets. Stand down immediately."

Everybody stops to watch General Thomas Loren walk up to them. He stands in front of Dennis and Paul.

"Please explain to me just what in the hell is going on here cadets?" says General Thomas Loren.

Paul breaks free from Dennis and the limousine driver. He calmly straightens out his uniform.

He looks at General Thomas Loren, and says, "I checked the calendar today and discovered it's Brawl with Mexi-Bahamian Bastard Day. I'm celebrating."

Mr. Dean looks at General Thomas Loren.

"General Loren, I come here in good faith to discuss our ongoing legal issues, and I end up being insulted and having my driver attacked by your cadets. I hope you know I'm leaving this instant. I have no desire to discuss anything while facing such hostility at this academy," says Mr. Dean.

Mr. Dean gets back into his limousine as General Loren looks at Paul and Dennis. The driver gets back into the limousine and it heads toward the academy's front gate.

"Explain yourselves cadets, and it had better be good," says General Loren.

Dennis says, "Sir, some guys who work for Dean jumped Cadet Wildman the other night. They took a gold money clip given to him by his grandfather. He was just trying to get it back."

General Loren says, "Is this true Wildman?

Paul shrugs his shoulders.

"Yeah, and for the record, I was willing to offer a decent sum of money for the return of my money clip. When he didn't want my money, what was I supposed to do? Offer him a ride in my sports car? I don't think that would have worked."

General Loren looks at Paul and then at Dennis. He is very upset as he tries to speak but stops himself.

General Loren suddenly says, "I don't think either of you realizes what you've just done. Wildman, I want you to report to James Hall tonight at Twenty hundred hours for punishment. Is that understood?" says General Loren.

Paul stands straight and says, "I will be there sir."

General Loren seems disgusted by Paul.

He looks at Dennis who is also standing at attention and says, "When I made him your roommate Cadet Martinez, I had hoped you would be a good influence on him. I hate to think that what has happened is him becoming a bad influence on you. You know better. I'm very disappointed in you Cadet Martinez."

"Sir, I am sorry to have disappointed you."

General Loren then turns and walks back to the main building without saying another word.

Paul looks at Dennis and says, "What's James Hall?"

"It's where they send cadets who are discipline problems. It is a lot of exercising and crazy stuff."

"Ah, no big deal, right?"

"Depends on the mood of Sergeant Samson."

"Not a problem. I'll just use the old Wildman charm on him. How hard could it possibly be?"

Dennis starts laughing. As they resume their walk to the mess hall, Paul thinks about what just happened. He realizes this is the first time he was ever angry enough to become physically violent with someone in public. Paul realizes his experiences here at the academy are making him different. He tells himself maybe this change will be a good thing.

# Chapter 11

## *Military Discipline*

Being ordered to go to James Hall in the evening is something every cadet at Saint Michael's Military Academy tries to avoid. It is a physical and psychological experience proven effective in getting cadets to obey all the academy rules, regulations, and not challenge authority.

Some cadets think less of a person who has been required to go to James Hall for discipline. It is a label of being a cadet whose behavior is a problem. At the academy, if one cadet is a problem, his entire squad may have to pay the price for their bad behavior. Paul J. Wildman has no idea what awaits him. Upon seeing the large and impressive building where the punishment will be held, Paul laughs to himself and wonders if it might be a place where a secret academy spa is hidden.

Once inside James Hall, he and other cadets are put into formation and marched into a gymnasium. Once in place, all of them stand at attention and look straight ahead with blank stares trying not to think about what will soon happen. They all have on shorts, a plain white T-shirt and tennis shoes. A very muscular forty-one-year-old man is walking back and forth in front of them. He is dressed the same way as the cadets and is known as Sergeant Samson. All cadets at the academy have heard the horror stories of how Sergeant Samson is tough during these discipline classes. It is said he has made the toughest cadets cry and leave the academy.

As Sergeant Samson walks back and forth in front of the expressionless cadets he appears angry and very intense. Behind Sergeant Samson are senior cadets who will help him with the evening's festivities. His expression suddenly turns to an angry scowl.

"Each of you little shitbags is at my party tonight because you seem to have a problem obeying academy rules and regulations. Tonight will be just a little taste of what you get when you don't grasp the concept of obeying the rules," says Sergeant Samson.

He notices Paul looking around and not paying attention. Sergeant Samson quickly turns, walks up to Paul, and leans so close to his face their noses almost touch.

He screams, "Do you understand what I'm talking about you dumb, stupid, ugly-looking piece of shit?"

Paul struggles to hide the fact he's disgusted. He turns his face away from Sergeant Samson. Taking his hand, Sergeant Samson moves Paul's face, so they are again looking straight at one another.

"What in the hell is the matter with you little boy? I want you to tell me what's upsetting your bonehead ass," says Sergeant Samson.

Paul responds, "Sir, ah, yeah, it's just obvious from my position at this moment you like to smoke cigars and drink a lot of coffee and might need to improve your oral hygiene."

Does 'da 'widdle "bitty 'baby 'boy 'not 'like 'da smell of my big 'ole 'nasty cigars and coffee?"

"Well sir, this 'widdle, 'bitty baby boy believes enjoying a good cigar is an absolutely wonderful thing. Coffee is great. The problem is right now the 'widdle, 'bitty baby boy is hoping your breath, that appears to have been corrupted by cheap cigars and store brand coffee, doesn't give him acne, or tobacco poisoning, or something."

Thomas Samson takes a deep breath, opens his mouth wide, and exhales into Paul's face. Paul groans and starts coughing.

Sergeant Samson points to the floor and says, "Now drop and give me twenty push-ups 'widdle, 'bitty baby boy asshole."

Paul is confused.

He says, "Push-ups? Twenty of them right now? I guess you're serious about this? Is this negotiable?"

"You'll do this unless the 'widdle, 'bitty baby boy wants me to breathe some more of my nasty, wasty, cheap cigar and store brand smelling breath on him."

"And if I refuse?"

Sergeant Samson yells, "If you don't do what I tell you tonight, then get your sad, stupid, ugly ass out of my academy, 'cause if you don't finish this, you're finished with this academy. You'll be out of here faster than a toupee in a hurricane. Do you understand asshole?"

Thomas Samson points at the front door. Paul takes one step toward the door and sees a vision of his father and grandfather pointing at him and laughing. Paul blinks his eyes and the vision is gone. He then sees a vision of his mother with a look of disappointment caused by him. He turns back and looks at Sergeant Samson with an expression of determination. Paul slowly gets down and starts doing push-ups.

Sergeant Samson smiles and starts to walk back and forth in front of the other cadets yelling, "That's more like it. As for the rest of you pieces of shit, we're going to have an exercise party, a weapon drilling party, and then a little special party at the end. I'm sure you'll love all the festivities I have planned for you. Party, party, party my little shitheads."

Paul finishes doing the push-ups. When he stands up, his face is red, and he's breathing heavily.

Sergeant Samson then says, "I want all of you to do as I do starting now."

He then gets down and starts doing push-ups. The senior cadets behind Sergeant Samson start doing push-ups. Paul groans and slowly gets down and starts doing more push-ups.

After this, Sergeant Samson has the cadets do various exercises. They are then required to hold rifles and move them as Sergeant Samson is moving a rifle in front of them. They are then required to run around the gymnasium and stop every so often to do more push-ups.

As they are running, the senior cadets are running beside the other cadets. They are yelling as well as swearing at them and saying insulting things. It is believed this will separate those who have strong minds and can learn to discipline themselves from those who can't. Two cadets fall out and run to buckets placed in the gymnasium and lose their dinner.

Paul is not having any problems. At first, one senior cadet is beside him yelling and screaming. Then two and eventually three senior cadets are running beside Paul. They are saying things to demean him, threaten him, and degrade him. Breaking Paul and making him fall out is becoming important to the senior cadets.

What is being said to Paul by the senior cadets doesn't bother him. Being yelled at, screamed at, and having the most horrible things said to him is nothing new to Paul. He has trained himself to ignore it. When Paul was younger, he saw the top salesperson for his family's company get screamed at by customers. Paul asked the salesperson why he wasn't upset. He told Paul everyone gets to choose what has power over them. He refused to let words said by others have power over him. It inspired Paul to remain calm no matter what is said to him. This is frustrating the senior cadets yelling at him. Some are screaming at him so much they are struggling to not strain their voices. Paul is hiding his pleasure at seeing their frustration.

After a few hours of this, Paul and the other cadets find themselves standing at attention in the same spot where they started. All of them are out of breath. Their faces are red, and they're all sweating profusely. Sergeant Samson gives each of the cadets a cup of soapy water and a toothbrush. He is smiling as sweat rolls down his face.

Sergeant Samson starts to walk back and forth in front of the cadets and says, "For the last and best part of our entertainment pleasure tonight, you will be cleaning the gymnasium floor with the party favors you've just been given."

All the cadets look down at the water and then at each other. They seem bewildered. Paul shakes his head and is angry. He raises his hand holding the toothbrush.

"Sergeant Samson quickly walks over to him and yells, "What? What could you possibly want at this time? Is there something the 'widdle, 'bitty baby boy doesn't understand?"

"Sir, I'm not sure you're aware of it or not, but a toothbrush in most parts of the civilized world are items used for dental hygiene, not gymnasium floor cleaning."

Paul clears his throat as Sergeant Samson's face becomes red with rage.

Sergeant Samson gets nose to nose with Paul and screams, "They're used for whatever purpose I damn well say they're used for. Do you understand this my 'widdle, 'bitty baby boy cadet?"

Paul makes a fist as if he's about to hit Sergeant Samson. The two look at each other with rage showing on their faces. Suddenly, Paul lets out a huge sigh and appears calm. He tells himself he can't let his father and grandfather win.

He says, "Yes sir."

Sergeant Samson then resumes walking back and forth in front of the cadets and says, "All of you useless pieces of shit get down and start scrubbing this damn gym floor with the party favors you've just been provided. I don't want to hear any complaining. If I hear one person complain, I will give all of you back your rifles, and we'll have some more fun with them."

The bewildered cadets look at each other with confused expressions. They slowly get down on their hands and knees and start scrubbing the gymnasium floor with their toothbrushes. Paul tries to hide his anger. He thinks it is time for him to do something completely unexpected. Paul begins singing in a deep voice as other cadets try to hide their laughter when hearing him.

Paul is singing, "Swing low, sweet chariot, coming for to carry me home, swing low, sweet chariot coming for to carry me home."

Sergeant Samson goes over to Paul and looks at him as if he's disgusted. Paul stops singing and Sergeant Samson walks away. Paul then starts whistling very softly.

Paul doesn't realize how his behavior this night gives him a great reputation among the other cadets. They admire how he didn't break no matter how Sergeant Samson and the senior cadets tried. Paul is now considered someone who is tough. He has earned the respect of many cadets. After this night more cadets stop and talk to Paul. When they see him, cadets often acknowledge him and include Paul in more things. Paul is confused by this new attention. He just assumes they probably learned about his family's wealth or they discovered he drives a sports car.

# Chapter 12

## *An Unexpected Turn of Events*

Paul has unknowingly developed a mental and emotional connection with the academy and other cadets. As he gets ready in the morning, he looks out of his window at the academy grounds. There are many cadets marching in formation going to class, a work detail, or some other destination. It's a sight that calms him. There are also other cadets walking and holding books as they make their way to the library or some other place. He now feels part of life at the military school. Paul is feeling good about himself. He is starting to believe he'll survive his time at the academy.

Paul is confident that when he's done at the academy, he will make money like he did when at the different colleges. He doesn't like being dependent on his controlling father and grandfather to access money in his trust fund. It is a struggle to push the thoughts of them out of his mind. Paul knows giving in to his anger has caused him to do bad things. He knows neither his father nor grandfather has had to face what he is facing at the academy. Thoughts of being stronger than either of them make Paul very optimistic about the future.

After putting on his uniform and making sure every crease is correct on his bed, and everything on the uniform is in accordance with academy regulations, he feels ready for the day. Each morning Paul makes certain his shoes have a nice shine on them, his uniform is correct, and everything is in proper academy order. He looks at himself in the mirror one last time to make certain his uniform is correct. Paul almost doesn't recognize his reflection. It's the first time in his life he can remember feeling real pride in something other than his family's name or money. He is accomplishing something without resorting to lying or cheating. This has never happened with him before.

Dennis walks into the room and notices Paul's bed is made according to academy standards. He looks at Paul's uniform and corrects something. Paul then looks at Dennis and corrects something on his uniform. They both laugh before leaving the room. They are heading to the mess hall for breakfast.

On their way to the mess hall, they see Peter Barnett walking toward them. Dennis and Paul give him a proper military salute. Peter responds with a salute and smiles at Paul. After breakfast, all the cadets stand in formation outside of the mess hall building waiting to march off to their classes.

Peter Barnett comes out and gives the orders for the cadets to begin marching to class. As they go toward the building where classes are being held, a sergeant sees Paul and gives him a thumbs-up for how he is marching. When the sergeant walks away, Paul puts his arms out and does some crazy moves while marching. He stops when another sergeant comes near. The other cadets see this and struggle to hide their laughter.

* * * * * * * *

It's the evening and Paul is in his room studying. It feels strange for him to take studying seriously, but he is finding he likes it. Dennis walks in, stands in place for a minute, and just looks at Paul. After turning his head to look in an opened book on his bed, Paul notices Dennis.

Paul says, "Why are you just standing there looking at me? I don't believe I owe you any money."

Dennis goes over to his standup locker, opens it, and begins changing his clothes.

"You always got to do your bullshit. You can't ever be real. I know you and how you try to act like you're this, I have an insult for everyone and enjoy pissing people off, kind of guy. You want people to think you don't care about anything. I've seen how you've been lately," says Dennis.

"Oh, and how have I been?" says Paul.

"I see you not complaining about things like before, and you're marching, saluting, taking care of your bed and uniform like we supposed to do at the academy. You even doing good in your classes. Face it, Wildman, I think you starting to like being a cadet."

"Nothing could be further from the truth. I'm simply protecting my future financial assets currently being held by my evil father and grandfather. Both of whom have obviously graduated with honors from the school for ruthless financial dictators."

Dennis walks over and nudges Paul on the shoulder with his elbow.

"There you go again with your bullshit. I don't believe you. I think you like it here. You like the mess hall food."

"I like it because that food inspires me with great business ideas. I believe a business I might soon start will be selling antacids to other cadets at a dollar an antacid. I know it's a bit of a serious price markup, but I believe after a mess hall meal, the other cadets will be motivated to pay my price. I'm going to make a fortune."

Paul looks up behind Dennis. He then stands at attention and yells, "Attention on deck."

Dennis has his back to the door. He doesn't see Peter Barnett walk into their room.

"Man, you think you are going to fool me again? You always say that and walk into the room laughing because you fooled me. I ain't falling for that one again," says Dennis.

"He's not trying to fool you this time," says Peter Barnett.

When Dennis turns around, he is shocked. He stands straight up at attention and says, "Sir, I apologize for my indiscretion. It will not happen again, sir."

"At ease cadets," says Peter Barnett.

"Sir, what is the reason for your unexpected and very stealthy visit to our room?" says Paul.

"There is an emergency meeting for all cadets in the auditorium immediately. You are to put on your uniforms and go there right away," says Peter Barnett.

"Why?" says Paul.

"Because you were told to, that's why. Now carry on, get changed, and get over to the auditorium. I have to inform all of the team leaders," says Peter Barnett.

Peter Barnett turns and walks out of the room.

Dennis is upset and says, "This isn't good."

"What could it be?" says Paul.

"I don't know, but the last time there was an emergency meeting at the auditorium some cadets were found cheating and were thrown out of the academy."

"Is that all it takes to get thrown out of here is a little innocent cheating? I may quit studying immediately."

Dennis laughs and throws a t-shirt at Paul who laughs and throws it back. Paul has Dennis down on his list as a strong consideration for his inner circle.

* * * * * * *

Paul and Dennis get to the auditorium and stand in a long line of cadets who are entering the building. They are all making their way to a long line of seats in the auditorium. Everyone has a solemn expression. Once all the cadets are seated, there is silence.

Dennis looks at Paul and says, "It is going to be something bad. This wasn't scheduled. We're about to hear something awful. I'm afraid it's going to be real bad."

"Relax. What could we possibly hear that would be so bad? Sergeant Samson is the new cook at the mess hall. I admit that would be pretty horrible."

Dennis rolls his eyes at Paul. They both look toward the stage in the front of the auditorium where Peter Barnett walks to a podium. He is motioning for a few standing cadets to quickly find a seat. When the auditorium is quiet, he looks to his left and then back toward the cadets sitting in the audience.

Peter yells, "Cadets, attention on deck."

All the cadets get up and stand at attention. General Thomas Loren walks onto the stage. When he reaches the podium, General Thomas Loren and Peter Barnett exchange salutes. Peter Barnett turns, walks to a chair on the stage in military fashion, and sits down. Thomas Loren motions for the cadets to sit down.

"At ease cadets. Please sit down. Good evening to all of you. It is a pleasure to see everyone gathered in one spot. I wish the reason you were here right now would be for good news. Unfortunately, that is not the case. It appears a local business organization has won a court case against the academy. They now have the legal right to seize our school's property. To avoid any further legal and financial difficulties our governing board has agreed to close Saint Michael's Military Academy effective at the end of this school year. This decision is final pending any drastic events that would change the situation. I know many of you will be deeply upset by this news. I hope you will face this challenge in your life with the same courage and conviction you have used while a cadet here at Saint Michael's Military Academy. That is all and thank you," says General Thomas Loren.

Peter Barnett walks up next to the podium. Peter Barnett faces General Thomas Loren and salutes him. General Thomas Loren then turns and walks to the back of the stage.

Peter yells, "Cadets, attention."

All the cadets get up and stand at attention.

Peter Barnett goes over to the podium and says, "Cadets, dismissed."

The cadets begin to slowly make their way out of the auditorium.

Dennis whispers to Paul and says, "I knew this would be awful. This is bad for me. This is really bad for me."

Paul doesn't say a word. In his mind, he is thinking this may be some of the best news he's heard since he was eighteen and given access to his trust fund. All he has to do now is deal with this academy stuff until the school year is over. Then he'll be free. His mother will be happy since he lasted the school year. He can tell his father and grandfather he has proven he can handle anything they throw at him. Nobody will suggest he return to an academy that is closed. Paul remains quiet and struggles to hide his smile. The attitude he had before attending the academy is trying to take control of him.

* * * * * * * *

The next morning in the mess hall most of the cadets eating breakfast are quiet. There is very little conversation. Depression seems to be felt by everyone. Paul and Dennis are sitting at a table by themselves. Paul is happily eating as Dennis only plays with his food.

Paul leans over to Dennis and whispers, "I don't know why everyone is so upset. I mean going to a new school isn't that big of a deal. Trust me when I tell you, I know all about going to new schools. This little turn of events means I get to keep my money and no longer have to worry about being sent back here. It's a great day."

Dennis Martinez throws down his fork on his plate.

He looks at Paul and says, "You just don't get it, do you?"

"Get what?"

"You leave here and you go back to your rich world and drive your sports car. Do you have any idea of the world some cadets are going back to?"

"I don't know. It's none of my business. I just assumed everyone here was wealthy."

"Sometimes you can really be an asshole. Look around at the cadets here. We're not the best of the best like West Point or any of those other government-run military schools. This is a private academy that provides a great scholarship program for kids with difficult lives. Every scholarship cadet who attends here has issues."

"So? What do you want from me?"

Dennis points to a cadet eating who has scars on his face.

"Look at Spivey over there. Born addicted to drugs. His mother put cigarettes out on his face when he was a baby. In all kinds of trouble before he got here. Now he's one of our best."

Dennis points to a female cadet.

"Helen over there ran away from her foster home to keep from getting raped by the drunk man her mother let live in their house. She'll tell you how this place is better than foster care. There are a lot of rich people here but there are also many who have some kind of story. Most of these stories don't involve being rich."

Paul shrugs his shoulders and says, "Why are you telling me this?"

"Because you need to know what this place means to some of us. Like a Puerto Rican boy so deep into gang life, his relatives thought he'd die before he reached eighteen. Now, look at me. I'm in the running to be named this year's best cadet. How about that rich kid?"

"I'm sorry if I upset you. But this is how I feel about it."

"That's okay. You are just a typical rich person who doesn't know what it's like to not be rich. Guess what? Most people aren't. If your friends saw where I come from, I bet they'd think I was a criminal. When I wear the same uniform as someone like you, people will forget where I come from and give me respect. Going to this school makes me, and other scholarship cadets like me, so proud."

"You graduate this year. How does this cause you trouble?"

"My little brother wanted so badly to come here and be a cadet. Now, he can't. When you put this place down, it feels personal."

"There's nothing I can do for any of you. I'll feel sorry for you if that's what you want."

Dennis sighs then stands up and takes his tray.

Before he leaves, Dennis turns back to Paul and says, "You didn't feel sorry for us the night we kept Dean's thugs from giving you a serious beating. It was us who felt sorry for you that night."

After Dennis leaves, Paul sits at the table brooding.

All of a sudden he slams his fist on the table and yells, "Damn it."

# Chapter 13

## *The Creation of Mr. Dean*

He is born Julio Antonio Dean in a poor section of El Paso, Texas. Julio is the youngest of four boys. The name of Julio's mother is Leticia and his father's name is Montez Rodrigo Dean. His parents are very proud and protective of all their children.

During the early days of his childhood, Julio is a very happy child. He enjoys playing basketball and soccer at the playground across the street from his family's apartment building. Julio has many friends. He easily switches from speaking Spanish to speaking English without much effort. Julio is often asked to translate for his mother and his other Spanish-speaking relatives. He is thought of as a good boy by his family. They also consider him to be nothing but average in all aspects of his life. Julio gets average grades; he is average in sports and is even average when it comes to his height and weight.

Julio does excel in one thing that amazes other children and adults. He can think through situations and create detailed steps to achieve future goals. It is more than thinking about how to accomplish something. Julio can make detailed plans in his mind. He has the patience and discipline at a young age to follow his ideas to completion. It does not matter the length of time required. This ability makes him stand out among other children.

At the beginning of the school year, he is tasked by his family as the one who makes plans for the holiday breaks that will occur. Julio always has a list of things for his family to do and figures out ways to make them happen. Most times his family has no idea what they should do, so they usually do the things Julio suggests. This gives him a special place in his family. Julio realizes it also gives him the confidence to make things happen in other areas of his life.

Most people believe Julio has been born with this gift. If any of them had taken the time to ask Julio, he would have told them it was not a gift. It is something he learned from his grandfather. Julio and his family referred to his grandfather as Yayo. This is a man who became wealthy over a short time on his own and then lost it just as quickly. His failure is not due to anything he has done wrong. Julio's grandfather was cheated out of his business by his two business partners. These men presented a falsified copy of their partnership agreement to a court. The new one gave them the power to eliminate Julio's grandfather from the business and pay him nothing. His grandfather protested but could not prove to the court that his two former partners had presented a falsified copy of their agreement.

This is when Julio's grandfather began focusing all his energy on devising a plan for revenge. It would take time, but he was determined to one day get the company back and kick out the two partners who cheated him.

His desire and determination for revenge consumed the grandfather daily. Success came a little bit at a time. It took him a few years to achieve his goal. Julio's grandfather started a competing business. It took patience, but he is eventually in a position to purchase his old business and combine it with his new one. His old partners learn too late they are unable to successfully operate their business without Julio's grandfather. Their clients start leaving and going to the grandfather's new business. When his old partners apologize and ask for his forgiveness, Julio's grandfather laughs at them. They are very angry. The two former partners leave the last meeting with Julio's grandfather claiming they will get their own revenge. In a few weeks, someone causes a fire that destroys the business of Julio's grandfather, but he doesn't care. He takes the insurance money and does not rebuild the business. Once he discovers who has started the fire, he notifies the authorities. He provides them with all of the proof they need. His two former partners are convicted of arson. Julio's grandfather now has money and none of the worries that go with having a business. He is also able to see those who had done him wrong serve time in jail. Julio's grandfather is satisfied with what happened and considers his revenge to be complete.

Julio watched and learned a lot as Yayo worked to get revenge. It is something his grandfather shared with nobody else but Julio. He paid special attention to the things Yayo did to make it happen. Julio helped his grandfather for years with his revenge. He discovered how to do things one step at a time. He learned from Yayo how to maintain focus on his goal. He tells Julio revenge comes to all who plan, execute, and wait. His grandfather inspired him to make detailed plans and to carefully prepare for things in the future.

*  *  *  *  *  *  *  *

Many years ago, Saint Michael's Military Academy was a place that had the prestige and respect of other military academies around the country. The majority of young people who attended it had families that paid all the expenses associated with being a cadet at Saint Michael's. The academy's board of governors eventually decided to offer scholarships to young boys and girls whose families didn't have the financial resources to attend it. These scholarships would be awarded based on academic achievement, physical ability, and moral character. These same standards did not apply to those who had families able to pay the costs of being a cadet at Saint Michael's Military Academy. This double standard created an environment of resentment toward the scholarship students from those who had parents able to pay for a Saint Michael's Military Academy education.

One young man who attended Saint Michael's Military Academy on a scholarship was Julio Antonio Dean. The choice for a scholarship came down to him and two other young boys from his school. Julio frightens one of the boys away from wanting to attend the academy. He tells the young man many horror stories about military life, and the boy believes him. Julio lies and says he knows this is what happens because he has relatives who previously had been cadets at the academy. The boy drops out of the competition for the scholarship. Julio then only has to deal with one other boy. He realizes it will be difficult but not impossible to eliminate him from the competition. Julio develops a plan to get this boy to drop out of the scholarship competition.

Julio knows the boy has a crush on a girl. He also knows this girl really likes him. The girl means absolutely nothing to Julio. He decides to talk the girl into pretending she likes the boy who is his competition for the scholarship. After the girl gets the boy interested in her, Julio lets the boy know he will not be able to see her when attending the academy. He tells the boy when he is at the academy another young man will certainly get his girlfriend. Julio then tells the boy he could lose the girl forever. The young boy drops out of the scholarship competition. This results in Julio being awarded the academy scholarship.

On the day before he leaves for Saint Michael's Military Academy, the girl who had such strong feelings for Julio comes to see him. She feels certain he will now love her since she has done what he wanted with the other young boy. Julio laughs at the girl. He tells her to go back to her new boyfriend. Her heart is broken. She yells and screams that she will tell the boy what Julio has done. Julio shrugs his shoulders and tells her he doesn't care. He got what he wanted. She asks Julio why he has done this to her. Julio tells her it doesn't matter. He will soon be at the academy. She now has this young man all to herself with his blessings. Julio's friends come to save him as the girl begins hitting him and swearing. After Julio walks away, she sits down on the ground and cries.

* * * * * * *

During his first year at the academy, Julio does well. His grades and performance in all areas are considered average. Julio feels this is a success for him. Being a cadet is not easy for anyone. He excels at military tactics and making mission plans. Julio continues this level of performance for the first two years.

Julio's time at the academy often consists of spending time with the other scholarship cadets. The non-scholarship cadets often act as if they believe they are smarter and better than the scholarship cadets. Julio knows this is not true and simply tolerates their behavior. He is often thinking of the plans he has made for when he is done. An academy education will open many doors in the business world for him. During his junior year at the academy, his life is forever changed. Nobody who is involved with what happens anticipates the outcome. Young people seldom think of consequences.

It starts with the only cadet at the academy Julio does not like; his name is Thomas Loren. The future academy Commandant is a wealthy kid who has a big ego. Thomas Loren doesn't excel at anything but is average or below in most things. The reason for this is he never gives his full effort. Thomas Loren knows his parents can pay his tuition at the academy. They also contribute quite a bit of money to the new building fund and other organizations designed to get money for the academy. Thomas Loren believes he can do anything he wants at the academy without the worry of ever facing consequences. He doesn't realize Julio is not a person to be pushed around. Julio thinks of himself as a person who may lose a battle, but he will always win the war.

* * * * * * * *

It is a typical day at the academy when Julio is stopped in a hallway by Thomas Loren. Thomas recently had his girlfriend break up with him. He has also been yelled at by his father because his grades are nothing but average or below. Thomas is in a very bad mood.

Since he is in his last year as a cadet, Thomas is a senior cadet. It is the right of all senior cadets to stop any underclassmen and ask them questions. The questions have to be about the rules of the academy and nothing more. Julio is walking down the hallway when Thomas spots him. He stands in front of Julio and begins asking him questions about the rules and regulations of the academy. Julio calmly answers all of them.

Thomas yells, "Do you think you know everything, scholarship cadet?"

"Sir, I know what all underclassmen cadets are required to know," responds Julio.

"Is that so? Do you know what it states in the cadet handbook in section 28 paragraph 3?

"Sir, there is no section 28. It only has 27 sections."

"Wrong, the cadet handbook will be updated with a new section this coming year. It will be section 28. If you would have paid attention to the latest memos from the administration, you would have known that fact."

"Sir, when was the latest memo from the administration sent?"

"I don't know. I do know it was sent and cadets are responsible for knowing about it."

"Sir, if you saw it, please tell me what is in it."

"That's not my job. Scholarship cadets are required to know everything about the cadet handbook like paying cadets. Do we understand one another?"

Julio is angry. He knows Thomas is just making his life difficult for no reason. Julio hopes this will be over soon.

"Yes sir."

"I don't like your attitude, scholarship cadet. It has earned you a trip to James Hall tonight to enjoy the nightly fun festivities that take place there."

"Sir, I didn't do anything wrong."

"I don't think you are in a position to argue with me. Be there tonight, your name will be on the list. Do we understand one another?"

Julio struggled with his anger, but he calmly said, "Yes sir."

Thomas walks away feeling relief from some of the anger and frustration he was feeling. Julio begins to plan his revenge against Thomas. He has many ideas.

* * * * * * *

When at James Hall for his punishment, Julio looks around at the other cadets. All of them, with one exception, are scholarship students. This is the first time in the years he has been at Saint Michael's Military Academy, Julio has been punished for anything. He keeps thinking of how Thomas will have to pay for doing this to him. Revenge will not just be for him but for all the other scholarship students who have been treated unfairly.

He doesn't complain about all the exercises he and the others are forced to endure during the night. When they are made to clean the gymnasium floor with a toothbrush, he doesn't complain. When it is all over, Julio is very motivated to get revenge on Thomas Loren.

The first step is to watch Thomas and make mental notes about his activities. Julio carefully asks those who are friends with Thomas about certain past situations. The bad ones where Thomas was involved. In a short time, Julio is aware of the routine and habits of Thomas. He knows bad things Thomas has gotten away with doing. This is information he keeps to himself. It is an essential part of making a plan for his revenge.

# Chapter 14

## *A World of Revenge*

Julio is very angry about being sent to James Hall long after it is over. His mind keeps telling him a terrible injustice had been done to him. He must dedicate himself to obtaining revenge. Yayo would expect nothing less of him. It must not be the type of revenge that is quick and easily forgotten. This will take time and planning. It will be done when the individual who is the focus of the revenge least expects anything to occur. Thomas Loren will pay for his actions toward Julio as well as the other scholarship students.

Julio never talks with anyone about all the things he and the other cadets were forced to do during the night at James Hall. He wants nobody to know what he is feeling. He acts as if it were nothing. There are those who would enjoy him being upset and complaining about it. They would enjoy the sight of him being broken by such an experience. This is a pleasure Julio refuses to give any person. As he and the others were made to clean the gymnasium floor with a toothbrush, Julio struggled to control his anger. After it was all over, he became very focused on getting even with Thomas Loren.

The first thing Julio does is watch Thomas and make mental notes about his routine. Julio also secretly listens to the conversations of all the cadets who are friends with Thomas. He is always just behind them during their time in the mess hall or simply hanging out on the academy grounds. Julio positions himself near their tables when it is time to study. Doing this provides Julio with a significant amount of information about Thomas. In a short time, he becomes aware of the routine and habits of Thomas Loren. He knows some of Thomas' history as well as certain things Thomas likes and dislikes. This is information Julio keeps to himself. It is an essential part of his plan.

Julio is in the library and asks Thomas Loren's roommate for help on a certain subject. The roommate takes a piece of paper and writes some notes to help Julio. Julio thanks him. He is happy to now have a sample of Thomas' roommate's handwriting. Julio will practice writing this note until he learns to write like Thomas Loren's roommate. It is all part of the plan for revenge that is coming together in his mind.

Several weeks after the James Hall incident everyone has forgotten about it. This is when Julio is ready to make his move. A clown wig and makeup are secretly brought into the Academy by him. It is a hideous-looking clown wig. Julio is careful to make sure nobody notices them. They are carefully hidden. After hearing stories about Thomas from his friends, Julio knows Thomas likes to dress up as a clown for children. This is also key to his revenge. Thomas will suspect nothing.

* * * * * * *

It is a Saturday during the early spring and the cadets who don't have duty are free to do as they like. Julio decides this is the day he will put his plan for revenge into action. Julio gets the note he created the night before in the handwriting of Thomas' roommate. He then places it under the door of Thomas Loren's room. It tells Thomas some children are going to be at the academy's main hall after dark. The note describes how the Academy's Commandant has asked if Thomas would greet the children in his cadet uniform dressed as a clown. It is common for people to bring children to see the academy. The note also tells Thomas where a clown wig and makeup are located.

Julio has duty on this particular day. He is responsible for sweeping the hallway outside Thomas' room. A short time after placing the note under the door, Julio hears Thomas laugh and say out loud in his room, "What the hell, I'll do it."

It states in the cadet handbook the cadet uniform is never to be worn in any way other than according to the regulations. Julio smiles at the arrogance of Thomas. A cadet who feels he is above every other cadet and doesn't have to follow the rules.

Julio's grandfather also taught him the power of a rumor. They don't need to be terrible. A rumor only needs to be strong enough so people have the desire to pass it on. Julio knows the cadet who is the biggest gossip at the academy. He simply tells this particular cadet a rumor that cadets need to meet at the main academy hall for some surprise entertainment in the evening. The lights won't be on, but they are to stand in the dark. When the surprise occurs, the lights will then be turned on. Julio says he has no idea if it is true and asks the cadet to not tell anyone until he can confirm it. The gossiping cadet simply smiles and begins telling the other cadets. Julio's plan is now in motion.

* * * * * * *

Later in the evening, Julio watches Thomas as he happily leaves his room and heads to the main academy hall. He has on clown white makeup, a hideous orange clown wig as well as a bright red nose. Thomas is wearing his uniform. Julio moves quickly to the main building and goes through the back door. He turns off the lights. Several cadets are standing in the dark. Some of them are senior cadets. Thomas enters the building and doesn't understand why no lights are on in the main academy hall.

The other cadets can't see who has just entered. Cadets start complaining about it being dark. Julio suggests to a cadet he turn the lights on for just a second. The cadet flips the switch and the main hallway is filled with light.

When the cadets see Thomas wearing his uniform and dressed as a clown, they are shocked. Some cadets start laughing while other cadets begin laughing and pointing at Thomas. Humiliation at this level is not something Thomas has ever experienced during his life. He is starting to get very angry.

Thomas screams, "Will you guys stop laughing? My roommate Allen left me a note that there would be children here, and I was to entertain them."

"Yeah, you are certainly entertaining. You broke a big rule by wearing your uniform," says one cadet.

"Hey, you got a clown jeep you drive around in?" says another cadet.

"Maybe we'll make you the official academy clown. You have the look for it," says another senior cadet.

As they continue to laugh, Thomas is getting angrier.

Thomas yells, "Who set me up? Who did this? You guys know me, and you know my family. Somebody is going to seriously pay for this one way or another."

As Thomas walks around, the cadets continue laughing at him. Thomas is struggling to deal with the comments he hears. He wants to begin hitting every cadet around him. Thomas notices Julio in the back of the hall near the light switch. He is simply smiling and struggling not to laugh. Thomas goes up to Julio and points at him.

"You, you did this. You are going to pay for this you stupid, backward, ignorant, piece of crap, scholarship cadet," says Thomas.

Julio looks at him and smiles.

"I don't know why you would believe I could have done such a thing. I am a mere scholarship cadet. How could a scholarship cadet, such as myself, possess the necessary intelligence and planning skills to have done such a thing? No, you may want to begin your search for a non-scholarship student. I'm sure they are the only ones with the intelligence necessary to pull off such an elaborate scheme as this."

Thomas looks at Julio and his face shows all the anger and rage he is feeling. After turning and heading toward the door, Thomas lets loose a vast array of expletives. The other students simply continue to laugh as Thomas leaves.

* * * * * * * *

Julio is brilliant at making plans. He has proven this on more than one occasion. His problem is a lack of understanding concerning the consequences of his actions. Julio is not able to anticipate what retribution may come his way. Thomas Loren and his family are part of the wealthy class of society. His father regularly plays golf and meets with the academy's Commandant, and other members of the academy's board of directors, in social settings. The Loren family considers the academy Commandant, and his family, to be close friends.

When the news about Thomas Loren's humiliation begins to make its rounds, the academy Commandant reaches out to speak with Thomas. As he struggles to remain calm, Thomas claims he knows it is Julio who did this to him. Many non-scholarship cadets are asked by Thomas to become involved with exposing the person who is guilty of setting him up. They discover it was Julio who purchased a clown wig and makeup at a local store. One of the cadets has a cousin who works at the store and confirms it. Another cadet claims he saw Julio put the note under the door to Thomas Loren's room. They believe it was him, but they have no actual proof.

Julio soon learns someone who has power will use it to get what they want in any situation. The Loren family meets with the academy Commandant's family. It is decided Julio will be covertly punished for what they believe he has done. Certain non-scholarship cadets, the academy Commandant, and the Loren family all agree to work together so Julio regrets what he has done to one of their own.

* * * * * * * *

The reprisal for the humiliation of Thomas Loren starts with certain cadets watching Julio. Some try to become his friend. The goal is always to find a weakness that can be used against him.

The academy's cadet handbook clearly states any cadet caught cheating will be expelled. Julio now only has a few months left before graduating from the academy. During a final exam, Julio is informed he must go to the Commandant's office immediately. He is told to leave his test on his desk. Julio finds this unusual. Cadets are required to always give the teacher their test papers before leaving the room for any reason.

Julio goes to the Commandant's office. This is when someone goes over some paperwork he needs to complete for his graduation. Julio knows this is also strange. This is not something normally done before a cadet passes the academy's final exams. He goes back to the classroom to continue taking his test. Julio knows something is very wrong.

When he walks into the room, it is quiet, and not a single cadet looks up at him. Julio is convinced something has been done to his test. He returns to his desk and continues taking the test. Julio is finished and the teacher comes to get his paper. When the test is removed from Julio's desk, a sheet of paper with the test answers falls to the floor. No cadet turns to look at Julio. He instantly knows he has been set up. He struggles to control his anger.

The teacher says, "Cadet Dean get your things and come with me. I must report this cheating to the Commandant immediately."

Julio stands up and says, "I didn't do this. You cadets have set me up. All of you must admit what you've done."

No cadet says anything. They all look away and ignore Julio. After getting his things, Julio follows the teacher out of the room.

Before he is out of the door a cadet says, "Maybe you shouldn't be clowning around so much and focus more on studying."

Julio walks back into the room and says, "All of you will pay for this, I promise you."

* * * * * * *

When the teacher goes into the Commandant's office, Julio feels as if the Commandant has been waiting for him. They go right into the Commandant's office as his office door is open. This has never happened during the years Julio has been a cadet at the academy.

After hearing what the teacher has to say about the cheating accusation, the Commandant says, "I'm very disappointed in you Cadet Dean. I had hoped you would be part of our graduating class this year."

"Sir, I did not do this, I was set up. I was told to come here in the middle of the test. When I returned, someone had tampered with my test paper. The teacher did not take my test paper when I left. I do not know why."

The teacher looks at Julio with an angry expression and then looks at the Commandant and says, "I assure you, Commandant, he was gone for a very short time. I easily kept an eye on his test paper. You can ask the other cadets. None of them touched Cadet Dean's test paper."

"Please have the cadets who were taking the test in that classroom come to see me immediately. If none of them support Cadet Dean's version of things, I will have no choice but to hold an expulsion trial for him. Now both of you return and carry on with your classes."

Julio calmly walks out of the Commandant's office. He is not angry at just one cadet or the Commandant. His rage has grown to include the entire academy.

* * * * * * * *

None of the cadets from the class support Julio's version of things. All of them claim nobody touched his test paper. The Commandant tells Julio he is now forced to hold an academy expulsion trial.

During the trial, the teacher and all the cadets claim nobody touched Julio's test paper. The truth was never told. A plan went into action the minute Julio left the room. After he was gone, the teacher gave a signal. This is when one of the cadets slipped a piece of paper with the answers under Julio's test paper. The cadets struggled to not laugh when Julio returned. The teacher had the sheet of paper with the answers discovered under Julio's test and claimed nobody touched it when he was gone.

Julio struggles to control his anger during the trial.

"Cadet Dean, do you have anything to say in your defense?"

Julio stands up and says, "This isn't right. It is all wrong. I did not do this. All of you know I did not do this. I am being blamed for something I have not done. A cadet made a comment to me about being a clown when I left the room. Am I also being blamed for what happened to Cadet Loren? There is no proof. How could I get test answers? Why am I being persecuted in this way?"

"Please sit down Cadet Dean," says the Commandant.

"Yes sir, but this is very wrong."

The Commandant looks around the room, takes a deep breath, and says, "Cadet Dean, there is no evidence to prove you are innocent. All the cadets in the room, and the teacher, have stated your test paper was never touched. I have no choice other than to expel you in your final year here at Saint Michael's Military Academy. Your records will reflect it was for cheating on exams. You must now go and clean out your things from your room. You must then make arrangements to return to your home. In other circumstances, a scholarship cadet who is expelled must pay back all the costs associated with their time at the academy. Until this time, you were a good cadet. For that reason, I am not going to require you to pay the academy back the costs associated with your education up to this point. This trial is hereby concluded."

Julio can no longer control himself. He stands up and yells, "You will pay. All of you will pay for this moment. I don't care how long it takes me. Revenge will be mine. I hope none of you ever forget what I'm saying right now. I will remind all of you at the appropriate time."

Julio then quickly leaves the room hitting the door violently with his hand causing it to open wide.

# Chapter 15

## *Clash of the Titans*

Paul decides he must pay a visit to Mr. Dean and discuss the closing of the academy. He believes when it comes to dealing with a person like him, the military minds of those in charge at Saint Michael's Military Academy are out of their league. To handle an individual as devious and underhanded as Mr. Dean requires someone who is just as devious and underhanded. It must be a person who has no business morals, no emotional feelings, and no concern for the damage it could cause their fellow human being. Paul figures since his father and grandfather won't be interested in helping, it's up to him to put such valuable family traits to use in this situation. The realistic business lessons he learned from seeing what is involved with being part of his family's very large and successful corporation will come in handy.

It is Monday, and Paul has gotten permission from the academy to take care of some personal business in town during the day. He decides to utilize public transportation for the first time in his life. Paul gets on a bus that travels from the academy to the downtown area of the local town. It is a very humbling experience. After being on the bus, Paul figures a bus line with well-maintained buses would be another profitable business for him to start in this town. He wonders if the bus he is on could have previously been a prison bus. It seems to Paul the individuals who run this bus company must have developed their management skills from bus lines serving third-world countries.

Paul has a conversation with the bus driver and discovers the location of Mr. Dean's office. It seems everyone he speaks with knows about Mr. Dean and where his office is located. It is in the largest and most visually appealing building in the town's business district. This structure is known as the Grand Tower. Mr. Dean has an office at the very top of the building.

The security guard at the front desk of the building's lobby is an older woman dressed in a nice white uniform. She has gold badges on her shoulders. Her uniform also has a silver metal badge hanging from a front shirt pocket.

Paul goes into the building and approaches the security guard.

She looks up from a book she is reading and says, "Can I help you?"

Paul smiles and says, "Yes, I would like to be directed to the office of Mr. Dean."

"He know you here?"

"Oh, he and I are such good friends we don't need the formalities of a scheduled appointment. That isn't necessary with people who are as close as the two of us."

"Okay, I'll just call up there. His secretary's name is Ruby. Tell me your name, and I'll see if you can go up."

"Did you say, Ruby?"

"Yeah. Between me and you, she don't look like no secretarial type, but I'm told that's what she does."

"Oh, this is now a very awkward situation. Do you know why?"

"Why?

"A short time ago Ruby was madly in love with me. I had no interest in her whatsoever and rejected her advances. I did my best to be kind considering the circumstances. She still relentlessly pursued me in a romantic way. I'm certain she hates herself for being so desperate and pathetic when it comes to me. The mere mention of my name could cause her broken heart to burst. It could result in her crying and sobbing. Why don't we avoid all of that unpleasantness and simply let me go up to Mr. Dean's office?"

"Well, if she is so upset by just hearing your name, how is she going to react to seeing you? Don't you want to avoid that unpleasantness?"

Paul smiles and says, "You're right. I've coddled her feelings far too long. It's time she grow up and faces the fact this stud muffin isn't interested in her. She needs to deal with reality. Call Ruby and tell her that Paul J. Wildman of Wildman Holdings is here to see Mr. Dean."

The security guard looks at Paul, resists the temptation to call him crazy, and says, "What? You look like just a cadet from the academy."

Paul leans closer to the woman, gives his best attempt at sincerity, and says, "I know what you must think. Please make the call. It would mean a lot to me."

The security guard picks up the phone on her desk and presses a button.

She says 'Paul J. Wildman is here to see Mr. Dean. Claims he is from some Wildman Holdings organization."

The security guard then smiles and hangs up the phone.

"What did she say?"

"I guess the good news is she seems to be completely over you."

"Really?"

"Yeah, I mentioned your name and not only did Ruby not start crying, but she started laughing. I guess you got nothing to worry about now."

"Well, it's good to see her mind and emotions have been able to recover from my rejection. That ole' Ruby is so resilient. I'm feeling proud of her right now. So, can I go up to the office?"

"According to her, he isn't in the building ."

"Can I go up to the office and wait for him?"

"No, but you can wait in the lobby for him. Ruby said she knows nothing about you and Mr. Dean being friends. Think you can keep your animal magnetism from breaking out on another girl while you wait?"

The security guard chuckles and points to some chairs in the lobby.

"Thank you. Most people don't like to acknowledge those of us who possess such power over females. It can be both a blessing as well as a curse."

Paul goes over to the lobby chairs and sits down. He can still hear the security guard struggling to hide her laughter. Paul replays in his mind what he is going to say to Mr. Dean. He tries to synchronize his mind to how his grandfather and father would handle this situation. Paul embraces their attitude to win at any cost.

Mr. Dean eventually walks through the door. He is wearing a beautifully tailored blue suit, a white shirt, and a yellow tie. Expensive dress shoes complete his ensemble. As Mr. Dean walks into the lobby, Paul stands up and gets in front of him.

"Dean, I would like to talk to you," says Paul.

Mr. Dean looks at Paul, smiles, and says, "What would you like to talk about?"

"I think there is a little matter of the academy and lawsuits you may have recently won."

"How does this concern you? Why should anything you have to say on the matter be important to me?"

"Mr. Dean, I'm Paul J. Wildman. Do you know what that means?"

"You know your name? I'm not following you right now."

"Oh, your wit is overwhelming. It means I have some rather strong influence on how business is conducted within Wildman Holdings. You could benefit greatly from our meeting."

"Okay, this is interesting. I'd like to hear what you have to say. Just follow me."

"Mr. Dean, I don't think you realize how this meeting could change your life for the better."

"Yeah, yeah, yeah sounds good. You have no idea how often I hear that during a typical business day. Are you sure you don't want to simply talk about that gold money clip given to you by your grandfather? I'd like to remind you the one I have was a gift to me. There is really nothing to talk about."

"Now that you mention it, I think that should be part of our discussion."

Mr. Dean motions to the security guard that it's okay if Paul goes with him. The security guard says something under her breath about stud muffin and struggles not to laugh before the elevator doors close.

"I wonder what she's talking about?" says Mr. Dean.

Paul shrugs his shoulders and says, "I have no idea"

Nothing more is spoken between the two of them during the elevator ride.

When the two men get off the elevator, they go into Mr. Dean's office. Ruby is sitting at a desk in the reception area.

She looks up, notices Paul, and says, "Well, well, well, if it isn't the CIA cadet here in our office. A guy so cheap he wouldn't even buy a girl a cup of coffee. I see you recovered from the beatdown you got last time we met."

Paul looks at Mr. Dean and says, "I do admire how you permit members of the local call-girl service an opportunity to have an honest profession. I'm sure with a little effort, you could easily replace this one with a more socially acceptable female for your office. Having her here tells me you do have a kind spot in your heart for low IQ individuals with loose morals."

Ruby is angry. She slams her hands on her desk, stands up, and points her finger at Paul. Before she says anything, Mr. Dean motions for her to calm down. He then opens the door to his office and tells Paul to go inside.

Mr. Dean's office is filled with beautiful furniture. It has windows that provide a stunning view of the local town and the surrounding areas. It has been designed to impress all who see it. The office provides the image of success, wealth, and power. Paul wonders about the reality behind the image this office provides. Mr. Dean goes over to a bar in the corner of the office and pours himself a drink.

"Could I interest you in a drink Mr. Wildman?" says Mr. Dean.

"No thank you. I would like it if we could just begin our discussion," says Paul.

"Have it your way."

Mr. Dean goes to his large desk and sits down. He motions for Paul to sit down in one of the chairs located at the front of his desk.

"This is a very nice office. Have you ever been to the headquarters for Wildman Holdings?"

"No, but I'm sure you are more than willing to provide me with a detailed description of its grandeur. I'm not interested. Please tell me why you came here to see me today."

"It's very simple. You are a big fish in a little pond and my family are the blue whales in the ocean of business. Let us agree to stop the usage of aquatic references. I'm sure your entire operation would not be a problem for my family's company to absorb. Let us purchase the lawsuits from you."

"Do you have the authority from your family's company to negotiate such a business deal on their behalf?"

"Let's just say, I have a significant influence on certain aspects of Wildman Holdings.

"That's very interesting."

"Why do you find that so interesting?"

"You see Mr. Wildman; I have many contacts within the academy. This makes it possible for me to get a good deal of information I need on cadets who attend there. I know you are at odds with your father and grandfather. Something to do with your trust fund. You've got a history of being kicked out of colleges. Some say you've never spent a day working in your family's business. I don't see where you are in a position to negotiate anything on behalf of Wildman Holdings."

Paul becomes angry and says, "I'm sure you know that family is family. We all have our problems. The mere fact my father and grandfather are destined to be inducted into the Asshole Hall of Fame doesn't mean they won't back me up if I make a good deal for our company. This is just how it works in my capitalistic family."

"Why would I believe such a thing?"

"Make a deal with me. If it doesn't happen, then you've lost nothing. You still have the potential to become an even bigger elephant in a small game reserve. Coming up with that original cliché was difficult, but I did it. Now, it's your turn."

Mr. Dean smiles, sits back in his chair, removes a gold money clip from a pocket in his suit, and shows it to Paul.

"I'm sure you remember this item that has come into my possession," says Mr. Dean.

"Yes, that is the gold money clip given to me by my grandfather."

"That is your claim. You've been so motivated to get this material possession back. It almost seems like an obsession. You know such focus on one thing can easily prevent you from seeing the bigger picture of a situation."

"Yes, the gold money clip is important to me, so what? What's your point? I want it back."

Mr. Dean finishes his drink and says, "Mr. Wildman, you are like every rich person I've ever known. You see, when anybody wants to get something from a rich person, they simply obtain a valuable material thing that person wants. When you show it around, rich people often focus on it. They eventually will forsake everything else to get it. That gives a distinct advantage to someone, such as myself, who has figured out a way to obtain it. I can see what is happening and they cannot."

"Sorry, I didn't come here to listen to a corrupt business person's bedtime stories. What are you saying?"

Mr. Dean holds up the gold money clip and says, "This material thing you have invested with so much of your emotion owns you. It calls to you, and you come for it. Now, you come and talk to me about the academy but your mind is still on this object. Money controls rich people. You are at the academy and forcing yourself to endure being miserable for money. Rich people are so controlled by their monetary desires they will lie, cheat, or even kill for it. You don't even realize how much of a prisoner you are to money and material things. You are oblivious to everything else of value around you."

"Pardon me, but when I look around here, I suppose the same could be said of you."

"I suppose that is true, but I spent many years without money. I know what it is like to live the life of a poor person in a bad neighborhood. I wouldn't change a moment of it. I learned more about people than someone like you will ever know. If I lose everything, I have the skills to get it all back. Can you, a trust fund baby, say the same thing about yourself? I think your life experiences have been limited."

Paul is hit with a flood of emotions he doesn't understand. He is both angry and scared by what Mr. Dean has just said to him. Paul thinks to himself this is probably how the world works. He then looks at Mr. Dean's desk. There is a file with the name Wildman on it. Paul decides to act as if he has not noticed it. He doesn't realize Mr. Dean is aware he has looked directly at the file.

"Thank you for sharing your socio-economic views of society. If I can get the backing of my family's company, would you consider selling your interests in the academy?"

"I will agree to take a look at any proposal that is in my best interest."

"Then we have a deal?"

"We have a deal for me to consider a proposal. Make it good. If it is bad, you will be dead to me.

Paul stands up and says, "No need to show me out. I know the way."

As he goes out of the door and into the reception area, Paul looks at Ruby.

He opens the door to the hallway, turns back, and says, "Do you have a taxi meter on your bed? If not, you might consider getting one. I'm sure it would help with being properly compensated for the many services you provide."

Ruby starts swearing and stands up. Paul quickly leaves and closes the office door. He decides to go down to the hallway and remain out of sight. Paul wants to get back into Mr. Dean's office and look at the file with his name on it. He's also hoping Mr. Dean has forgotten about his gold money clip sitting on the desk.

Paul waits for an hour. He then sees Ruby and Mr. Dean leave the office. They are focused on their conversation and don't seem to notice Paul watching them from down the hallway.

When both of them get on an elevator, Paul slowly makes his way to the office. He tells himself he is the James Bond of cadets and a sports car owner. Paul thinks about how he'll try using a credit card to open the door like in the movies. He is surprised when he turns the door knob and the door opens. Paul looks around and goes into the reception area. The door to Mr. Dean's office is also open. The file with his name on it is still on Mr. Dean's desk. He opens the file and begins reading. His gold money clip is there but Paul doesn't touch it.

In the file are various papers concerning Wildman Holdings. Paul is shocked when he sees a letter from his father. He knows the signature at the bottom of the letter is that of his father.

*Dear Mr. Dean,*

*As per our previous conversation over the phone, I would like my son Paul to be toughened up. Please stage a small robbery and rough him up a bit, but don't hurt him. Experiencing such violence may help him appreciate his home more. Bill me for the agreed-upon amount.*

*Just want you to know our plans to put a shopping center where the academy is now located are on track. I'm sure my son will be glad to only stay at the academy for a short time. I'll be in touch.*

*Sincerely,*

*Walter Wildman.*

When Paul finishes reading the letter, he pounds his fist on the desk. The sense of betrayal is overwhelming. He sits down. His confused mind attempts to process what he has just read. Paul knew his father and grandfather had issues with him. He never believed they would go so low as to stage a fake robbery in the misguided belief it would toughen him up. Paul struggles with the shock he's feeling. He decides to put it out of his mind for right now and focus on saving the academy.

Paul goes to a copier in the corner of the room and makes a copy of the letter. He returns the original to the file and leaves. Paul puts the gold money clip in his pocket. He quickly takes an elevator to the first floor and makes his way out of the building. Paul then heads back to the academy.

* * * * * * *

At a local restaurant, Mr. Dean and Ruby are enjoying a nice lunch.

"Do you really think that asshole went back into the office to look at the file and get his money clip?" says Ruby.

Mr. Dean swallows a mouthful of food, carefully wipes his mouth with a napkin, and says, "I can almost guarantee it. I know this kind of person. He doesn't care about rules or regulations. People like him only care about getting what they want. They believe consequences are for people who are not wealthy."

"What are you going to do if he took the gold money clip?"

"Let him have it. That money clip is of no value to me. There may come a time when I can use his theft against him."

"Seems like everything is going according to plan."

"Yes, everything is proceeding according to plan. I was very surprised when his family contacted me soon after I won the appeals for the lawsuit. Building the shopping center on the academy grounds was their idea. Even more amazing is Wildman's grandfather sits on the academy's board of directors. These people have no business morals at all."

Ruby and Mr. Dean enjoy their meals at the restaurant. Paul rides the local bus back to the academy. He is too upset to look at the letter. Paul keeps thinking about the money clip. He has never told anybody the truth about it. His grandfather never gave it to him. He took it hoping for the opportunity to admit to his grandfather he took it. His grandfather would then be forced to pay attention to him for once and not just his cousins. His grandfather never even realized the money clip was missing. He still never got any attention when told his father he had taken it. Paul used to fight the belief that he was as unimportant to his grandfather as the money clip. Its value to him was not based on happy memories. The money clip reminds him his grandfather didn't know him and had no desire to know him as a person.

# Chapter 16

## *It's What They Represent*

When he gets back to the academy, Paul decides to spend some time walking around the grounds. He can't get out of his mind that Mr. Dean knows about the type of relationship he has with his family. Embarrassment is experienced by this realization. After finding the letter, Paul realizes Mr. Dean was probably laughing the entire time he was in his office. It will take time for Paul to think of a way to change things. His family taught him there is a solution to every problem. Paul is determined to find it in this situation. The feelings of anger and rage toward his father and grandfather are starting to overwhelm him.

Paul makes it to a bench near the woods surrounding the academy and decides this is where he will sit and think. It's a place that is quiet and where he feels free from outside influences. Paul sits there for a long time. Everything he believed to be true about his life has now turned out to be a lie. He asks himself what exactly in his life is real. Paul struggles to not think about his father paying someone to rob him and assault him. He is experiencing the type of anger that stays inside a person and doesn't leave. No matter what someone does, says, or how happy they appear, this type of anger is always part of their thoughts.

After spending a long time alone on the bench, the sun starts to set and it becomes dusk. Paul knows it is time to get back to his room in the barracks. He is too upset to even make a trip to the mess hall for the evening meal. When gets to the barracks, he hears a lot of talking in a room at the end of a hall. Paul decides to investigate.

He walks down the hall and sees an open door. Paul looks in and Peter Barnett is talking to a large group of cadets. He's using his official military tone of voice. Peter is pointing to a map of the academy grounds that has been pinned up on a wall. Jane Westin, Dennis Martinez, and other cadets are wearing camouflage uniforms and their faces are covered with camo paint.

"Cadet Martinez, I need you to take your squad and set up a parameter around the building with the trophies. You and all of your people are to use the whistles you were given in case you experience any complications. This will get the other cadets to come to where you are located. If this happens contact me using the two-way radio you were given. You are not to engage anyone. Is that understood?" says Peter.

Dennis salutes and says, "Yes sir."

Peter nods his head and says, "Now take your people and get set up outside."

After a quick about-face move, Dennis leaves the room as a group of cadets follows him.

Peter Barnett looks at Jane Westin and says, "I want you and your people to set up near the trophy case and record any attempt to open it and get any of the trophies. If they do get the trophies, you are to then follow them at a safe distance. Make certain to see where they take them. Do not engage anyone. Do you understand?"

"Yes, sir," says Jane Westin.

Jane Westin and Peter Barnett exchange salutes. She also does an about-face move. As she leaves, a group of cadets follows her. After the last cadet leaves, Paul enters the room. Peter Barnett turns around and notices Paul but does not react.

"I hope all is well with you Cadet Wildman. What do you want?"

"I want to know what's going on. What's with all this do not engage stuff and the camo-painted faces? I have to admit, it does make the female cadets look rather erotic but on the male cadets it doesn't work the same."

"Again with smartass comments. I don't want to talk about it, and you don't want to know. Just go back to your rich family, drive your sports car, pick out your next college to screw with, and forget about the cadets here at Saint Michael's. I heard how the academy closing doesn't bother you. I hope you realize it will affect many of us. We will take care of our academy until the day it closes," says Peter.

Peter Barnett then turns away from Paul and starts putting camo paint on his face. Paul grabs Peter Barnett's shoulder and turns him around.

Paul yells, "I want to know what's going on."

"Why?" Peter screams.

"Because if it has anything to do with that asshole Dean, I want to be part of it."

There is a silent moment as Paul and Peter exchange serious and intense expressions.

"You sure?" says Peter.

"I'm positive," says Paul.

"Okay, you can be a part of this insanity if you want. Ever heard the story of Dean's trophies?"

"Doesn't seem like something you'd find on the New York Times best-seller list. No, I've never heard the story."

"Years ago, Dean was a cadet here at the academy. He led the academy's rifle drill team in competitions. The team won the state championship three years in a row. A trophy was given to the academy each year they won. Dean has always felt he should have been given these trophies and not the academy. After he was kicked out, Dean was caught trying to steal the trophies more than once. Dean has sent many letters to the Commandant demanding the trophies and saying he will get those trophies one way or another. Plans have been made to preserve the trophies at the local museum. We know Dean is aware of this, and he still intends to steal the trophies he considers to be his before they are given to the museum. He has been unsuccessful over the years. Dean has tried to steal those trophies many times. Each time he has been stopped. The Commandant and those civilians sitting on the board don't seem to care anymore about the trophies. Cadets over the years have worked so hard to keep them from being stolen. This is a stupid game that has been occurring for years. It is now up to us cadets to make certain Dean doesn't get them. We will make sure they are given to the museum."

"But they're just cheap material things. They have little monetary worth. Why do you let a thing of such little monetary value get you so worked up? I've seen the trophies. They're not that valuable. You could easily put your money together and buy better-looking trophies. Why not just let Dean have them and forget about it?"

Peter yells, "It's not their monetary value. It's what they represent. They signify the success of previous cadets here at Saint Michael's Military Academy. They are a source of inspiration. We owe a debt to the memories of those cadets who worked so hard to inspire future generations with their hard work and determination. A flag is just a piece of cloth, it's what it represents that makes people value it so much. Some things in life are worth fighting for because they are a symbol of something important. That's why we care so much."

"That was good. For some reason, I now feel like voting for you in the next election. I don't even care if you're not on the ballot."

Peter sighs, turns from Paul, and says "You never take anything serious. Why don't you just leave and forget about this?"

Peter starts to walk away, but Paul stops him and continues to talk.

"So, you're willing to risk police, fighting, and physical harm over some cheap trophies?"

"Dean may be able to destroy our academy, but we're not going to let him have our history. Those trophies don't belong to him. They belong to all Saint Michael's Military Academy cadets."

"And you people think I'm crazy. Does the Commandant know about this extracurricular cadet activity?"

"I hope not. We have no idea where he is right now. Guarding the trophies is now up to us. Someone from town told us Dean is going to try to steal them tonight. We plan to take pictures of anyone who tries to take the trophies and then follow them wherever they go and try to get them back. If they want to get physical, we're ready for that as well. We must do it off academy grounds."

Paul smiles and goes over to where Peter resumes putting camo paint on his face. He starts to smear stuff onto his face.

"I'm definitely in. Can we use guns and rocket launchers and stuff like that?"

"Your idiotic comments are not helping. We have everything covered. The goal is to avoid confrontation if possible. We don't want to give Dean a reason to shut us down before the school year is over."

"Ah, you forget I come from a long line of business people who owe their success to having an ethical bypass at birth. I think I've got a plan that might make things go more easily.

"Oh, yeah? What do you think we should do?"

"It's important to realize criminals who do such things as this are not the sharpest tools in the shed. I consider my well-developed ability to take advantage of such people's stupidity one of the many services I provide."

Peter laughs and says, "You can be really strange, but, okay, you can be a part of this if you want. I'd like to hear your plan."

When Paul turns around, Peter can see Paul has both brown shoe polish and green camo paint on his face. When Peter points it out, he and Paul begin to laugh."

* * * * * * *

Paul is standing in the dark with Peter Barnett. They are hiding near the trophy case. On the opposite side are Jane Westin and a few other cadets. They've just finished placing a covering over the trophy case. A sign was put on it that says 'Trophies from display case moved to room 121' with an arrow pointing down a hallway.

They hear a voice coming from the walkie-talkie Peter is holding. It's Dennis saying, "Papa one nine this is Mike two five, the actors have come over the stone fence at the southern end of the academy. It appears there are approximately three of them."

Peter speaks into his walkie-talkie and says, "Roger Mike two five, and good work. Make sure they don't see you or any of your people. Make certain they only came to get the trophies and not cause any other harm. Follow them until they get to the building. We'll take it from there."

"Roger Papa one nine and concur."

It's dark and there is silence where Paul and the other cadets are standing. Suddenly, they see flashlights being shown in the lobby area from the glass of the front door. Peter is shocked when he realizes the people trying to get the trophies have a key to the building. They are simply unlocking the door. Once they are inside, they go directly to the trophy case. One of the intruders lifts the covering and sees there are no trophies in the display case.

A young male voice speaks in a low voice and says, "This doesn't make any sense. Why would they move them?"

A young female voice says, "Who cares? Let's just get the stupid trophies and get out of here. I hate this place."

They then follow the arrow to a hallway and another sign with an arrow pointing to room 121. The intruders go down the hallway and see a sign on a door that reads 'Temporary Trophy Storage.' The three slowly go into the room. Paul, Peter, Jane, and the other cadets quietly follow behind the intruders as they go into the room. The intruders don't notice them.

Once inside, a light is turned on. The three intruders suddenly realize they are facing over a dozen cadets. Jane orders a cadet holding a video camera to continue filming. It is Jake, Seth, and Ruby.

"What are you people doing on academy grounds at this time of night?" says Peter.

"Hey, we thought it was a beautiful place for a late-night stroll. I got a key to this building, and I thought I'd use the bathroom," says Seth.

Jake looks at Seth and yells, "Shut up."

Paul looks at Ruby and says, "Does the madame where you work know what you're doing right now?"

Ruby goes to lunge at Paul, but Jake grabs her and pulls her back.

"So, what now? Are you little punk cadets going to beat us up or something? That would be a mistake," says Jake.

"Oh, I would love such a thing, but the police have been notified. They'll be here any minute. You will soon be their problem," says Peter.

Jake laughs and says, "Good move. We'll be out in less than an hour. You guys should just consider giving the poor man his trophies. He's going to get them eventually. Why do you want to waste your time with this nonsense?"

"They're not his trophies. They belong to all cadets. That's why they're going to the museum," yells Jane Westin.

Paul steps in front of Jane. He looks at Seth and says, "Yeah, and we consider spending any evening that involves preventing you three stooges from committing an act of larceny a good time."

"Says the boy whose father is willing to pay to have someone beat his ass," says Ruby.

All the cadets look at Paul and Peter says, "What is he talking about?"

Paul says, "Nothing, never mind, it's nothing."

Seth, Jake, and Ruby start laughing. Paul then turns and heads toward the door.

"Where are you going?" says Jane.

"I am going to bet there is a limousine parked nearby. I'd like to talk to the well-dressed man who is sitting in the back. He is always nearby when things like this happen," says Paul.

Paul leaves the building and goes down the walkway to the academy entrance. As he is walking, two police cars with flashing lights go past him toward the main building where the empty trophy case is located. After walking out of the academy, Paul sees the limousine parked down the street from the academy. He goes up to it and knocks on the rear window on the driver's side. When the window comes down, Paul sees Mr. Dean sitting there.

"Ah, Mr. Wildman. It is a surprise to see you. I hope all is well," says Mr. Dean.

"I hate to be the bearer of bad news, but it seems the trophies you want so badly will remain with the academy. Your trio of criminal misfits wasn't able to get them for you tonight. They will soon be in police custody."

"I assure you I have no idea what you are talking about."

"Yeah, it's just a lovely night to sit in a limousine outside an academy you hate. It makes perfect sense. I have something for you."

Paul takes out his money clip and places it in Mr. Dean's hand. He then closes Mr. Dean's hand over it and smiles.

"This is the money clip you claim to be yours. You stole it from my office. Why are you giving it back?"

Paul thinks of his painful memories of being ignored by his grandfather even after taking the money clip.

"Because it's not what something is that matters, it's what it represents to you. Let's just say there are things in my past associated with that money clip I just need to let go."

Mr. Dean is quiet as Paul turns around and starts walking back to the academy. He starts whistling. Paul can't remember when he has felt this free from a past hurt.

# Chapter 17

## A Kindred Spirit

Paul slowly begins to realize his views of the world have changed drastically since he has been at the academy. The other cadets probably wouldn't understand the world he lived in since he was born. Before becoming a cadet, Paul had only associated with wealthy people and their families. It was the only socializing he'd ever known. Paul spent his life in an environment where material things and wealth were highly valued. They were what provided a family and its members with status and social ranking. The amount of a family's wealth and material things often determine social acceptance and business success.

People, where Paul grew up, knew about the importance of belonging to certain private clubs and attending specific social functions to maintain status. The appearance of friendships with the right wealthy and influential individuals was an essential part of maintaining an image. Being invited to the right private gatherings was a strict requirement for obtaining social positions of influence.

Equally important was having the right people attend any social event someone provided. If the right people didn't attend, the gathering could be labeled as a disaster. In this world, status equals power and influence. Impressing the right individuals could provide contacts that could make an average company become large and a large company develop an impressive worldwide reach. Family, personal feelings, and dreams all had to conform to the goal of maintaining status. Those who want to succeed must never lose focus on this. Everyone must be willing to sacrifice anything to get and maintain status. An individual's identity and self-worth were always based on it and these unspoken rules didn't change for anyone. Should an individual or family lose their status in this world, they would become a social and business pariah.

Dennis Martinez is the first person Paul has ever had as a friend who didn't come from his world. He constantly struggles to understand why Dennis seems so content to not be wealthy. Dennis never talks about going to a famous person's party or knowing someone who is extremely successful. He has shared many stories with Paul about happy times with his family. Dennis often talks about his younger brother and two sisters. He writes to them often and occasionally calls them on the phone. Dennis' father is a plumber and his mother works as a secretary for a small manufacturing company. It appears to Paul that Dennis' family worries more about one another than being wealthy. Paul had heard of such people and now he knows they do exist.

Paul begins to realize Dennis has something he doesn't. A family that values him more than money and status. They don't seem focused on having an image within their world. Dennis has never had any real wealth by Paul's standards. He doesn't know what it's like to go skiing in Aspen, Colorado on a whim or go to the Bahamas for a long weekend. Dennis is saving money for a car. What fascinates Paul is how Dennis can be so very comfortable and happy with his life.

Paul looks at himself and realizes the anger and hatred he has for his father and grandfather has made him a typical obnoxious rich kid. He's become a stereotypical wealthy brat. One of the three women his father has divorced claims she gave birth to his father's child. Paul knows this is his half-brother. His father has made no effort to introduce the child to Paul. He never mentions the little boy. Paul knows the boy's mother always hated him. He just tries to not think about it. Part of him does wonder what it would be like to have a relationship with this little person who has the same father as him.

Peter Barnett has also shared some things about his family with their small group. He and his older sister are close. She is very important to Peter. It appears the Barnett family was quite wealthy when Peter was growing up. A series of bad things happened. Their family's business failed and Peter's father went to jail for a few years associated with the failure of the business where he worked. There is a rumor Peter's father did drugs and alcohol and had been in and out of rehab a few times. Peter often says many wonderful things about his mother. She means quite a bit to him. The way Peter talks about his family, it seems they've accepted his father's mistakes and have chosen to forgive him and move on with their lives. Paul knows no such thing would happen within his family. A lot of effort would be made to hide such things and pretend they never happened. It would be a scandal if anyone discovered it. This is something that would be used as a social weapon against his family.

There are so many different types of scholarship cadets Paul has come to experience at the academy. Most of them are nothing like the people he has previously known. He sometimes thinks it may not matter if you have money. When he has this thought, Paul tells himself it may not matter to these people, but it matters to him because he doesn't have the necessary skills to survive without it. Being rich is all he knows.

* * * * * * * *

It is a typical weekend at the academy. Some cadets have duty. This means they will be responsible for cleaning things, maintaining the academy grounds, and more. This is done on a rotation basis. All cadets have duty at least one weekend a month.

One of the things Paul has noticed about weekends at the academy is how many friends, parents, and relatives of cadets come to visit. Those who don't get visitors often leave on Friday to go and be with their families and return early on Monday morning. Not too many cadets spend time at the academy on the weekends. Paul hasn't had any visitors except his mother since he came to the academy. He's not been contacted by any friends from his neighborhood, his father, or even his grandfather. Paul refuses to think about also being ignored by his grandmother. None of them has ever made any attempt to contact him let alone come and see him.

Paul did try to contact a few people he thought were his friends, but they always claimed to be too busy to come and see him. He knows these friends are probably laughing at his situation. Paul understands it is probably now a source of mocking and ridicule with them. It's just how things are in his world. He'd do the same thing to them if one of them was a cadet. Paul feels he has no real reason to go home for a visit.

After catching up on his schoolwork, Paul spends the afternoon at his favorite bench near the woods. It is the weekend and few people ever come to this part of the academy grounds near the woods. There is a quiet and relaxed feeling Paul experiences sitting on the bench.

The warmth of the afternoon sun takes Paul. Without realizing it, he falls asleep on the bench to the sound of birds singing and the wind pushing new leaves forming on the trees. After some pleasant dreams of driving his sports car filled with beautiful women, Paul is awakened by the sound of loud female voices. They are yelling at one another. He sits up and tries to awaken and gather his senses. The sound of the loud female voices are behind him. He turns around to see Jane Westin and an older woman arguing. The woman is a bit shorter than Jane and is standing with her hand on her hip in a rather rigid stance. Her eyebrows and pushed together and there is an authoritative tone in her voice.

Jane yells, "I told you, Mother, I didn't want to go to a government-run academy. When you are finished there, you have to be in the military for six years. I'm only at this place to appease you. I thought you understood this and agreed it was a fair compromise."

Jane's mother takes a deep breath and says, "Your sister was one of the first females to graduate from the Air Force Academy. I served for years in the Army as an officer. I'm telling you; we weren't treated very fairly in those days. I didn't have the opportunity to go to the Air Force Academy like your sister or the Naval Academy like your brother. Your aunt Sarah was one of the first female cadets to graduate from West Point. What is wrong with you? This is our family tradition."

"This is your tradition. I told you I didn't want to come here. After I'm done at this academy, I'm going to art school. Isn't that enough for you? You'll have pictures of me in my uniform and you can tell all your friends I graduated from a military academy like your other kids. Isn't that enough of a sacrifice for you?"

"Not really. You could have gone to one of the federal military academies. We have all the necessary connections."

Jane screams, "Sorry if this is not good enough for you. It's all you are going to get from me. Do you want me to quit? Every day I'm tempted to walk away from here."

"Don't be ridiculous. It's too late. You graduate in a few months. Then it will all be over for you. Then you can go live some hippie artist lifestyle in the back of a van or something."

"I said I'm going to art school."

Paul watches Jane arguing with her mother and feels close to her. He knows what she is feeling. There is a desire to please her mother combined with the need to be her own person. Paul can sense Jane's frustration, anger, and desire to simply quit. She wants to scream. Paul knows the hurt from such a lack of acceptance. He thinks about how he can now relate to Jane more than she knows.

Jane's mother notices Paul sitting on a bench and yells, "You, on the bench, get over here immediately. I want to have a word with you cadet."

Paul stands up, shrugs his shoulders, puts his hands in his pockets, and walks toward where Jane and her mother are standing. He whistles a happy tune as he walks. Sarcastic comments begin to flood his mind. When Paul gets there, he looks at Jane and smiles as she looks away.

Paul smiles at Jane's mother and says, "I apologize as I had simply fallen asleep on the bench. It is such a nice warm day. I had no idea this part of the academy grounds would be used for some type of family intervention. I don't understand how anyone could be upset with your daughter. She is one of the best cadets Saint Michaels has ever had."

Paul holds out his hand to Jane's mother to shake. She only looks at Paul's hand and clears her throat. She takes a deep breath and shows her indignation.

"Cadet, You need to mind your own business. The discussion between me and my daughter does not concern you. I may report you to the academy Commandant. I can tell you those who run this academy take a very dim view of cadets spying on people. Who are you?"

"Spied on? I was on the bench sleeping before you got here. I'm Paul J. Wildman. My family is the owner of Wildman Holdings. You can always read articles about us in any top business publication."

"Do you realize you are talking to a woman who was an Army officer as well as a parent who has children and other family members serving in the military? Without us people like your family would have nothing."

"Without people like my family, the military wouldn't receive enough tax revenue to pay for anything. Maybe you should respect the hand that pays for all those guns, bullets, ships, and airplanes."

Jane's mother is about to yell something when Jane screams, "Enough, stop it. Both of you."

Jane turns her back to her mother and then stands in front of Paul and gets face-to-face with him. She is struggling to hide her smile.

Paul says, "Sorry. I don't mean to be disrespectful, but I am having a hard time dealing with your mother's attitude. You don't deserve this."

Jane speaks softly so her mother doesn't hear. She says, "Look, I appreciate the smartass attitude and comments more than you know. Please leave now and just go back to your barracks. We'll talk about this later."

"Okay."

"Thank you."

Before Paul turns to leave he waves at Jane's mother and says, "It was a pleasure to meet you. I almost feel like calling my family and ordering the Army another tank in your honor. I think we may name it Big Mother Westin."

Paul turns to leave as Jane's mother is about to say something. Jane stops her. She watches Paul walk through the meadow toward the barracks and smiles. It's the first time she has ever seen anybody stand up to her mother and is surprised at how good it feels.

# Chapter 18

*Nothing Is What It Seems*

When Paul returns to his room in the male barracks, he laughs remembering the expression on the face of Jane's mother. It was a mixture of rage and shock. Paul doesn't have any hope Jane Westin will actually come to see him. She is an upperclassman and isn't supposed to fraternize on academy grounds with cadets in the lower classes unless necessary. Females aren't even permitted in the male barracks.

Most of the women in his past only came to see him when they wanted something. It may have been transportation with his sports car, paying for them to get into a club, or simply because they had nothing else to do that night. The only exception was Monica. She was always nice to Paul. He realizes she cared for him. The frustrating thing was that his mother cared more for Monica than he did.

He is surprised when there is a knock on the door of his room.

Paul opens it, Jane Westin leans in, smiles, and says, "Hello, is there a Paul J. Wildman here? The Paul J. Wildman of Wildman Holdings?"

Paul panics and moves past Jane. He looks up and down the hallway outside the door to make certain nobody saw Jane. Paul quickly pulls her inside his room. He then closes the door and locks it. Paul struggles to control his shock.

"Are you crazy? Females aren't permitted in the male barracks. You could get in real trouble if somebody sees you here."

Jane smiles and says, "Oh, relax already. I know Tommy who is on duty downstairs. He and my roommate are an item. You're the only one on this floor who stays the weekend. It's okay, don't worry."

"I'd hate to see you get in trouble. It doesn't matter if I get in trouble. It's sort of my favorite hobby. I got family money. You are almost done with this academy. It would be a shame if something happened to you."

Jane walks over to Paul and lightly kisses him. She then pulls away and just looks at him as she smiles. Paul doesn't say a word as this is a moment he doesn't want to ruin. He is trying to be as pleasant as possible. Paul decides to be quiet and fight the urge to say something sarcastic.

Jane puts her arms around Paul and says, "You are so sweet. Thank you for standing up to my mother for me today. Nobody has ever stood up for me like that when facing her. She is such a domineering person. People just tend to give her what she wants or run away in fear. My mother has scared off more than one boyfriend with her attitude. In my family, things are crazy. My brother and sister didn't want to go to those federal academies, but they did it to please my mother. I stood up to her and came here to a private military academy. I still feel so guilty about it. I thought coming here would at least give her pride in something I'm doing with my life. I'm not really a military person."

"I know what it is like when nothing you do is good enough for your family. Sometimes you just quit trying to please them. Getting people angry at me is how I rebel. I hope you realize being a smartass to authority figures is just one of the many services I provide. I wouldn't recommend it as a career."

"I'm sure."

As Paul looks at Jane, he can't help the attraction he's feeling. It is the first time he has seen her as just a girl who is his age and shares common family experiences. The fear of her treating him like an underclassman goes away. His mind has those hopes for the two of them. He gives in to making a smartass comment to hide his feeling of vulnerability.

"Would this be a really bad time to make a sexual innuendo or suggest a mutually beneficial physical experience between us?"

"Take it easy, tiger. Trust me, now is not the time. It would not be in your best interest to mention those things."

"Well, I'm glad we cleared that one up. I will keep those very vivid thoughts to myself until the time is appropriate."

"You do that. Keep hoping for an appropriate time to occur. Hey, why don't you come over to my room? I have something I want to show you. It is nothing sexual."

"I'm going to agree. I intend to hide my disappointment and frustration for my own benefit."

"Good."

"I take it your roommate is not an issue."

"Nope, she has been gone the entire weekend like she is almost every weekend."

"Oh, I love a good clandestine meeting."

As Jane and Paul leave his room, they go down the back staircase of the male barracks. Jane takes out a key and unlocks the door at the bottom.

"How did you get one of those keys?"

"Don't ask. I'll tell you someday."

The two of them make their way across the academy grounds. They get to the back of the girl's barracks. Both of them look around to see if anyone is watching. Jane uses her key to open the barracks door. Jane and Paul go up the stairs and into Jane's room. Paul sits on her roommate's desk chair. Jane goes over to an air vent in a corner of the room. She takes off the grille and pulls out a jar containing a dark liquid.

"This is some whiskey I got last time I went home. I was able to smuggle it in here. Would you like some?"

"You are certainly full of surprises. Yes, I would. I am struggling to believe this is the same Jane Westin who was Major Hardass to me my first day here."

Jane gets two plastic glasses from a drawer in her desk. She carefully pours some whiskey into each one.

She hands a plastic cup to Paul and says, "You have to admit, the first day here you acted like a whiney, arrogant, smartass, rich kid."

"Just being true to myself. What's with this whiskey and going into the male barracks with a key? This is not how I believed the female senior cadets at Saint Michael's Military Academy conducted themselves."

"Oh, don't be shocked. There are a lot of things that go on here that most people don't know about. It's like this at all the academies. Dennis and Peter are two of the few cadets who take the rules seriously. They avoid problems because they really want to have a piece of paper someday that says they graduated from here."

"What do you want?"

"To get done with this place so my mother can cut down on her guilt trips with me. I'm never coming back here when I'm finished."

"How does your father feel about all of this?"

Jane looks away and says in a low voice, "He died in a helicopter accident during an Army mission. I was pretty young. I don't remember him much."

"I'm sorry. I shouldn't have brought it up."

"It's okay. I've had years to learn how to deal with it."

Paul holds out his plastic cup and says, "We seem to have similar goals once our time at the academy is over. Here's to finishing and never coming back."

Jane taps her plastic cup on Paul's and says, "To never coming back."

She and Paul drink all the whiskey in their plastic cups. Jane looks at Paul and says, "Hey, I do have some stuff I want to show you."

Jane pulls out a large leather case from behind her bed. It is filled with papers. She opens it up and starts putting the papers on her bed. They are paintings and drawings. They're beautiful images of people and landscapes. Paul looks at them and his eyes open wide. He's impressed by what he's looking at."

"These are great. You have talent. Did you make these?"

"Yeah, I've not had any real training. I took some art classes in high school. I know I could do much better if I had some art lessons. This is where my mind and heart are at all times."

"Your mother doesn't get you, does she?"

"No, she doesn't. My mother isn't a bad person. She has been good to me. Her claim to fame is that when she was a nurse in the Army, she was working at a hospital in some remote place in South America. Some bad guys tried to kill the people in the hospital. My mother and two other local guys grabbed guns and fought them off until the good guys arrived. She got wounded and was given a medal for it. My mother has a purple heart. She and my father met during their time in the Army."

"Was your father as intense and serious as your mother?"

"I don't know. I do know he flew the helicopter that evacuated the people from the hospital that was attacked. My mother looked him up when she recovered from her injuries. I'm told it was almost love at first sight."

"That's quite a story."

"Yeah, I know. Everybody knows because she always talks about it. I feel guilty because I'm tired of hearing about the day the hospital was attacked. In my family, you are labeled as bad if you don't listen to my mother's Army stories and do what she wants. I just can't do that anymore. I'm tired of hearing about her life. So, what's your story?"

Paul decides he shouldn't talk about his family's wealth. He is not going to mention his sports car or trips to locations around the world. Paul is tempted to mention how his father paid those three people working for Mr. Dean to beat him up but decides against it. He believes he should just talk to Jane without making any of his sarcastic comments.

"I would have to say I am a non-conformist. My father believes I should have a piece of paper from an institution of higher learning, so he can parade around his educated son in front of his friends and business partners. I don't believe that is for me, but my father doesn't seem to believe I should live my life the way I want. I've enjoyed being told to leave every university he's tried to make me attend. This academy has been the exception."

"I noticed you aren't trying to get kicked out of the academy. Is there a reason?"

"It's simple. I was put on a guilt trip by my mother to stay here. You know what mother-initiated guilt trips are like."

"Wow, I can relate to that in many ways. I guess we're a lot more alike than we realize."

As the whiskey starts to take effect, Paul notices how Jane's hair is not carefully pinned up under a cadet cap. She has long blonde hair that cascades over her shoulders. He realizes her figure and blue eyes are stunning. Paul knows now is a time to control himself.

Paul is feeling good and says, "Yes, our parents are a lot alike and it seems we've come to resent them in very similar ways."

Paul and Jane spend a long time talking and drinking whiskey. Jane suddenly notices the time and remembers her roommate will be back at the academy very soon. She and Paul go down the back stairs of the barracks. Jane uses her key to open up the back door.

Before Paul leaves, she kisses him and says, "Thank you so much for standing up for me and everything."

"Thank you for the whiskey. I had a great time. It is great to see there is more to you than a tough-as-nails female cadet who gives the impression her favorite two words in the English language are male castration. We should do this again real soon."

Jane smiles and says, "Real soon. Please remember we are still cadets. If you see me you must salute and give me the respect due a senior cadet. If not, I will come down on you."

"I am going to clear my mind of any sexual image your statement may have caused me to experience. I agree in principle with what you requested."

Jane laughs and says, "Good, now go back to your barracks and behave."

Paul walks back to the male barracks whistling a happy tune. He tells himself there are times when being an arrogant, smartass, rich kid, as well as being quiet, can be a benefit. He thinks about having the illegal whiskey with Jane and all the things he has learned about the academy. Paul's grandfather was right when he told him nothing in this world is what it seems.

* * * * * * *

The relationship between Jane and Paul develops into regular secret meetings at various places around the academy. Their hidden moments together become more important and exciting. He believes this may be the first relationship with a female where his emotions are starting to be involved.

Paul was taught early in his life that everyone has secrets they do not want to be revealed. The discovery of these secrets is what can provide important leverage when negotiating with anyone in the business world.

At one of the colleges that expelled Paul, he made friends with a guy whose father was a very successful private detective. His friend is a young man who greatly benefited from one of Paul's many business ventures closed down by the police. The influence and financial power of Paul's family are what kept both of them from going to jail. This is a guy who once told Paul if he ever needed a favor, he should simply ask.

Paul's goal is now to prevent the academy from closing and punish his father, grandfather, and Mr. Dean for what they have done. The only way to handle these people is to get information about them they don't want anyone to know. Paul decides now is the perfect time to call in his favor. None of the people he wants to punish feel threatened by Paul. They don't think of him as anything more than an arrogant, obnoxious, rich kid. Paul thinks their misguided perception of him may be what causes their downfall.

# Chapter 19

## *Sins of the Past*

General Thomas Loren is standing by the large window in his office. He is looking out at the stately old structures and beautiful landscape of the academy grounds. During his time at the academy he has always been so busy, he's never taken the time to really see it. The stone buildings, plush green meadows, and colorful gardens are stunning. Thomas is viewing everything outside his window for the first time as an observer. He looks at what happens on a typical day at this school and feels Saint Michael's Military Academy is truly a special place. He is thankful to have been part of it for so long.

Thomas lets his mind remember all of the events that have taken place at the academy. High-ranking members of the military, US Senators, and more have come to speak at graduation ceremonies. The many graduations that took place on the back lawn of the academy. His heart becomes heavy when he thinks this year will be the last graduating class of Saint Michael's Military Academy. Everything he is now looking at will soon be torn down and turned into a shopping plaza. The old buildings, the stone fence around the academy, and all the property will soon be turned into retail stores in a shopping complex and a parking garage. There are even plans to turn the academy's large open training area into a golf course.

Thomas thinks about when he was a child. Family members would tell him many stories about being at the academy. His great-grandfather was a member of the academy's first graduating class of cadets. Thomas' father, older brother, as well as cousin, and uncle all graduated from Saint Michael's Military Academy. His father and grandfather have served on the academy's board of governors. Now, Thomas is the school's Commandant.

Things started going badly years ago after Thomas graduated. He returned to work at the academy after spending time as an infantry officer in the Army. He was given the academy rank of general. This is when Mr. Dean showed up in town with a real estate license. Nobody thought much of him until he started buying businesses. Dean created a stock and real estate investment company that quickly grew. After a few years, he began to file frivolous lawsuits against the academy. In the beginning, they were just annoying and easily dismissed or settled. Then the lawsuits slowly became larger and more serious. The academy was forced to pay more and more money to defend itself against them.

The academy hired an expensive accounting firm to make certain they carefully followed all the requirements of the lawsuits and complied with all of the tax requirements. Money soon became very tight. In time, the academy could no longer afford the large accounting firm. To save money, they hired an accountant who promised he could do the same as the large accounting firm for much less money. It was too late when they learned the accountant didn't pay the academy's property tax or other taxes. Everyone on the academy's board of directors trusted this accountant. He had excellent references and was a graduate of Saint Michael's Military Academy. The accountant kept his lack of tax payments hidden. This resulted in the academy being sued by governmental agencies for not paying taxes. A payment plan was worked out with the taxing agencies. Then one of Mr. Dean's lawsuits succeeded. It was too much of a financial blow. This is when Dean moved in and convinced members of the academy's board of directors to accept his offer of purchasing everything associated with the academy. James Wildman was a strong voice in convincing other board members to accept Dean's offer. The school's tax problems would be over and Dean would never again file a lawsuit against the academy. It also meant Dean would now own everything associated with the academy.

He agreed to take control of the academy's grounds and property in the late summer. It would be a time after the current school year had ended. This would give members of the academy, as well as the academy's board of directors time to clear everything out. General Thomas Loren hated feeling he had let down his family and future generations of cadets. Accepting defeat is never an easy thing for a soldier.

* * * * * * * *

Thomas Loren has been taught the ways of warfare. He does not understand how to fight lawsuits and lawyers. It all seems so cowardly to him. Thomas realizes there is not much he can do to change the situation the academy is facing. The only thing he has left to defend the academy is his words. He has made an appointment to meet with Mr. Dean. It required quite a bit of self-control and discipline to make the call and request a meeting. He was then subjected to hearing Mr. Dean's condescending and arrogant attitude. The sound of Mr. Dean's laughter is forever etched into the mind of Thomas. He keeps telling himself he is speaking with Dean for the sake of the academy.

* * * * * * * *

The meeting takes place at Mr. Dean's office. It could not be at the academy since Mr. Dean refuses to step onto academy grounds. He brings up what happened the last time he went to the academy and was confronted by Dennis and Paul. This is the reason he will not go there.

The meeting is tense even in the beginning. There is no formal greeting or handshake. Thomas walks into Mr. Dean's office and begins to talk about the academy right away. Sitting at his desk, Mr. Dean calmly continues to sort papers as he listens.

"Look Dean, I don't know why you did what you've done. Don't you think you should try to understand the big picture of your actions? Over half of the students at the academy are scholarship students. Do you realize what this will do to them, their families, and their education?" says Thomas.

Dean slams his hand on his desk, stands up, and yells, "Yes, I do understand. They will only benefit from getting away from that pathetic excuse of a military academy. It is now and has always been controlled by the rich who treat scholarship students like dirt."

"How would you know?"

"You don't remember me, do you? I guess you have forgotten. I suppose my time at the academy was too insignificant for a cadet from a wealthy family like yours to remember. I was scheduled to be in your graduating class at the academy. I did not graduate. I was tossed out because you rich kids decided it was easier to get rid of me than deal with the reality I was smarter than all of you. I'm sure if you try you can remember."

Memories of Dean suddenly flood Thomas's mind. He takes a step back when he realizes this is the same Julio Antonio Dean who was dismissed from the academy many years ago for cheating on an exam.

"Is that what this is all about? You got caught cheating years ago and were dismissed from the academy. You've done nothing with your life since then except work on getting revenge for something that happened so long ago? You are sick."

"You are the one who is sick and must be taught a lesson. You see Thomas, I did not cheat. That one incident sent my life on a downward trajectory. It brought me and my family shame. When some people heard the story, they would not hire me for a job. I had to leave my home and start again in a new place. My desire to right the wrong done to me so many years ago has brought me wealth and notoriety. It has turned out to be a good thing. I have honored the memory of my Yayo."

"You are really disturbed. This is completely insane. You need help."

"What I need is for you to remember the moment you dressed as a clown and then were made to be a clown. A special moment in time when you experienced the humiliation of so many cadets laughing at you. It is a special memory for me."

"That was you, wasn't it? I got over that and moved on shortly after it happened. You should try to do the same."

Mr. Dean yells, "You got over it because you got your revenge. You set me up to be kicked out of the academy my senior year. You had your revenge, now I get mine. Maybe now, I'll be able to move on as you say."

There is silence as the two men stare at one another. Thomas is fighting his desire to grab Mr. Dean by the throat. Mr. Dean is trying not to laugh at how upset he has made Thomas.

Suddenly Ruby's voice is heard from the phone on his desk saying, "Mr. Dean, your backers are here for the meeting."

Mr. Dean turns, goes to the phone on his desk, and presses a button.

"Excellent, please show them to my office."

"Maybe I should go," says Thomas.

"Nonsense, I think you would like to meet my financial backers for the acquisition of the academy. You may know them."

The office door opens. James and Walter Wildman walk in. They shake hands with Mr. Dean. The three of them look at Thomas who recognizes Paul's father and grandfather. He is confused and can't think of anything to say.

"Walter, James, this is an old friend of mine from the academy. He is now known at the academy as General Thomas Loren, the school's Commandant."

Mr. Dean looks at Thomas and says, "This is James and Walter Wildman. I'm sure you know them. This is Paul Wildman's father and grandfather. I believe he is a cadet at the academy."

There is no effort by anyone to shake hands.

Thomas looks at Walter and says, "Aren't you on the academy's board of directors? Isn't doing something like this considered a conflict of interest?"

"Yes, I am. It's only a conflict of interest if you don't have your contract to serve on the board of the academy altered by your attorney to make it possible. We've had quite a bit of work to do with closing down the academy," says James.

"How could you do this? You sat on the board of directors and instead of working for the betterment of the academy, you worked for the betterment of yourself and your company. Do you have any idea what you've done to the lives of the cadets?"

James chuckles and says, "Oh, come on now. This is business. Schools close down all the time. This one was bound to close down eventually. You had too many scholarship students. You should have had more focus on families who can pay to have that education. You didn't realize what happens when you don't focus on the bottom line. Even if it is a private military academy; this is just another business to us."

Thomas struggles to speak and then says, "We had a criminal accountant who ruined our finances and then just disappeared. He's the reason we are in this situation. The academy used to have all the income necessary to operate with no problem. We were even able to deal with Dean's frivolous lawsuits. Do you know anything about this accountant?"

Walter, James, and Mr. Dean all look at one another and smile.

"I can say there is no proof any of us knew anything about this individual you have mentioned," says James.

The three men are struggling to not laugh.

Thomas Loren looks at James and Walter then says, "You shouldn't be doing this. Your company is so large and wealthy. Why do you need to destroy a small private military academy that has been helping young people for almost a hundred years? You couldn't be that desperate for money."

Walter looks at James as they both smile.

"Oh, don't be so dramatic. This is about business and nothing more," says Walter.

James says, "Our business is about making money and that is what we do. We are one of the best at it."

Thomas Loren yells, "Have you no honor or morals? Do you value anything other than money?"

Walter yells, "I guess you believe you have honor and high moral standards but guess what? None of that will stop us from turning your academy into a shopping plaza. Maybe if you valued money a little more this wouldn't have happened."

Thomas Loren yells, "You are all despicable and cowardly individuals who hide behind your wealth. That is all you have."

Mr. Dean smiles and says, "It's all we need. I bet right now you wish you had some to keep this academy of yours from going away, but you don't. So suck it up, Loren. You lose. You thought you were so superior to me all those years ago, but look who is superior now. Face it, you and your wealthy family have been taught a painful lesson by a former disgraced scholarship cadet. I bet that burns in you like fire."

Thomas Loren's anger grows quickly as Mr. Dean starts laughing. The anger quickly turns to rage and is reaching a point where he doesn't know if he can control it. Thomas quickly goes toward the office door to leave. He is being subjected to laughter from James, Walter, and Mr. Dean. It is the type of laughter intended to degrade and humiliate. Laughter done by individuals who feel the power of their victory and a desire to grind it into those they have defeated. With such people winning is just not enough. They only feel completely triumphant when the spirit of those who have lost to them is broken.

Thomas Loren opens the office door and walks out. In the reception area, Ruby looks up from her desk and says, "Do you want me to schedule another meeting for you?"

"That won't be necessary."

"Isn't it strange how those two well-dressed guys in there have Paul Wildman as a son and grandson? I don't understand why he behaves the way he does."

"I think I now understand Paul Wildman's behavior more than I ever thought possible."

Thomas leaves the office. Standing in the hallway he presses a button for the elevator. As he is waiting, Thomas is praying something happens to save the academy.

# Chapter 20

## *The Sword of Truth*

Paul learns about the power of truth when he is young. It can be positive as well as cause people significant fear. Telling the truth about what he sees occurring in his family often gets him in trouble as a child. Agreeing with his family's illusions usually gets him acceptance. They teach him how avoidance of having an uncomfortable truth revealed is something that motivates people in many ways. It can be a useful tool. His family teaches Paul how knowing the truth about people can provide an important advantage when dealing with them. It is something individuals can accept or reject, but it remains a powerful tool when used properly.

It is Paul's grandfather who taught him all people present a facade to the world around them. Sitting on a chair in an office furnished with dark leather furniture and colorful paintings on the wall, Paul would listen to a man he admired so much. With an impressive view of the city from the window behind him, his grandfather explained how this is done so people can ignore the negative truths in their lives and protect their highly-valued image. Paul hears how obtaining knowledge about the truth behind the façade of a person, company, or institution is important. The resources used to obtain it are always a worthwhile investment. His father and grandfather have used truths they've discovered about people and organizations many times and in many different ways. They consider it simply a cost associated with running a large and successful company.

Paul believes his father and grandfather are the same as every other big top executive in the business world. They have paid money and done a variety of things to protect their façades. The two of them always have one standard for themselves and another one for everyone else.

The truth is Paul's façade. He never denies doing the things people accuse him of doing. Paul works to help people see these things in a positive way. Paul feels emboldened by owning his present and past behavior. He decided when he was young embracing the truth about yourself is power. It has always provided him with a sense of freedom. Nobody could say anything about him he didn't openly admit was true. Paul has come to understand how this makes his life much simpler and less expensive.

Paul knows his father and grandfather have always underestimated him. They've dismissed all the businesses Paul started during college and labeled them as worthless. These unusual businesses were part of the reason Paul was thrown out of three colleges. His father and grandfather could never see their value or how they provided Paul with a significant amount of money. No legal action has ever been taken against Paul because of his businesses. His father and grandfather always assume Paul only has the money from his trust fund to spend. They fail to realize Paul's business success has put him in a position to purchase many things without his trust fund. To Paul, his trust fund is much more than money. It is a symbol of something he is entitled to have and worth fighting to get.

* * * * * * *

It is a Saturday at the academy and Paul doesn't have duty. He is free for the weekend. Jane has gone back to her family's home and will return Sunday. She has become a big part of his life. They are now experiencing the excitement of a new relationship. Jane and Paul are developing a comfortable routine of secret meetings and acting indifferent to one another around other cadets. He has never told her about his plans to save the academy. Paul is afraid she may not approve. He has decided she won't know anything about them until the time is right. Jane may not understand why his plan is what's necessary to save the academy.

The father of Paul's friend from a former college is a private detective. His name is Ted. Paul prefers to call him Mr. Istina. He has been a private detective for over two decades. Ted has worked for a large private investigative firm and various companies for many years. He recently started his own detective agency. When he gets a call from Paul about a job, it is good news to him. The name Wildman Holdings always brings hope for a big payday. Ted needs the money. Paul sets up a meeting and is very vague about the details of what he wants.

Ted and Paul meet at a local coffee shop. A busy place with white walls and red leather stools positioned next to the counter. There is a large glass window next to the booth where they are seated with views of the sidewalk and a busy road. Ted is enjoying pancakes and Paul is simply having coffee. Paul noticed a sweat stain on the cook's hat and decided to avoid their culinary offerings. He looks around hoping nobody from the academy sees them. There would be questions and Paul would not tell the truth about this meeting. It is why he asked Ted to pick him up away from the academy. Paul chose to meet at a place in a town several miles away. Ted is a tall, thin man with white hair and a beard. He is dressed casually but is wearing expensive clothes.

"Is there a reason we had to come to a coffee shop so far from the academy?" says Ted.

"It's the only place near the academy that has the special imported Peruvian coffee beans I prefer. They are grown at a special temperature in the Himalayas," says Paul.

"Don't you mean the Andes? The Himalayas are in India. Peru and the Andes are in South America."

"Sorry, I'm not a geography major. I appreciate your knowledge on the subject, but I hadn't anticipated discussing the topographic and coffee-growing industries of different continents. I was hoping we could talk about you gathering some information for me."

"What kind of information are we talking about?"

"You know, the usual. Who someone knows, associates with, or any substantiated rumors of behind-the-scenes legal troubles. The sort of stuff most people don't want anyone to know about."

"You want me to dig up dirt on people."

"Digging up dirt on people sounds so harsh. Let's think of this as removing a person's façade so I can see their truth. It may be something that could help these people reconnect with their inner selves."

"My but you have a well-developed line of BS. It's still digging up dirt on people."

"Okay, have it your way."

"Do you have a list of people you want me to remove their façade, so they can reconnect with their inner selves?"

"Yes, the list is short but distinguished."

Paul takes out a business-size envelope and hands it to Ted. The envelope is opened and a sheet of paper is removed. Ted takes his glasses from his pocket, puts them on, and begins to read.

"Hey, two people on this list have the same last name as you."

"Isn't that an amazing coincidence? We live in such a small world."

Ted puts the list down on the table. He then puts his glasses back into his pocket.

"I don't know about this. I thought I'd be working for your family's company. I don't know if I want to get involved in some domestic family situation. Besides that, I've been doing this for a long time. I charge quite a bit of money. I'd expect to be paid and have my expenses covered. I may not be the right guy for this job."

Paul smiles and then takes out a large business envelope bulging with money. He hands it to Ted. After the envelope is opened, Ted looks inside and is amazed at the amount of cash it contains.

"Can I ask you if this now makes you the right man for the job?" says Paul.

Ted's eyes widen and he makes a faint whistle sound.

He then takes the envelope, puts it in his pocket, and says, "That is a lot of money. Where did you get all this?"

"Do you ask all of your clients the source of their funds or do you just take your payment and do the job? I think there is enough in that envelope to get you started and working on things for a few days."

"If this is from doing something illegal don't tell me. I don't want to know."

"You have nothing to worry about. I'm simply a cadet at the academy who comes from a wealthy family."

"A wealthy family you want me to get information about."

"Yes, and I think this proves we are a family that could be categorized as dysfunctional at the highest possible level. With the type of family I have this should not be considered unusual."

Ted smiles, shakes his head, and says, "Okay, you got a deal."

They spend the afternoon discussing Ted's history of working as a private detective. Paul is careful not to reveal too much about himself. People don't seem to want to hear about spoiled rich kids and their sports cars.

* * * * * * * *

Jane has been with her mother for only a day. She is not having a good time. The closer it gets to graduation, the more her mother expresses her displeasure with Jane having attended Saint Michael's Military Academy. Jane now dreams of leaving her mother's home and never coming back. Her thoughts turn to her siblings. On the counter is a cutting board her brother made in woodshop class during high school. The dark wood is uneven and the stain is gone, but they still use it. The window has a stained glass ornament her sister made in a high school art class. Her artwork was removed from around the house. Her mother didn't want to encourage Jane's desire for art school. She misses being around her brother and sister.

Jane's mother walks into the kitchen. She sees Jane enjoying a cup of tea and says, "You know Neil has called here more than once asking for you. I don't know why you aren't interested in him. He is crazy about you, and he is going to graduate from the Air Force Academy this year. What is wrong with him?"

"As I've told you before, he is pompous, he is arrogant, conceited as well as very controlling. He's not for me. I wish you would leave it alone."

"Okay, so I'll leave it alone. All men have rough edges. He may just take some time to iron out his difficult spots is all. He comes from a good family. A military family. It would be such a great match."

"It would be a great match for you. I suppose you don't want to consider the fact I don't like Neil. If you like him so much, why don't you go out with him? You haven't been on a date since Dad died. It's been over two decades."

"Watch your mouth young lady. Don't you talk to me that way. This isn't about me."

"Everything is about you in this house. Neil isn't a good match for me, he's a good match for you. He is the kind of guy that interests you."

"What kind of guy interests you? Someone like that smartass who gave me lip when I visited you at the academy? That asshole was a piece of work."

Jane looks away and says, "Please drop it."

Jane's mother walks around Jane looking closely at her.

"You have nothing to do with that obnoxious individual, right? Please tell me you have nothing to do with him. He is not our kind of people."

"What is our kind of people? Are you saying because he and his family have nothing to do with the military; he is off-limits for me? That's ridiculous. I like him and he is now what I think of as my people. I don't want to talk about this anymore."

Jane gets up and walks toward the staircase to go to her bedroom.

Jane's mother yells at her as she walks away, "I don't want to think you have gone so low as to be interested in a mouthy little rich jerk like him. If you are interested in him, I don't want to see him in this house. Do you understand? He has to apologize for how he talked to me first before he is permitted to be anywhere near this house."

Jane goes into her bedroom. She takes out a box from under her bed. It is filled with brochures for art schools. Jane begins to look at them. She's not certain how she feels about Paul. Strong feelings are growing between them. Jane does know she loves the reaction he causes in her mother. That thought makes her feel a bit better about her visit.

# Chapter 21

## *A Sense of Justice*

The closure of the academy has cast a sense of impending doom over all the cadets. Most of them are quiet and less energetic than before. The cadets and the staff seem to be only going through the motions of daily academy life. There is a feeling that all of them are simply waiting for the academic year to be over. They are putting in their time until they move on from graduation or to a new school. Everyone seems to be struggling to deal with the deep sadness they're feeling.

Paul is in his room working at his desk. Books are open and he is writing in a notebook. He is wearing a white T-shirt and regulation blue shorts. Paul has not shared his plans to save the academy with anyone. This may be the biggest thing he has ever undertaken in his life.

Dennis is sitting across from him and gets Paul's attention.

He says, "You know the worst part of the academy closing? I have to face my little brother. He has been talking about coming to this academy since my first days as a cadet. When I go home, he puts on my uniform and walks around the house. He makes me laugh. I now feel bad for him. When I told him the academy was closing, his eyes filled with tears."

Paul looks at Dennis and listens quietly. He doesn't remember the easy-going Dennis ever getting this upset about anything.

"I think the worst part for you must be the feeling you have no control over what is happening," says Paul.

"That is what sucks the most. They think I am a good cadet around here. My little brother would have put me to shame if he could've been a cadet at this academy. That little man is motivated."

"You really like your little brother, don't you?"

"Yeah, he is the coolest little guy in the world."

"I don't think we should give up yet."

"Are you serious? The general made the announcement. I know plans are being made to move the academy's stuff out of these buildings and off of the property after graduation. Unless you know something I don't, I'd say the academy closing is a done deal."

"I just may know something you don't"

"Oh, yeah, what?"

"That things are never as good or as bad as they may seem."

"When did you become such a philosopher?"

"There was a very attractive girl majoring in philosophy at one of the schools I attended. I learned a few things."

Dennis laughs and says, "You are so crazy. Did it pay off?"

"It took me several attempts to get her attention. She wasn't too interested until I picked her up for a date in my sports car. A bit of philosophy, a sports car, and dinner at a nice place, it was the perfect combination. It turned into a rather interesting dating experience."

Dennis laughs even louder.

"How long was she your girlfriend?"

"Less than a week. I had other prospects. The point is I didn't give up. It looked pretty bad when her boyfriend threatened me, and her sister said terrible things about the time I dated her."

"The girl had a boyfriend and you dated her sister?"

"Yeah, it's a bit complicated. Look, the point is with all that going against me, I didn't give up on my quest to date this girl. I was lucky when her boyfriend started dating her sister, and she needed a shoulder to cry on. His actions didn't cost me all that much. It wouldn't have happened if I had quit. I don't think we should give up on the academy."

"You paid a girl's boyfriend to date her sister so you could date her? You are one crazy dude or an insane romantic."

"I think the word crazy is harsh. I'd like to think of myself as goal-oriented, and a creative problem solver."

"I still think you're crazy."

"Have it your way. I simply suggest things are going on behind the scenes concerning this academy not known by many people."

"How do you know?"

"That is top secret classified information for authorized people only."

Dennis laughs and says, "Oh yeah, right. I'm sure you know everything."

Paul and Dennis continue talking. They eventually return to doing work at their desks. Paul resists the temptation to tell Dennis how he is putting his problem-solving skills to work to save the academy. Most people don't seem to agree with his methods, but they won't be able to deny their success.

* * * * * * * *

At a rather large park in the town outside the academy, Paul is sitting on a bench and waiting for Ted. He will be giving Paul the results of his investigation. The sky is clear. The grass and trees provide the outdoor aroma of spring in the air. The bench where Paul is sitting isn't too far away from a wooden pavilion where a family is celebrating the birthday of one of their children. There are colorful hand-decorated signs located around the pavilion as well as some balloons with colorful streamers tied to the posts. The adults are talking and playing outdoor games as children run around laughing and yelling. An outside grill on the side of the pavilion is being put to good use as hot dogs, hamburgers, and more are being prepared. The sizzling sound of various foods being cooked is loud. The smells are intoxicating. A table inside the pavilion is covered with many types of food as well as condiments, buns, and desserts. Another table is filled with presents. Everyone seems to be having a good time.

Watching these things brings back a powerful memory to Paul from his childhood. He thinks about the time he was eleven and forced to attend his family's company picnic. It was something he always hated doing. Paul's father would give him an annual speech at the picnic. Walter explained since he and his grandfather are the owners of the company, many people would be watching what Paul does during the picnic. He was told to be on his best behavior. Walter then takes out a significant amount of money from his pocket and shows it to Paul.

He smiles and says, "If you behave yourself, and don't get into trouble with anyone today, you will earn a reward. Should you make me and your grandfather proud of you today, then all of this will be yours. Do you understand?"

"Paul is angry and yells, "Why can't I just have fun? I don't care about behaving and getting money. I want to have fun."

Paul's father quickly puts the money back into his pocket.

He gets down on one knee, looks directly into Paul's face, and yells, "Now you listen to me, young man. You are a Wildman. With that comes certain responsibilities that will follow you throughout your entire life. I didn't like it either when I was your age but it's what we must do. Now, don't get dirty, talk nice to people and behave. You can go on a shopping trip tomorrow if you earn this money. Do we understand one another?"

Paul is looking down and mumbles, "I guess so."

"Good, now you have a golden opportunity to make your family proud of you. Run along and enjoy yourself."

Paul walks away feeling sad and angry. He goes to another part of the picnic and sees a man yelling at his son.

"Do you understand the family having this picnic are the Wildmans? They can really make things much better for our family. You will act in a way that impresses them or else," screams the boy's father.

The boy looks down and says, "I don't want to."

The boy's father slaps the young man's face. When he is about to cry, the father kneels, grabs him by the shoulders, and yells, "Now you stop that right now. Do you want people to say my son is a crybaby? Is that what you want?"

Fighting back his tears the boy sniffles and says, "No."

"Then don't act like one. Now go out there and play nice. Don't get dirty and find a way to impress these people and especially the Wildmans."

The boy's father stands up and walks away. The boy has his head down and starts walking.

This is the moment when Paul experiences an epiphany that changes his life. There is a feeling of rage deep within him caused by a hatred of bullies. It's the first time he understands his father and grandfather are bullies. He wants bad things to happen to the young boy's father. Paul wants the father to be punished for what he has done to his son. He knows he is too small. Paul is determined to figure out a way to deal with this bully. He will do something to make him pay. Paul decides right now he is going to make a new friend.

Paul walks over to the boy and says, "Hi, my name is Paul. What's your name?"

"Tony, Tony Jenkins."

"Your dad is an asshole."

Tony lifts his head and looks angry.

"Don't say that about my dad."

"It's okay, my dad is an asshole too. I don't like my dad or my grandfather."

"My dad scares me."

"Hey, how about we go explore the woods, play some games, and have some fun? We can talk about how our dads are assholes."

Tony smiles and says, "Okay."

Tony and Paul go and explore the woods. There are dirt paths and green ferns covering open spaces. There are tall pine trees and even a rushing creek. Tony and Paul look under rocks and find broken branches they use as walking sticks. After leaving the woods, they go on the pony ride being provided at the picnic and more. Both of them are having fun. When it gets late, Tony decides it's time for him to find his father. On their way back to where the adults are talking, Tony trips and falls into a mud puddle. His shirt is a mess. Tony is in a panic and tears start streaming down his face.

"My father is going to kill me. He hates me. He is going to hit me so hard. I don't know what to do."

"I know, we'll go to the bathroom. You can wash up, and we'll trade shirts. They look almost the same. Then your father won't be mad at you."

Tony stops crying and says, "What about your dad? What will he say?"

"Oh, he'll be upset, but he'd never hit me. My grandmother would be furious with him. Nobody wants my grandmother mad at them. Especially not my father."

"You sure?"

"Yeah, let's go."

The two boys head to the bathroom. Tony washes up and gets as clean as possible. They trade shirts and Tony smiles. The two boys decide it's time for them to find Tony's father.

As they're walking, Paul looks at Tony and says, "Did I ever tell you my last name?"

"No, you didn't"

"It's Wildman. I'm Paul J. Wildman. My father and grandfather own the company where your dad works."

Tony's eyes widen as he says, "You're one of them. The rich people. The ones my dad always wants to impress. I never thought a rich kid would be so much fun."

"Yeah, some of us can be fun. Don't be impressed. You don't know my family.

"My father will be happy I made friends with you."

"I'd like to meet your father."

As the two boys walk through the crowd, they spot Tony's father.

Tony walks up to him and says, "Dad, this is my new friend Paul. He is one of the Wildmans. The rich people who own the company where you work."

Tony's dad sighs and says, "You don't need to make a public announcement. I'm sure everyone is aware of that fact."

Paul puts out his hand to Tony's father. He smiles and shakes it.

"Mr. Jenkins, I would like to say it was certainly a pleasure to meet your son. We had a great time playing together. I am impressed by how he can keep clean when outdoors. You can see by my shirt, I tried to keep clean, but I just couldn't do it."

Paul points to the mud-stained shirt he is wearing. Tony's father looks down at his son, puts his arm around him, and smiles.

"I'm glad he met you, Paul Wildman. I'm also glad you both had a great time with my son."

Tony's father turns to walk away, but Paul stops him. He motions for Tony's father to get close so he can talk to him. Paul is controlling his disgust for this man.

Paul whispers, "Mr. Jenkins, I would also like to let you know if some young boy were to see an employee hit their son, and this young boy was then to share what happened with their family, the person who did it would really be in quite a bit of trouble with our company. Especially if they were an employee. I hope you understand if given a reason to inform them of such a thing, it will be done. This will result in your life at our company being quite unpleasant. I'm sure we understand one another. Right?"

Tony's father steps away from Paul and is shocked as well as angry. Paul smiles at him.

Tony's father says, "I can't believe you would say such things to an adult. Let's go, Tony."

As Tony and his father walk away, Paul yells, "I'm glad to have met you, Mr. Jenkins. I can't wait to tell my family all about you."

Mr. Jenkins turns and looks at Paul with a rather angry expression. Paul smiles at him. He then puts his hands in his pockets and walks to where his father is standing. Paul is wearing Tony's dirty shirt and whistling a happy tune. His father looks at Paul and quickly becomes angry.

Paul's father yells, "I told you to remain clean and presentable, and look what you've done."

Paul looks at his father and smiles. His father tells Paul he is ashamed of him for walking around so dirty. Paul is told he can forget about shopping tomorrow. Paul sighs. His father is furious with him. Paul is still happy and tries to communicate he had a great time at the picnic. These remarks are ignored by his father. Paul begins to realize how much he hates bullies. He keeps thinking his father didn't ask him what happened or realize he wasn't wearing the same shirt as when they arrived.

* * * * * * *

A brown sedan pulls into the parking lot across the road from where Paul is sitting. He gets up and walks toward the car. When Paul is next to the brown sedan, the driver's side window comes down.

Ted says, "Get in, so we can have a talk."

Paul gets in and sits in the passenger seat, looks at Ted, and says, "Did you get everything I asked?"

"Yes."

"I assume that includes all the real estate information I requested. I hope I provided enough money for your work?"

"Yeah, the real estate information is pretty interesting. About the money, it was a little too much actually. Do you want the rest of it back?"

"No, consider it as part of your retainer. I may need you to do some more work for me in the future. I'm anxious to see what you discovered."

Ted gets a briefcase from the back seat. He puts it on his lap and opens it. He takes out a large manila envelope filled with papers. After handing it to Paul, he closes the briefcase and returns it to the back seat. Paul notices there is an emblem on the briefcase from Soward Industries. This is one of the biggest competitors of his family's business.

"You work for Soward Industries?"

"I did work for them for a few years long ago. I just moved up to bigger and better things. They were assholes."

"I would have to agree. Have you ever worked for my family's company in any capacity?"

"No, I have not."

"Good, if you had I would request a refund, formal apology, and an embarrassing picture of you to put on T-shirts that I would give away for free."

"What?"

"Never mind. Is this everything?"

Ted is feeling confused and says, "It's all there in the envelope. All my research and findings. I'm sure you'll have some surprises. I did a very extensive public record search as you requested, interviewed people, and provided reports from some of my informants in different places."

"Excellent."

Ted drives Paul back to the academy. Paul asks him to park quite a distance away from the front gate. He'll get out there. Ted is curious about what is going on with Paul but feels it's better if he doesn't know.

# Chapter 22

## *A Time of Discovery*

A clear blue sky reveals small green leaf buds starting to open on the branches of trees surrounding a large house. Birds are making their voices heard. It will soon be time for Jane's mother to get busy planting her summer garden. Beautiful flowers and a nice vegetable garden will be placed on the land directly behind her home. She is making plans to get everything ready for the fast-approaching warm weather. The anticipation of future summer holiday celebrations taking place here makes her excited. This is a great time of year.

Jane is going to be graduating from the academy in a few months. She has spent a lot of time during her current visit thinking about the direction of her life. Jane has developed some strong feelings for Paul Wildman. He is very loyal and considerate of her. She loves how he is fun and makes her laugh. It can be difficult to get past his attitude about being a spoiled rich kid. Paul's desire to challenge people in authority worries her. It's obvious he has authority issues. This makes Jane curious about his past.

Paul seldom talks to Jane about his parents or life at home. Her curiosity about the man she is starting to care about overwhelms her. He never shares much about himself. Jane has tried more than once to learn about Paul and his life before the academy. He simply avoids her inquiries by making jokes or asking questions about her until she forgets about it. Jane hates that he keeps so many things about himself from her. She wants Paul to know he can trust her.

Jane's mother is unaware of her daughter's recent decision to return to the academy earlier than planned. As Jane loads things into her car for the drive back, she has a plan to learn more about Paul. There is a small brown suitcase and some food in a small brown box. A jar containing stolen whiskey is among the items in the box.

Paul seems to only mention things from his past intended to shock or impress Jane. It doesn't work. She believes he is simply telling stories like all guys. At times, it seems as if Paul is unknowingly pushing her away out of fear. She can sense the deep hurt and suppressed anger within him. Jane sees it with every smart remark he makes or attempts at humor. It's how Paul hides his true self from her and the rest of the world. There is probably much more to Paul Wildman than anyone realizes.

After the brown box and travel bag are in her car, Jane walks into the backyard. Her mother is sitting at a glass table located on a patio and writing on a notepad.

"Mother."

Jane's mother stops writing and looks up. She shifts her mind from the world of determining what plants, and new patio furniture to purchase to what her daughter is now saying.

"Yes, what is it, Jane?"

"I think I'll be leaving to go back to the academy soon. There is really nothing left for me to do here. I want to go and get things ready for the week."

"Are you certain? It's no problem if you want to stay."

"I understand, I think I just want to get back."

"Okay, if you need some help with anything let me know."

"Sure."

Jane can detect the disappointment in her mother's voice. She has a plan to learn more about the spoiled rich kid who is starting to mean something to her.

* * * * * * * *

After a two-hour drive, Jane finally arrives in the town where Paul grew up. She is amazed at all the expensive houses with well-manicured lawns, high-end restaurants, and shops in the downtown area. Gardeners are working on lawns and most of the vehicles being driven around are expensive. She is out of place driving her twelve-year-old car around this place.

After going in circles, Jane finally gives up and realizes she has no idea where she is going. She is lost. Jane pulls over into a parking lot next to a park. She gets a map from her car's glove compartment. Jane gets out of the car, spreads the map on the top of the car, and starts looking at it. As an attractive female, Jane is used to being noticed by men. She can ignore the stares and comments. It has happened so many times to her. There are people at a nearby park. A thin guy wearing glasses who appears to be around her age soon walks over.

"If you need help finding someplace around here; I can help. I've lived around here all my life," says the young man.

"That is very kind of you. I'm trying to find the easiest way to get back to the interstate."

"Where are you trying to get to?"

"I'm a cadet at Saint Michael's Military Academy."

"Really? I have a friend who goes there. Do you know a Paul Wildman?"

Jane is stunned. It's a few seconds before she replies.

"Yes, I do know a Paul Wildman. Are you a friend of his?"

The guy smiles and says, "This is so crazy. You could call it that. I've known him since we were kids in kindergarten. His father lives about two miles down the road. Paul's grandfather lives up in the Glens. His grandfather's house is so big, it's the only one in the area. He lives there with just his wife and house staff. My name is Charles, but everyone calls me Chuck."

Jane smiles and the two shake hands. Chuck tells her stories about Paul and the neighborhood. She finds all of it very interesting. He tells Jane where Paul's mother works. Chuck also shares some of the difficult stories about when Paul was younger. After some more conversation, Jane knows what directions she needs to travel. She thanks Chuck and leaves. Jane is glad for the opportunity to speak with him. She has enough time to stop off where Paul's mother works. It's important to her she learn as much as possible about anyone she has feelings for and there is nothing wrong with asking questions.

* * * * * * * *

An upscale art gallery is located about an hour's drive away from the park. The outside of the art gallery has impressive paintings in the window. She walks in and is instantly overwhelmed by all the amazing artwork on display. It also has expensive fixtures and decor. It appears to be more of a museum to her than an art gallery. Jane begins to feel a little insecure. She wants to be part of this world. Her artwork will be displayed in an art gallery just like this someday. She'll have supporters and give showings of her work. Jane walks around and tells herself how that day is not today. She is losing her nerve. Jane turns and begins heading to the door.

She hears a friendly female voice say, "Can I help you?"

Jane turns around to see a woman in her late 40s with blonde hair and blue eyes that appear to be like Paul's. She is wearing expensive clothing and nice jewelry. Her outfit is very tasteful and a bit elegant. Jane has on blue jeans and a simple knit top with tennis shoes. She is now aware she must look very out of place in such an upscale art gallery.

The woman walks closer and says, "Is there something I can help you find?"

Jane smiles and says, "Oh, I just saw this art gallery and I like art. I decided to come and look at a few things. I'm a bit of an artist myself. I like to see what other people are selling."

"Well, if you want to know anything about a particular piece of artwork you see just let me know. I'd be glad to help you."

"Thank you very much."

"Are you attending an art school at the moment?"

"Not at the moment. I would like to go after I'm done with the current school I'm attending."

"Really? What school are you currently attending?"

"It has nothing to do with art. I'm currently a cadet at Saint Michael's Military Academy."

"I know someone who also goes to school there."

"What is their name?"

"It's my son. His name is Paul J. Wildman. Do you know him?"

Now that the moment has presented itself to her, Jane isn't sure what to do next. She is determined to learn more about Paul and won't let herself back down.

"To be honest with you, I know him quite well. I may have come in here to see art, but having the opportunity to speak with you is much more important to me. I guess you could say, I'm kind of his girlfriend. I don't know anything about Paul, and I want to know about him. Can you understand my frustration?"

"Yes, I do. My name is Mary Alon. Paul's father and I are divorced and I'm now using my maiden name. It's funny, Paul actually mentioned you in the last conversation I had with him. He said something about how there is a female cadet who made him realize there is quite a bit of money to be made by hosting a female cadet beauty contest. He didn't know if one existed, but if not, he was thinking of starting one. That is his way of saying he has found someone special to him. I don't know what to say other than that's my Paul."

"Yeah, that is definitely Paul Wildman."

"I bet you can see there is more to him than the obnoxious persona he displays to those around him. There are so many good things about Paul that nobody knows. He has helped a lot of people in his unique way. You can call me Mary if you'd like. There is a room in the back where we can have a cup of tea and a chat. Does that work for you?"

"Yes, it does, thank you so much."

After going to the back of the art gallery Jane and May enjoy a few cups of tea and pleasant conversation. Neither one of them is aware of how long they've been talking. Suddenly, Mary's boss asks her to get back to work. Before Jane leaves, the two of them agree to keep in touch with one another.

When Jane is in her car going down the interstate toward Saint Michael's Military Academy, she has many thoughts about Paul. The recent conversation with his mother has caused her to have even more strong feelings for him. Jane decides to not mention this meeting with his mother until the time is right. She is beginning to believe her relationship with Paul J. Wildman has a good future.

# Chapter 23

## *Losing an Illusion*

Paul is alone in his room at the academy. Dennis is away for the weekend with his family as usual. It is a time when Paul doesn't have to worry about being interrupted by unanticipated visitors of any rank. He can now focus on some very important things.

Paul carefully takes out the folder given to him by Ted and places it on his desk. He knows it contains information capable of destroying people's lives. It's what he paid to get. The information is the type that has power over those who act as if their mistakes in the past will always remain unknown. Paul realizes this will make it possible for him to crush the illusions many people project about themselves. These are truths that required quite a bit of effort to hide. In the business world, when someone is unable to maintain their illusion, they can lose everything. The truth can be quite dangerous when it comes to exposing a person's carefully concealed transgressions.

Once the folder is open, Paul looks at each of the papers it contains. He is determined to read everything at least three times. Paul knows exactly what he will do with much of the information. He doesn't know what he will do with some of it. Paul believes innocent people don't deserve to have their past mistakes exposed. There are some things in life that just need to be forgotten.

* * * * * * *

Paul visits a print shop in the local town. He has made more than one copy of the documents he intends to use. They are an essential part of his plan to save the academy. Paul has hidden copies of the documents in various places where only he knows their location. The documents he has determined play no role in saving the academy will be eliminated at the academy's incinerator. Most of the cadets don't know or care about the location of the academy's incinerator. It is a large red brick structure located far away from all the main academy buildings. This is a place that has always been ignored by most of the administration at the school. It is unknown except by the few who are responsible for it and the person who works there.

Paul discovered the incinerator building during one of the many times he was exploring the academy grounds. He made friends with the only man who works at the incinerator. His name is Edward Partan. He is a tall thin man with a thick gray beard and wears well-worn work overalls. Paul learns Mr. Partan is a very soft-spoken and gentle person who looks to be in his early 60s. He seems to enjoy Paul's visits. The two have many discussions. Paul learns important things about the academy's history from Mr. Partan. Things nobody else talks about or has any idea exist. It is some of the most valuable information Paul has come to know. It will be part of his plan to save the academy. Mr. Partan doesn't realize the importance of what he has shared with Paul.

* * * * * * *

It is a dark and overcast Sunday. Mr. Partan is spending his free time at the academy's incinerator doing some work. During their previous talks, Mr. Partan let Paul know about his wife who died, his children who are all grown and moved to other states as well as his three grandchildren. Sometimes he comes down to run the incinerator just to get out of his empty house.

On this particular Sunday, Paul wants to use the incinerator but prefers to be alone when does. He doesn't want to risk any questions concerning what he is burning. Paul knows this man is lonely. He gladly listens to all of his stories and this seems to make Mr. Partan happy. Paul has a plan to be alone with the incinerator.

Paul smiles and says, "It's a shame you are here on a Sunday Mr. Partan. I think you work too much."

"Aw, it don't bother me none. I spend a few hours doing some work today, and I will have an easier week."

Paul has the folder with documents he intends to destroy in his hand. He opens it up and pulls out two gift cards and hands them to Mr. Partan.

"I want you to take these two gift cards for free chicken sandwich meals at the Chicken Hot Spot restaurant in town. My father's company gets these all the time, and I've had enough. I thought you'd enjoy them."

Mr. Partan's eyes open wide, and he has a smile.

"Are you serious? You remembered that is my favorite place to eat. I'm going to enjoy this. Thank you so much. I don't know what to say."

"I would like you to say you are going to go down there right now and get your favorite chicken sandwich meal. As a fellow single guy who doesn't like to cook, I understand what it is like to need a nice lunch. What do you say? Go on and get your food."

"I sure would like to but I got the fire going in the incinerator. It's not supposed to be left alone."

"I'll be here to take care of it while you're gone. It's an incinerator. I'm certain it will burn fine while you enjoy your lunch. I'll be right here, so it's no problem."

Mr. Partan looks at the gift cards and then at Paul and shows his excitement.

"Are you sure? I would really like to go get this food."

"I will be here so you can relax and know everything will be fine until you return. Go and say hi to Trixie for me."

"I didn't know there was a girl working there named Trixie."

"There has to be. I think it is a requirement for all fast food restaurants to have someone working for them named Trixie. Might be a federal regulation or something."

"You are a nice guy Paul, but you can also be very strange at times."

"I agree with you completely and consider it my trademark. It's how I stand out from the crowd."

Mr. Partan laughs as he gets his coat. He then makes his way to the door, and says, "I will be getting the food to go, so I won't be gone too long. Should I get you something from the restaurant?"

"No, I've given up eating fast food for lent."

"I think you may have missed your chance. Lent was over a month ago."

"Well, see, I didn't give up anything for the real lent. So, I figure by giving up fast food now I'll be making up for it."

"I don't know if that's how it works."

"You may be right, I'm not a religious studies major."

Mr. Partan smiles and then looks at Paul as he leaves. He tries to not reveal he thinks Paul is a good guy but a little on the crazy side.

* * * * * * * *

The heavy metal door on the incinerator squeaks loudly as Paul slowly opens it. The yellow flames are dancing around in the metal container and the heat is intense. He takes the folder and removes some papers.

This is information Paul believes is best forgotten.

The first few papers show Peter Barnett was arrested during high school for having marijuana in a car he was driving. Paul tosses the papers into the incinerator. The paper turns brown and then black as the flames consume it. Nobody needs to know about this.

The next few pages cover the older brother of Dennis Martinez. It appears he's been in trouble with the law many times and is in jail. Their father was suspected of helping him, but the charges against the father were dropped. It is a family situation. This is their business. Paul throws all the papers associated with this into the incinerator.

Then there is the information concerning the school's Commandant. He is everything he claims to be in his speeches. The Commandant has earned every medal and military commendation he claims to have been given. He also spent some time in an alcohol rehabilitation center. Paul quickly takes these papers and puts them into the mouth of the incinerator's fire. Whatever problems the Commandant has had in the past have been resolved. Paul knows how some people deserve to be free of mistakes they've worked hard to make right. There is no benefit to anyone knowing about such things.

The last few pages concern Jane and her mother. Paul has read these pages more than once. This information causes him to experience a real dilemma. There are things about her mother Jane doesn't know and may not want to know. Paul struggles to contain himself. He has a deep dislike for family members who project a false image and work hard to hide their reality. It is something he's had to live with his entire life. Paul closes the folder with the information about Jane's mother still inside. He decides this is not the right time to get rid of this information. Paul tells himself it may be done sometime in the future. He knows he has feelings for Jane. This information may make Jane's mother think twice before becoming a problem for him. It could also turn Jane against him. Paul decides he will do something about it later.

In a short time, Mr. Partan returns. Paul enjoys a few French fries and half of a chicken sandwich. After some conversation, Mr. Partan tells Paul he will be ready to leave the academy when it closes. He listens to the stories of Mr. Partan's decades of service to the academy. Paul learns the long and involved history of Mr. Partan's family and the academy. With the folder containing saved documents in hand, Paul leaves the incinerator building.

He intends to put the information about Jane's mother with copies of the other information in a special place tomorrow. It will be with all the paperwork he has on Mr. Dean as well as his father and grandfather. Paul feels he can achieve what others believe is impossible. He is confident saving the academy from Mr. Dean is something that can now happen.

# Chapter 24

## *Destroying a Stereotype*

Paul is sitting at a desk in class. He is thinking about the folder he has in his room containing documents from the private detective. He must decide what to do with them. Paul looks out a window and realizes the dark asphalt roads and tan stone wall surrounding the academy are kept in perfect condition. The large black wrought iron gate at the entrance is an impressive design. It shows there is a high level of dedication to the academy by the people in charge of it. This has always impressed Paul. It is more than just a school to them. To the cadets and administration, it is a common identity that gives them pride and a sense of belonging. They value it more than money. Saint Michael's Military Academy means so much to the cadets and staff, Paul can't help but feel the hurt and pain caused by its closing. Paul knows he is doing the right thing by doing what is necessary to save it

It's Friday and Dennis has once again left to spend the weekend with his family. After returning to his room, Paul looks at the closed folder on his desk. He tells himself it must be locked up as soon as he changes his clothes. His plans for saving the academy are slowly coming together. Not many people seem to know Saint Michael's Military Academy has a good chance of not being turned into a land of retail stores and office buildings. Paul thinks about his father and grandfather being part of the deceitful business dealings involving the academy. He is disgusted by them. Nobody running the academy seems to have any idea how the world of money controls the school. They are unable to stop those who know how to use money.

Paul looks at his watch. It is now time to get ready and meet Jane. He always gets excited about seeing her. She called the male barracks earlier and left a message for him to meet her at the front gate in about an hour. Jane wants to go to the Coffee House tonight and watch a local band performing.

Paul hates to admit he misses Jane on the weekends when she goes back to her mother's house. As he gets ready, Paul is careful to put on some nice civilian clothes but nothing that shows wealth. He forgets about the folder sitting on his desk. He is not aware of the papers sticking out of it that have the name of Jane's mother on it. These things have been pushed to the back of his mind. Seeing Jane is now his focus. He doesn't think about how information in the folder has the potential of being seen by anyone who comes into his room. It could cause serious problems if discovered.

* * * * * * * *

Jane meets Paul at the front gate. He is a little surprised by her car and slowly gets in it. This is the first time Paul has ever been inside a yellow 1971 Ford Pinto. As they drive away, Paul keeps looking around. He seems a bit uncomfortable sitting in her car. Paul grew up in a world where he was taught the inside of a car must be as impressive as the outside. An image must be maintained.

Jane says, "Oh, it's not an expensive sports car, but it's mine. Quit looking at everything."

"It's just that I don't know if I've ever been in a car with such accommodations. The empty bottles in the back do complement the empty food wrappers in the center console and other items sticking out from the edge of the seats. The dirt on the floor brings out an earthy feeling. The clothes, books, and other stuff in the back seat are perfectly arranged to bring out the true rebel girl motif. I'm impressed."

"Okay, Captain Sarcasm. I just had a long drive, and I haven't had a chance to clean my car out. You are an asshole."

"Yes, but I'm an exemplary one."

"I agree with you."

"I have always believed it is important to be the best at whatever endeavor you choose."

Jane looks at Paul and they both laugh. There is a bit of silence between them as they make their way into the local town. Jane wants to ask Paul about all the things his mother told her. She has so many questions she wants to ask him.

It is a struggle to find a parking spot near the Coffee House. When they do find a place, it requires Jane and Paul to walk several blocks to get there. Neither of them minds walking the distance.

"I've been looking into art schools to attend in the fall. There are a few that seem great. I can't wait to get into an academic environment where I can do art each day and not wear a uniform or salute people. It will be a wonderful change from being a cadet at the academy."

Paul smiles and admires her enthusiasm. He also likes how good she can look in apparel from a discount clothing store.

"You endured four years of being a cadet at Saint Michael's Military Academy to appease your family. Now you are going to do what you want with your life. I'm overwhelmed by your sense of dedication. I know I would never sacrifice so much for my family."

"No, you'd only sacrifice it for your trust fund. Just be glad you don't feel it's something you must do to live with your family."

They walk past a parking lot filled with cars and hear, "Paul Wildman, I need help. Please help me. I know your father Walter."

Paul looks at Jane who seems surprised. He then slowly walks into the parking lot with her behind him. When they get to a dead end, a young man in his twenties is sitting on some boxes. He has on a blue jeans jacket; a cigarette is in the corner of his mouth and his dark hair is unkempt. He stands up and takes the cigarette from his mouth and throws it on the ground. The young man then stamps it out with his leather boot as smoke exits his mouth.

"Do I know you? You don't look familiar. How do you know my name and my father's name?" says Paul.

The young man walks past Paul toward the edge of the parking lot to block them from leaving. He whistles and an older man comes and stands beside him. The older man is wearing a leather jacket and sunglasses.

He walks up to Paul and says, "You don't need to know who we are because the two of us know all we need to know about you."

"I never knew my notoriety would result in having parking lot-dwelling fans. I guess this is the popular hangout for such people in this town. What do you think you know about me?"

"You are rich and you have access to lots of money. Me and my friend think people like you need to be more charitable with your financial success. We are in a bit of a financial bind and need some cash. We need it right now if you get what I'm saying."

"I am going to go out on a limb here. I don't think you are interested in a low-interest loan. By the looks of you two, I doubt either of you would even qualify for one. You could do credit card scams, but you would have to be somewhat intelligent for that one, so that's out. I guess you want to rob me. You believe I'm a terrified spoiled rich kid and will just give you money. Many people have made such an assumption. If I refuse, you will bestow violence upon me and my lady friend. I hope you are not working for my father or grandfather. They've sent lowlifes like you after me before."

The older man looks back at the younger man and laughs. They both display their confidence with smiles. When the older man turns back and looks at Paul, he seems angry.

"I don't know nothing about your dad or grandpa. Somebody told me your father's name. I know you got lots of money. Everybody knows you got money because you make sure everybody knows you got money. Lowlifes? I believe you've hurt our feelings. Now, that is going to cost you. It is going to be real expensive to repair our self-esteem. So, why don't you just give us your wallet, watch, and anything else you have of value? Then you can walk away. This doesn't have to end in violence."

Jane grabs Paul's shoulder and whispers in his ear, "Just give them the money and your watch so we can get out of here."

Paul looks at Jane, smiles, and says, "Don't worry, I got this."

Jane doesn't know what to do. She is in a panic and looks around for something to use as a weapon. Paul seems fearless. This is a side of him she has never seen. Jane is afraid his fantasy of being a tough guy will result in a beating from the current reality of these two guys. She is terrified for Paul.

The older man yells, "I want the money now."

Paul bends over and removes his shoes. He then moves his arms and torso as if he's warming up for exercise.

"You see gentlemen, here's the problem. You are not the first hoodlums who have tried to rob me, and you probably won't be the last. I've always had to deal with worthless pieces of excrement like you two. Guys who have always looked at me and thought I'm a spoiled rich kid who will be terrified of the big, mean-looking douchebags. We'll just take his money because it will be easy. Guess what? It doesn't work that way with me. If you think you are so tough and want my money then come and take it from me."

Paul takes out his wallet and places it on a box behind him. He then takes off his watch and puts it on top of the wallet.

"There is my money and watch. All you have to do to get these items is get past me. Think you can handle a spoiled rich kid for such a nice financial reward?"

Jane tries to say something but she can't because she's too frightened. The older man steps toward Paul and tries to punch him. Paul moves and the older man misses. Paul then rams his elbow into the older man's rib cage. After getting closer he puts his leg behind the older man's hip and throws him down. The younger man comes running toward Paul. He is met with a kick to his chin. This makes him fall back and hit the ground.

The two men stand up and Paul is now moving up and down on the ball of his feet.

"Oh, please try again, this is getting fun."

Jane is in shock. She can't believe what she's seeing. Jane wonders who is this person fighting these two guys. Who is Paul Wildman?

The older man lunges at Paul and is met with a kick to his ribs and then a kick to his face. The younger man tries to make a move on Paul. He is quickly thrown down to the ground and punched in the face. When he gets up, he lunges at Paul who spins around and kicks him in the stomach then turns and kicks him in the face again. The young man's nose is now bleeding and his eyes are swollen.

The older man takes out a knife and tries to stab Paul. He easily moves out of the way and the older man misses. Paul then grabs the man's hand with the knife and quickly twists his wrist until the knife falls. Paul kicks him in the face. He stumbles back and then goes down.

"Do either of you still want the wallet and watch? They remain on a box behind me."

The young man says, "I say we forget this, and next time we bring some bullet launchers."

He starts limping away with the older man slowly following him. As they're walking away, the older man suddenly stops.

He turns toward Paul and says, "I just don't think it's right you should have so much money and people like me have so little."

Paul yells at the men, "When I want your opinion, I'll beat it out of you. Is it my fault you suck at being a criminal? Try working at a job. I don't think there is too much career advancement in being a hoodlum."

Jane just keeps looking at Paul and can't hide her stunned expression. Paul gets his wallet, puts on his watch, and then starts putting on his shoes. The two men have left. Jane goes over to Paul and hugs him. She feels safe with him. He has stood up for her against her mother and fought off attackers. Nobody realizes Paul is brave. Paul is real. She doesn't understand why he hides so many things about himself from the world.

"That is one of the most incredible things I have ever seen. Who taught you to fight?"

"Bruce Lee and Chuck Norris."

"What?"

"Yeah, my friend Kenny and I used to watch Bruce Lee and Chuck Norris movies on the weekends. We'd practice the moves we saw in the movies. Kenny even had a stand-up dummy we used for practicing kicking and punching. There was also a student from South Korea who couldn't pay his franchise fee for a rickshaw business I owned at a college. He gave me some lessons in martial arts to pay off his debt."

"You had a rickshaw franchise at college?"

"Yeah, it's a long story."

"You are one in a million."

"I can't take credit for the line 'When I want your opinion, I'll beat it out of you.' That was from Chuck Norris in the movie "Code of Silence.""

"That first night in town you got in trouble. Why didn't you defend yourself then?"

Paul yells, "Because none of you would let me. All of you thought you would be the big heroes and rushed in to save the poor rich kid from getting beat up by some thugs. You were so full of yourselves and your perceived superiority. None of you asked if I felt I needed your help. None of you could give up the opportunity to play heroes."

Jane puts her head down and says, "I guess we shouldn't have made assumptions about you. We were wrong."

"On the one hand, those guys were just like these guys. They were brawlers and not fighters. If they ever send experienced fighters, we are all in trouble. On the other hand, I didn't have to take off my shoes or get warmed up that time in the alley so there is that."

"I have never met anyone like you, Paul Wildman."

"I'm glad because I have always thought of myself as an original never to be duplicated."

"You're like Batman's Bruce Wayne."

"I don't like being associated with creatures. I'd prefer to be called something like Lamborghini Man or Captain Rolex. That would fit my personality better."

Jane looks at Paul and rolls her eyes and tries not to laugh. She and Paul make their way out of the parking lot and toward the Coffee House. Paul starts to make conversation.  He shares his ideas for businesses he thinks would do well in the local town. Paul seems to have quickly forgotten the incident in the parking lot. Jane doesn't believe Paul's story about him and his friend Kenny learning martial arts from movies. The story about the rickshaw franchise at a college does sound like something Paul would attempt. She hopes to eventually gain Paul's trust. Jane begins to realize her feelings for Paul are stronger than for any man she has ever dated.

# Chapter 25

*Discovering Secrets*

Jane and Paul finally make it to the Coffee House and get a good table near the stage. After ordering some drinks, they aren't talking much. Jane reaches over and holds Paul's hand. He looks at her and smiles. Paul looks around to make certain no other cadets can see this. He doesn't want Jane to get into trouble. Paul may be experiencing feelings he has never had for any other female. It's a bit frightening. Paul is handling this situation like he does every time he experiences intense emotion. He jokes about it. Paul tries to tell himself these strong feelings are either caused by Jane or his desire to buy the Coffee House and rename it the Wildman Coffee House. Paul finds both things very exciting.

The band stops for a break. The lights come on in the small room and waitresses are busy going to the many tables getting orders. People are getting up and heading to the restrooms. Others are waving at a waitress to get their attention and another round of drinks.

Paul looks at Jane and says, "What would you think if I purchased this fine establishment and renamed it Wildman Coffee House?"

"I think it would be extremely egotistical of you."

"Yeah, I didn't see anything wrong with it either."

Jane has a growing desire to tell Paul she met his mother. The idea slowly starts to creep into her mind. She does fear Paul's reaction. There are some feelings of guilt. It was kind of sneaky of her. She tells herself she can't expect Paul to be open and honest if she can't do the same with him. Jane decides she must tell him. She wants to have an honest relationship with Paul.

"I have a little confession to make."

"You do realize I've never been a seminary student? Anything you tell me I can have published in a local newspaper and no religious police can come and arrest me or anything. You will be given the opportunity to change my mind as only you can."

"You always struggle to be serious about anything. It's like all the time you try to say something funny to distract from what is going on with you. I think this is how you shield yourself from anybody knowing about you. The wall of jokes and humor is something you use to protect yourself from people getting to know the real Paul J. Wildman. Why is that?"

"I'm no expert on confessions but this one seems pretty bad."

"Can we just be serious for a minute?"

"Sure."

"I left my home and instead of coming directly to the academy, I took a little detour. I went to the neighborhood of Ross Commons. I know you and your family live there."

"Why would you go there?"

"I just thought if I drove around your neighborhood for a while, I'd get to know you better. I wanted to gain a sense of who you are as a person."

"If you were at Ross Commons, you probably got a sense of me telling you the truth when I say my label of spoiled rich kid is well deserved."

"Yeah, my old car did stand out a bit. I stopped at a park and a nice young man helped me with directions. He told me he knew you."

"What was his name?"

"He said his name was Charles but everybody called him Chuck."

"Was he tall and thin? Did he wear Coke bottle glasses? Did it appear as if he could have been on the cover of "Nerd Illustrated?""

"Yeah, I guess you know him."

"Yes, he is a delusional individual who roams the streets of our neighborhood giving false information about the residents to anyone who stops for directions. He's a public nuisance. We've been trying to get rid of him for years."

"You're doing it again. Stop with the jokes."

"Okay. You're right, but you need to understand I've never gone through a sarcastic comment detox. I don't think there is a 12-step program for people like me."

"He gave me directions to an art gallery a few miles away. I like art, and I thought I'd stop and see what they have. I met someone there who knows you quite well."

"You saw my mother. Why would you do such a thing? She doesn't know you."

Jane smiles and says, "She does now."

Paul yells, "I can't believe you did this. You went behind my back to see my mother and dig up dirt on me? I know it is something I would do on you but that is completely different."

"Calm down, it's no big deal. Your mother had many nice things to say about you. I was impressed by how much she loves you."

"I'll be honest. I'm very upset with what you did. You know nothing about my family. You had no right to do this. Be thankful I have feelings for you, or I would be contacting my legal counsel right now. I may still write some derogatory things about you on a wall in the men's room."

"I don't know what you're upset about. She told me you are kind of a secret hero. I heard how you started a homeless shelter at a university that kicked you out. Most people don't know you told them about an abandoned building they had off campus and about federal funds available to turn the building into a homeless shelter. They only listened after you had homeless people living in the basement of that building. Now the school claims the homeless shelter was their idea. The homeless around there are now being helped."

"Can I make a sarcastic comment that might be considered funny to me?"

"No, now is not the time.

"Darn."

"At the other university that kicked you out, you stopped a guy from selling steroids to athletes. You also had a professor at that college who told horrible things about you during a meeting of the school's trustees. You showed up to the meeting with two girls the professor had been giving good grades to for sex. The investigation got a lot of bad people out of that place."

"I'm really struggling to not make a sarcastic comment. I may need to create a 12-step program to help me deal with these urges."

"My favorite one was spending the weekend with the girl who was being deported. You let people think things were happening between the two of you. Nobody knew most of the weekend was spent with an immigration attorney you hired and helped her legally return to the United States. This made it possible for her to be with her family. This was done at your expense. You paid for the attorney who helped that girl. You are a good person Paul. I am so impressed with you."

"She made the most incredible Argentinian food. I think it had something to do with the fact she was from Argentina. I plan to contact her when I open a restaurant serving Argentinian food. That one weekend I spent providing access to an immigration attorney is going to have serious financial rewards in the future. You have no idea how much better I feel right now. Sorry, you need to be more sensitive to sarcastic comment-making addiction."

"Again with the jokes. Will you ever stop?"

"Hey, I'm helpless over my addiction. What do you expect? This attempt at a detox program isn't working."

The lights of the room suddenly get dim and the band walks back onto the stage.

"You do struggle with people thinking good things about you. Are you still mad at me for visiting your mother?"

"Yes, but I'm willing to negotiate an appropriate settlement for this misgiving."

"What might that involve?"

"You'll find out when we start our negotiations. It could involve some physical compensation to begin with and then become more extreme."

Janet laughs and moves her seat closer to Paul. She holds his hand and they enjoy the music.

* * * * * * * *

When Jane and Paul make it back to the academy, the sun is slowly setting. It's a Saturday. Most of the upperclassmen and the administration are gone until Monday. Paul and Jane are friends with the person on duty at the guy's barracks. They know he won't alert anyone or officially record it if Jane is in Paul's room. Dennis isn't going to be back for a few hours. They plan to make the most of the limited time they are going to be able to spend together. Paul leaves to use the bathroom promising to be back quickly.

Anyone can forget something important. People do it all the time. Sometimes forgetting something important can result in serious consequences. On Paul's desk is a folder with papers sticking out of it. Papers with the name of Jane's mother on them. Information Paul was going to keep hidden and only reveal if he felt it was necessary.

Jane initially doesn't notice the folder. She occupies herself by walking around the room and looking at different things. The bed where Dennis sleeps is made perfectly and everything is in order. There are many pictures of his family. Pictures of him with his parents, pictures of him with his little brother, and one of his entire family. On his desk are school books, a copy of the Bible, and a book about Spain.

When Jane walks over to the part of the room where Paul resides, it is completely different. His bed is made but it could be much better. On Paul's desk, there are no family pictures. He has pictures of famous businessmen such as Andrew Carnegie, Sam Walton, and Steve Jobs. He has school books but also several books about creating wealth.

Jane notices the folder and the paper with her mother's name on it She picks up the folder and opens it. There are only a few pages. After reading them she gasps and covers her mouth. Jane puts the folder down and struggles not to cry. She hates Paul. The door to the room opens.

Paul walks in and says, "Well, I suggest we proceed quickly with our amorous activities as I believe Dennis will be back very soon."

Jane's eyes are red as she can't keep from crying.

She yells, "You dirty, rotten, bastard."

Paul clears his throat and says, "I'm not known for being a romantic. I do believe that would not be considered the way to set the mood for amorous activities. I assure you my parents were married to each other at the time of my birth. I can provide you with all the proper documentation if you'd like."

Jane holds up the folder and yells, "Oh cut the comedy crap asshole. I want you to explain this."

When Jane slams the folder down on the desk, Paul feels a bit lightheaded and swallows. He quickly takes the folder. Paul opens his locker, places the folder inside, and then closes the locker and locks it.

"It's complicated. You weren't supposed to see what was inside that folder."

"I'm sure I wasn't, but I saw it. What do you have to say for yourself? Where did you get this stuff?"

"I believe it is time we have a very serious talk."

"I agree."

"Just to confirm a hunch I have right now. Am I correct in assuming there is no longer any possibility of any amorous activities taking place between us?"

"Not while I still live and breathe."

"It's a shame necrophilia is just not my thing."

Jane sits down on Paul's bed. He then takes a chair and moves it so he is sitting across from her. Ignoring his strong desire to make jokes and sarcastic comments; Paul begins to speak. He knows this is a time when he must be very serious and it is something he is not good at.

# Chapter 26

## *The Past Never Dies*

The year is 1974 and the US military is conducting operations in a hot and steamy Asian jungle. A select group of American army troops are stationed at a remote location. It is a secret mission unknown by the American media and not acknowledged by the American government. There are several small wooden buildings with corrugated metal roofs being used as field hospitals. American troops are leading soldiers from the host country on combat missions. The goal is to neutralize the leaders of local armies hostile to the United States and its allies. It is a dangerous situation. The enemy is using sophisticated weapons and has been taught advanced military tactics.

One of the nurses attending to patients at the field hospital is the future Rebecca Westin. She will one day give birth to a daughter she'll name Jane. Rebecca does not like being in this place surrounded by jungle. It is hot and humid. There are strange smells and odd animal sounds coming from the surrounding area day and night. Bugs are constantly annoying everyone. There is no air conditioning. Only hot humid air. She is struggling to focus and avoid making mistakes as sweat constantly rolls down her face. The hospital is regularly attacked by an enemy and has always been easily defended by the soldiers on guard outside.

Rebecca becomes terrified when she hears a lot of gunfire in the distance that seems to be getting closer. It is a constant struggle for her to communicate with her patients. Most of them only speak their native Asian language. There are many interpreters available who help translate for the American doctors and nurses. All of the medical staff have gotten used to working very long hours with only minimal sleep.

Rebecca is finished treating a patient and throws away some blood-stained bandages. It is a struggle for her to ignore the increasing volume of gunfire outside. She is walking toward the hospital's store room to get some more supplies when it happens. A man with a gun emerges out of the jungle and Rebecca sees him through a window. He is an enemy soldier. Rebecca screams just as the man shoots at her. The bullet breaks through a glass window and lightly grazes her arm. It hits a glass container behind Rebecca. She is terrified and faints. Rebecca falls into the safety of the hospital's store room. She is lying on the floor in a dream state. She is unaware of the major battle occurring outside the storeroom where she is lying.

Members of the host country's army come from the back of the hospital and start shooting at the men coming out of the jungle. More men come out of the jungle and start shooting at the hospital. A soldier from the host country screams for the US Army nurses and doctors to grab guns from the weapons locker and start shooting back. There are too many enemy soldiers for the men to handle. The medical staff does as they are told. They grab guns and start shooting at the enemy soldiers attacking the hospital. Many of the medical staff are fatally shot. Bullets kill patients lying in beds and destroy medical equipment. An explosion occurs outside the hospital. Eventually, US Army soldiers arrive with more soldiers from the host country. They are able to drive the enemy away. Quite a bit of damage had been done to the hospital buildings. There had been a significant loss of life.

When it is all over many patients have been killed. They lay in their beds motionless and bloody. None of the American doctors or nurses survive. The exception is Rebecca. When she regains consciousness and opens her eyes, she is looking up at a US Soldier. Rebecca is bleeding from the cut glass she landed on after she passed out. She struggles to stand up. When Rebecca does, she goes out into the room where the patients are located. Rebecca is horrified at the carnage she sees. She almost becomes ill. Rebecca is evacuated to the nearest town in the Asian country. She is then flown to a US military hospital in Texas. The attack on the hospital would remain one of the most traumatic experiences of her life. It is also a secret she is not permitted to discuss.

There are questions and interviews by senior military staff concerning what happened during the attack at the hospital. Reports of the incident are made and distributed for internal review. Rebecca knows her behavior would not be considered appropriate with some of the senior Army officers. She fears this could get her removed from the military with a bad discharge. Rebecca believes her chances of career advancement have significantly decreased.

Things change when she speaks with a Major who has the power to make important decisions concerning Rebecca. Major Donahue is a man getting over a terrible divorce. Rebecca decides her best bet is to be his friend. There is a recommendation Rebecca be demoted and sent to a base hospital where nobody wants to be stationed for the remainder of her time in the Army. Rebecca knows Major Donahue can change everything for her. The bad reports about her can be eliminated and good reports could be generated. He could even recommend she receive medals for bravery. Rebecca decides to be the very best possible friend she can to Major Donahue.

Rebecca is awarded a Purple Heart as well as another medal for bravery. The negative reports in her file are exchanged with good ones. All of the negative reports are removed except one. This is kept by a US soldier who was at the hospital during the attack and now works in administration. It is someone who knows the reality of what happened during the attack and reported it to his superior officers. The effort to falsify military documents by Major Donahue is discovered. He is demoted and sent to a duty station in a remote part of the world. Rebecca is told it would be in her best interest not to attempt to reenlist in the US Army when her time is up. An order to take away Rebecca's medals is never carried out. A friend of Major Donahue's does him a huge favor to prevent him from being court-martialed.

All the information contained within the bad report was kept by a man who saw too much lying and falsehoods being believed during the war. He made copies of the report and kept it in his apartment. The originals were destroyed. These papers had remained untouched for many years.

The man had forgotten about them until he was approached by someone named Ted Istina. Ted explained how he was a private investigator working for a concerned client. Ted learned about members of the unit Rebecca had been with during her time in the army. He also knows about some of these people from working on previous cases. After learning this man was in charge of the administration of the unit, Ted approached him. The two discussed the information the man had and the terms of Ted getting copies of the bad report. Since Paul was so generous with his funding, Ted was able to obtain copies of the original bad report concerning Rebecca. He also had papers that provided detailed descriptions of her relationship with Major Donahue.

* * * * * * * *

Jane yells at Paul, "Do you know what you've done? My entire perception of my mother has changed because of you. I don't recognize her anymore."

"Facing the truth is never easy. I would suggest you never mention this to her."

"What are you talking about? I can never look at her in the same way again. All these years she has been telling a huge lie. She has maintained this image of being the bravest and best female soldier. I want to confront her with this."

"I'm sorry you saw those documents. You wouldn't have seen this if you had respected my privacy. You did this to yourself. Let me ask how you would benefit from confronting your mother with this information? How would your life be made better?"

"She would know I know the truth about her."

"And then what? Your relationship with your mother would be permanently damaged. Some things are best left in the past."

"It's already permanently damaged. How did you get this information?"

"Ah, I hired a private investigator. He's very good and extremely detailed."

"How many people did you investigate?"

"I don't think that's the real issue. The real issue is what am I going to do with the information I've obtained."

"So, what are you going to do with it?"

"Save the academy."

"How?"

"I know how my father and grandfather think. I know how they use information to their benefit. It is an essential part of how they do business. The two of them believe they know Mr. Dean, but they don't. My father and grandfather have not done the proper background checks on his personal or professional life. They've probably looked at his financial information, asked some business people in the area about him, and that is it. I have checked out Mr. Dean in so many ways only his proctologist knows him better."

"You will just threaten Mr. Dean and your family with stuff you discovered about them? That's your plan?"

"Look, nobody at this academy can save it. Who is going to do it? You? You put up with four years of academy life so you can appease your family and then go to art school. Dennis? He's one of the nicest people I've ever met in my life. He has no idea how to handle this situation. The Commandant or Peter? They're soldiers. They're trained to fight wars on battlefields. This is a type of warfare unknown to them. It's up to me. I was raised by these bastards. I think I've learned enough to out-bastard them at their own game. I have a plan."

There is a moment of silence before Jane hugs Paul and says, "You are putting yourself on the line again for others. Nobody knows you like I do. I would love to tell people about the real you."

"Only if I can tell them how you were caught by the police high on dope and naked with your date in the back of a car on your prom night."

Jane's eyes open wide and she says, "It didn't happen quite that way. Hey, those records were supposed to be sealed by the court because I was a first-time offender."

Paul smiles and lovingly covers Jane's mouth with his hand.

"It doesn't matter to me. I don't care. I destroyed copies of the arrest report and police report I was given. If there is a record of something, it can be obtained with the right resources no matter what anybody tells you. You need to learn this is how the real world works."

Jane shrugs her shoulders and sighs.

"Okay, back to my mother. You're saying I should just forget about her lies concerning her military career?"

"You can no longer use copies of the report. If I am asked about it, I will claim to have no idea what you are talking about."

"Why?"

"Because you would only use that information to punish your mother. It serves no useful purpose. It is best for everyone if you forget about your mother's past".

"Are you going to destroy it?"

"Probably, but it doesn't matter because I know it exists and can get copies of that report whenever I need it. The key word is need."

Paul and Jane notice the time. After things calm down between them, they're able to have a romantic time together. Dennis gets back to the room soon after Jane leaves. He lets Paul know how the academy closing is upsetting him and his family. Paul tells Dennis to never give up hope because miracles do happen.

# Chapter 27

---

## *Preparing for Battle*

Soldiers who are preparing for an imminent battle will carefully check their equipment. Everything necessary for the success of their mission must be in the best possible working order. They will also carefully check their uniform. The correct one must be worn. Detailed plans are made and discussed with all those involved before any type of battlefield engagement. This is done to make certain everyone knows their role and what will be expected of them during their engagement with the enemy. This type of preparation is something done by members of militaries around the world.

Paul has made certain his father and grandfather will be in Mr. Dean's office on a particular day. They have all been informed an important unscheduled meeting must take place. Nobody is happy about it. Paul explained to them how it would be to their advantage to hear the information he will be sharing during this meeting. To make certain they value the meeting, he tells them about a possible serious financial benefit that could be experienced from it. Each of the participants expressed their anger when Paul refused to provide them with any specific details.

He knows these people. All of them are always focused on making money. They will schedule the necessary time to attend the meeting if there is a possible monetary benefit from it. Paul believes Mr. Dean might be anticipating another opportunity to laugh at him. His father and grandfather never take him seriously and probably think this meeting is a joke. They also know Paul is unpredictable and understand it is important to know what he is up to.

Paul has carefully covered all the necessary details for the meeting. The correct suit, shoes, tie, and sunglasses have all been chosen. When he explains his plan to save the academy to Jane, she wants to be part of it. Paul has gotten her an expensive fashion business suit to wear and borrowed a friend's high-end sports car for the day. Everything must be done so his father, grandfather, as well as Mr. Dean, perceive he and Jane are their equals. Paul has made very specific and detailed plans for the day. He has gone over the paperwork located in Jane's, briefcase with her several times. Paul has had his hair cut and styled. After he puts on his suit, Paul is ready for war. He feels like a soldier experiencing an adrenaline rush before facing an enemy on a battlefield. Paul is glad this one will involve papers and not bullets. He knows when it comes to money and his family nothing is certain.

* * * * * * *

Paul is outside the academy waiting for Jane. He is standing beside a silver-colored Ferrari F40. He's wearing a black Giorgio Armani suit and has on his favorite Ray-Ban sunglasses. Jane walks out of the academy wearing a dark blue CC Button Dress and blazer. Her hair is pulled back and she is also wearing Ray-Ban sunglasses. Both of them look like very serious business people.

When she reaches Paul, Jane says, "Where did you get the Ferrari?"

"Let's just say I have a friend who has some rather negative feelings toward his father. He takes great pleasure in upsetting the man by lending this prized vehicle to me and other people. I guess it's a spoiled rich kid thing."

"When do you have to return it?"

"I would estimate when we are done with this, he will be waiting at the academy gate for us. Let's enjoy this vehicle while we have it. Oh, and by the way, you look absolutely stunning. I am glad the sister of my other friend and you are the same size. I will have the loveliest female assistant for this meeting."

"This car is certainly a good way to announce our arrival. You know, I would rather you think of me as your partner during this meeting."

"That will be a struggle for me, but I will try to remember you are my partner in this situation. I must warn you. Experience has taught me when you drive around in a high-end sports car and wear expensive clothes in a town this size; you get noticed. Women go especially crazy about it. I suggest you be prepared."

"How would you know this"?

"Let's just say that is a story for another time."

"I hope you know what you're doing."

"I never know what I'm doing. That is why I'm always such an adventure to be with."

Jane smiles. They both get into the Ferrari F40. Paul starts the car and is busy revving the engine and listening to it.

Jane yells, "Get going. We don't want to be late."

Paul smiles as he pulls out onto the road and heads toward Mr. Dean's office.

* * * * * * * *

The silver Ferrari F40 with Paul at the wheel pulls into the parking garage across from Mr. Dean's office building. Paul gets out and gives the keys to an attendant who is very impressed with the car. As Jane and Paul head toward the building they are unaware they're walking in unison. Each of them is carrying a briefcase and moving them in the same way as they walk. Paul and Jane don't realize they're marching together like they're cadets at the academy. With the expensive clothes and the car, each of them feels like a successful high-level business executive. They both have serious and determined expressions. People who pass them on the sidewalk notice them. Paul and Jane are only focused on getting to the meeting.

When they go into the office building, an older woman is at the reception desk. She is wearing a white uniform shirt with a gold badge on the front pocket. It also has the name of her company. The woman's name is Edna. She has lived in this small town all her life. Her dark hair is pulled back and formed into a bun. She has thick glasses and is known to talk slowly. Edna has spent the last two decades working at the building's reception desk. The farthest distance she has ever traveled from her home is approximately 500 miles. Edna only did this once. She is known for being fascinated by new things she has never before seen.

Paul and Jane go up to the reception desk. Paul looks at Edna and says, "Excuse me, but could you please let Mr. Dean know a Mr. Paul Wildman and a Miss Jane Westin are here for our scheduled meeting?"

Now Edna has never seen a car like the one she saw Paul driving. She has also never seen anyone wearing a Giorgio Armani suit. Edna has so many questions. She is not the type of person who is impressed with people who have power or money. Edna considers herself to be their equal in God's eyes. When other people have tried to project an image to impress her it never worked. She has told co-workers the only individuals impressed by an image are those trying to project one.

Edna looks at Paul and says, "I seen you drive up to the garage in that strange-looking car. What kinda car is that I see you driving in?" says

Edna.

"That is a Ferrari F40."

"A what? A Feerareeee. I ain't never seen no car like that before. Where you got it at? I know Bucks Cars and Linden Car dealerships don't have no cars like that one. You get it that at someplace like a big city or something?"

"I am curious about the part of your official job duties involves inquiring about the purchase location of a person's vehicle when they come into the building. Is this just a line of questioning you have to make me feel special for the day?"

"Naw, I am just curious is all. I hope you ain't stole it or nothing like that 'cause that would be a problem?"

"Now look, unless you are an undercover police officer who has a job of tracking down stolen expensive sports cars, I suggest you leave it alone. Why don't you perform your job duties? I think that might involve informing Mr. Dean Paul Wildman and his assistant, I mean partner, have arrived for our meeting. I assume that is what you are paid to do?"

"Okay, okay, no need to get all testy with me. Just asked a question about your car is all."

"I think it's possible a woman with your level of intelligence and people skills might best serve this company as a member of its janitorial staff."

Edna is about to say something when Jane yells, "Paul, stop."

Jane gets in front of Paul, looks at Edna, and says, "Please understand he is really excited about this meeting. Can you just give us our security badges and let us go up to Mr. Dean's office?"

Edna picks up the phone, presses a button, starts talking, and says, "Did you see that fancy car a boy and girl drove into the garage? The boy is here now and says it is something called a Feeraree. You ever hear of a car like that around here? Yeah, the boy who drove it is down here right now. Says he is here for some kind a meetin' with Mr. Dean. Oh, he got himself one super attitude. Okay, I'll ask him."

Paul's face is getting red with anger. It is obvious to him she is talking to other people in the office building. Paul is about to yell when Edna hangs up and looks at him.

"My friend's husband wants to know if he could take it for a spin. He like me, he ain't never seen no Feerareeee type car before."

Struggling to maintain his composure and not scream, Paul says, "Unless your friend's husband is a certified high-performance sports car driver, I can't allow it. I refuse to break the law. What does that have to do with us getting to Mr. Dean's office?"

Edna dials a number then laughs and mutters under her breath she accidentally dialed the wrong number. She does this a few times and seems to enjoy Paul's increasing aggravation. Finally, it's obvious she's talking to Ruby. She then puts the badges for Paul and Jane out on the counter and motions to the elevator.

"You good to go there Mr. and Miss Feerareee."

Paul says, "You are truly a very gifted and talented person. I think you bring many wonderful things to your job just like Typhoid Mary brought to the medical profession."

"What?" says Edna.

Jane grabs Paul and starts walking him toward the elevators. She puts her badge on and connects one to Paul's suit coat. Paul turns back to say something to Edna. Jane quickly grabs him and moves him into an open elevator.

Once the elevator doors close, Jane says, "You were very rude to that woman."

"What do you mean? I merely enlightened her on important aspects of a Feerareee and provided her with some excellent career advice. You really need to start focusing on the positive side of things."

Jane rolls her eyes and looks away. The elevator ride is quiet until they get to the floor where Mr. Dean's office is located.

# Chapter 28

## *It's Showtime*

In Mr. Dean's office, the sounds of strong words being exchanged between Mr. Dean, Walter, and James Wildman are loud enough to be heard in the hallway.

"I demand to know what this meeting is about. I refuse to believe you don't know," yells Mr. Dean.

"You need to watch your tone with us Dean. I would like to remind you that if you want funding for this project from our company you better have all the details addressed. I don't want to think my son could know something about this situation that you don't," yells Walter.

"I refuse to be insulted like this in my own office. I demand an apology at once."

Walter and James look at one another and laugh. The tension in the room is high.

When the elevator doors open, Paul and Jane make their way to Mr. Dean's outer office. Ruby is sitting at the reception desk. When she looks up at Paul, she sighs.

Ruby says, "I don't know what you did, but you got Mr. Dean as well as your father and grandfather yelling at one another. I hope this isn't about your paternity."

Paul smiles and says, "Ruby, you look a little hunched over as you sit there. I suppose having a job that requires you to work in a vertical position might be harmful to someone, such as yourself, who makes the majority of her income in the horizontal position."

Ruby goes to stand up. Jane yells, "Paul, stop it. We have important things to do right now."

"You are right. We can discuss Ruby's horizontal career later."

Paul walks past Ruby and goes into the office. Mr. Dean, Walter, and James are now shouting over one another. They all stop and the room becomes quiet when Paul and Jane enter. The two of them instantly become the focus of everyone's attention.

"This had better be something worthwhile. You may have gone too far this time," yells Walter.

"I am feeling very disrespected. I have other more important things to do right now than deal with the ignorant and rude behavior of your family," says Mr. Dean.

Paul and Jane calmly go over to a table, put their briefcases down, and open them. Paul takes off his sunglasses and carefully places them in the breast pocket of his suit. He calmly starts walking between his father and grandfather on one side of the office and Mr. Dean on the other. He opens his arms and smiles.

"Gentlemen, and with the three of you, I use the term loosely; I promise what I have to say is something all of you will find quite important."

"Then let's hear what you have to say," says James.

"I have always loved how direct you are, grandfather. Let us begin. As all of you know, Mr. Dean won a lawsuit against the academy. He then contacted you, the members of my family, in hopes of securing financing to build stores and other businesses on the property where the academy is currently located.”

“Yes, that is pretty much a done deal. Why are we here for something we all know about?” says Mr. Dean.

“I am here to provide all of you with very important information none of you seem to know,” says Paul.

“What are you talking about?” says Walter.

Paul smiles and says, “Because of Mr. Dean’s legal victory, he is now the alleged owner of all of the academy’s assets. Unfortunately for all of you, those assets don’t include the land where the academy’s buildings are located. I’m shocked at the sloppy due diligence work done by such knowledgeable and distinguished members of the business community. I’m sure a basic title search may or may not have been done after the lawsuit victory. None of you bothered to do a detailed title search. If you had done such a thing, you would have learned a little-known fact about the academy’s property. The school has been leasing the land where it sits for over 100 years to a particular family. With further detailed research, you would have learned the lease clearly states if the land is used for anything other than the academy, the lease is no longer valid and the family retains the rights to use the property as they see fit. These terms of the agreement extend to any person or entity they let have the property. You can see for yourself.”

Jane takes papers from one of the briefcases and hands them to Mr. Dean, Walter, and James.

“My lovely assistant, I mean partner, is providing you with a copy of the detailed title search and the lease signed many years ago.”

As James, Walter, and Mr. Dean begin reading the papers their eyes get large and they seem shocked.

“This is preposterous, I’ll sue the academy again,” yells Mr. Dean.

Save your legal fees, Mr. Dean. You can’t take anything from the academy it doesn't have to give," says Paul.

"We will simply negotiate with the property owner. I'm assuming you know who owns the property," says Walter.

"I'm glad you asked that question. That is a correct assumption on your part, Father. Here is the really great part of why we are all meeting today. It is a little complicated, so let me make it easy for you. The last remaining member of the family who owns the property where the academy sits is a man who works at the academy's incinerator. A very nice man with an obsession for fast food dinners named Mr. Partan," says Paul.

"Oh no, I assume you have spoken with him about this?" says James.

Paul laughs and says, "Mr. Partan and I have become good friends. We've discussed the situation at the academy concerning his family's property and the lease involved at great length. His wife is deceased. Mr. Partan's children are not at all active in his life. He plans to retire soon and move to another state. We came to what we both thought was a solution to his problems with owning the property."

Walter is angry and says, "Just what kind of solution?"

Paul nods to Jane who gets more papers from one of the briefcases and starts handing them out.

"As these papers will show you, Mr. Partan has signed the property over to me. I now own the property, and also the lease. I've decided to keep the property and maintain the lease as part of the academy. Since it is private property, I, as the property owner, have the right to decide who does and does not go onto my property."

Walter yells, "Why would he sign over his family property to you?"

Paul calmly says, "Wouldn't you like to know? Let's just say, I have that certain special something when it comes to making deals. It's like you with getting women to marry you."

Mr. Dean throws the papers onto his desk and screams, "Then I'll sue you and get the academy's land in my name."

Paul smiles and says, "That is very bold talk from someone who is under federal investigation. You may not be free long enough to do anything to the academy. Don't act like you don't know. The administration staff at federal agencies hear many things. Some have even been known to talk about it to strangers. You might also want to ask yourself why you have a private investigator working for you as a receptionist."

Mr. Dean walks closer to Paul and says, "What are you talking about?"

"Ask Ruby to come in here for a second."

Mr. Deans opens his office door and motions for Ruby to come into the office. She walks in and stands in the middle of the office with everyone looking at her. Ruby's eyes widen as she notices the serious expressions on everyone's faces.

"What do you want Mr. Dean?" says Ruby.

"Mr. Paul Wildman has made a serious accusation against you."

"What has that asshole been saying about me now?"

Paul walks over to Ruby and says, "Ruby, your private investigator license from the state is a matter of public record. Do you want me to have my lovely assistant, I mean partner, hand out copies of your private investigator license and resume? You try to pass yourself off as being in your early twenties and you are really in your thirties. To be honest, I wasn't shocked. I do wonder who is your client. Those who have hired you in the past say working with federal law enforcement is a specialty of yours. Is that true?"

Ruby's face becomes red as she says, "I have to go somewhere right now."

Mr. Dean yells, "What?"

As she heads toward the door Ruby yells, "I have to go right now. I'm sorry. I may not be returning."

Ruby quickly leaves the office and slams the door. Mr. Dean sits down at his desk and puts his head in his hands.

Paul looks at Mr. Dean and says, "I'm certain any nefarious business activities you have had Ruby participate in are known by federal law enforcement. I imagine nothing will happen to her, but you may not do so good."

In a soft mumble, Mr. Dean says, "I can't believe this is happening."

"So, what happens?" says James.

"Well, I know Wildman Holdings has not released any funds to Mr. Dean for this particular project. You will now be able to avoid this bad investment and all of the possible negative publicity that goes with it. The agreement you signed with him won't be valid since he falsely represented to you that he owned the land when he did not. The company will save money and avoid being associated with a man who will have some serious legal issues with the federal government coming his way. You can thank me later," says Paul.

Mr. Dean looks at Paul and says, "You have wanted to ruin me for a long time, haven't you? This doesn't end here."

"I see it as you've ruined yourself. I was just able to put it to my advantage. Here is a deal for you. If you stop your quest to destroy the academy, I will leave you to deal with your federal legal problems on your own. I will not volunteer any information I've discovered about your organization. You may want to focus your efforts in another direction."

"Anything else?" says Walter.

Paul then looks around and says, "I do have one last request of everyone here before we leave today," says Paul.

"What would that be?" says James.

Paul nods to Jane who passes out more papers.

Paul says, "I'm sure none of us want what was disclosed here today to get into the public's eye. I've prepared a non-disclosure agreement to make certain what has transpired will not leave this room. My lovely assistant, sorry, partner will sign one and then show all of you where you are to sign."

Jane signs one and hands it to Mr. Dean who quickly signs the paper and hands it back to Jane. After signing the agreement, Walter and James give it to Jane. Paul is struggling to not laugh.

Walter says, "What is to stop us from taking the property from you? If you want to play dirty, you can pay the price. Don't forget, we're not emotionally involved here. This is just business to us."

Paul smiles and says, "I know you and grandfather are involved in some very shady deals with various Asian countries. Should specific documentation about this situation be leaked to the press it could have a very bad impact on your reputation as well as that of the company. I've got that paperwork here today as well if you want to take a look. Like you said, if you want to play dirty, you can pay the price. We all know I'll do it. I'm not emotionally involved. This is also just business to me."

Walter and James look at one another in shock as worry comes over their faces. They never believed anyone would discover certain things about their company. Neither of them ever thought Paul would be smart enough to discover this type of information and use it against them.

James looks at Paul and says, "Well, you've certainly become quite the ruthless businessman. I don't know if I should be proud or horrified. To be honest, I'm experiencing a mixture of both."

"I learned from the best ruthless businessmen I know. I also did it without a college degree. Isn't that amazing?"

Jane gets the non-disclosure agreement with everyone's signature and puts it in Paul's briefcase. After this is done, Paul goes over to his briefcase, closes it, and locks it. He then takes his briefcase and starts walking toward the door.

"Do you intend to continue with your education at the academy?" says Walter.

Paul looks at Jane and smiles.

He then goes over to Walter and says, "At the end of this current school year at the academy, I will be finished with higher education. I'm not much of an academic. I think after our meeting today, you have to agree I'm more of a hands-on type of person. I also think it would not be wise for you and grandfather to never again try to interfere with me or my trust fund now or in the future. I'm not a good student. I'm more of an emotionless, cold-hearted, self-serving businessman like you and grandfather. The two of you may have taught me too well. Remember what Robert Frost said about the student becoming the master."

Jane yells, "That is a quote from the Greek philosopher Plato."

"Whatever, I never studied Greek."

"We're done here. Please leave," says Mr. Dean.

Paul looks around the room, smiles, and says, "Good day gentlemen. It's been a pleasure doing business with you."

Jane and Paul put on their sunglasses. Jane gets her briefcase and they both go out of Mr. Dean's office slowly walking in unison like they're marching at the academy.

* * * * * * * *

Sitting in the Ferrari as they head back to the academy, Jane and Paul can't help but smile at one another. Paul is quiet, but Jane wants to ask him so many questions.

"You did it. You saved the academy. Now, it will be open next year and who knows for how many years. I can't believe you pulled this off. "

"Pulled what off? I have no idea what you're talking about."

"Oh, don't play your games with me. You know what just happened."

"I would like to remind you the details of the meeting that just took place are not to be discussed with anyone. I would also like to remind you I have a nondisclosure agreement with your signature on it in my briefcase. I would hate to take legal action against you."

"You would do that to me?"

"Only if you give me a reason. So don't give me one. After what you saw today, I don't think you want to test me. I have an excellent private investigator and an even better attorney working for me."

Jane looks away for a second and tries not to be angry.

She turns back to Paul and says, "There were no more papers in the briefcases to hand out. What shady business dealings in Asian countries were you talking about? Your father and grandfather seemed pretty upset when you mentioned it."

"I don't know. My family's company has shady dealings with countries all over the world. I just picked one of the many rumors I've heard them discuss and got lucky."

Jane looks at Paul as he drives the Ferrari and they both start laughing.

"So, what are you going to do with the academy's land you own?"

"I will honor the lease. It is very specific. The academy pays nothing for the land as long as it remains a military academy."

"You mean you're not making any money on it?"

"I don't need to make money on it. Dennis Martinez, Peter, the Commandant, and many other cadets current and future being able to be at Saint Michael's Military Academy is enough for me. It's good karma, and I know it will come back to me in a big way. It always does."

Jane looks at Paul and realizes his jokes and spoiled rich kid routine are only a diversion. She now understands he is a very serious person. Paul has proven to her he is determined to help powerless people from being hurt by those with power. Jane knows it is very important to Paul that nobody be aware of the real Paul J. Wildman. He hides it well. She tells herself Paul probably believes he would not have such success if people knew him for real. Jane has her first strong feeling of love for Paul. It isn't because of his money, but because she now knows the real Paul J. Wildman. Jane finds him someone she wants to be with as much as possible.

# Chapter 29

## *The Paperwork*

Paul and Jane are standing outside of the main building at the academy. The upper floor is where the Commandant's office is located. They are wearing their academy uniforms since it is a weekday. The weather is exceptionally nice. The temperature is perfect and there are hardly any clouds in the sky. The shade provided by a large maple tree branch protects them from bright sunlight.

"Do you know if he has gotten the paperwork yet?" asks Paul.

"I talked with his secretary. She told me when to get it from the messenger at the gate. I got it. I'm going to be the one to give it to him. She also said he'll be getting a call from the academy's attorneys any minute now. I know you talked with them yesterday to coordinate everything and make it official. Once he gets the call we can go to his office. I'll tell him a messenger at the gate gave me this package and told me to bring it to him," says Jane.

"You are a great assistant, I mean partner,"

"This is so exciting. I guess you are really struggling with the idea of having a partner."

"You have no idea."

"Yes, I do."

Both of them are near the open window of the Commandant's office. They hear a phone ring.

The Commandant is heard saying, "Are you certain? That is wonderful news. I never thought such a thing could happen. This is a miracle. So many current cadets, future cadets, and their families will be anxious to hear about it. I hope you realize what fantastic news this is for all of us. Did you send the paperwork? Okay, so you're saying I should get it any minute now? I understand you're busy, so I'll let you go. Thank you for calling me and telling me about such an exciting turn of events."

Paul looks at Jane and says, "Let's do this."

They go into the building and climb the two sets of steps to the Commandant's office. Jane slowly opens the door to the outer office. The secretary in the outer office smiles at them and points at the door to the Commandant's office.

Jane knocks on it and says, "Sir, I recently was at the academy gate and was given a package to deliver to you. May I enter and give you the package, sir."

The Commandant's voice from behind the door is heard saying, "Yes, please enter and give me the package."

"Sir, Cadet Wildman is here with me. He was with me when I obtained the package at the gate. Is it acceptable for him to enter as well?"

The Commandant sighs and then says, "What is Cadet Wildman doing with you? It doesn't matter. I suppose he can enter as well."

When Jane opens the door, she and Paul walk into the room in military fashion and stop in front of the Commandant's desk. They stand at attention. Paul then puts his hands behind his back and opens his legs in a stance known as parade rest. He looks forward. Jane does this as well after handing the package to the Commandant. This is customary for any cadet who enters the Commandant's office. The Commandant opens the package, takes out the paperwork, and quickly looks it over.

He smiles and says, "It's true. This is all the proof I need. This is such incredible news." Do either of you know what this package contains?"

"No sir," says Jane.

"This is the paperwork that shows the academy is no longer going to close. It appears Saint Michael's Military Academy will be up and running next year and for many years to come. Isn't that fantastic news?"

"Sir, that is fantastic news," says Jane.

The Commandant looks at Paul and is struggling to hide his dislike.

"Is it safe to assume you will not be joining us here at the academy next year Cadet Wildman?"

"Sir, that is as safe to say as stating people need to breathe oxygen to live. My commitment to my family was to be here until the end of the school year. I will have met that commitment in two weeks. I believe the academy leaves much to be desired. I mean, these uniforms, what can you say? When I'm dressed in them, I'm not sure if I should hop on a truck and sell ice cream or drive a city bus. Your food here leaves much to be desired. The cooks at the mess hall must have all graduated from the Le Cordon Bleu culinary school of botulism."

The Commandant says, "Okay, you've made your point. That is enough cadet."

Paul continues talking and says, "Who designed these barracks? Maybe it was the same architects who are famous for making box enclosures for homeless people. Then there is this walking around all the time in unison like you are victims of some alien mind implant program."

"I said that's enough cadet," yells the Commandant.

"Yes sir," says Paul.

"Cadet Wildman, you are dismissed. I would like to discuss something with Cadet Westin in private."

"Paul says, "You got it. I mean yes sir."

Paul then turns around and walks out of the office in military fashion as the Commandant rolls his eyes.

When Paul is gone, the Commandant looks at Jane and says, "Cadet Westin, I have heard rumors you may be romantically involved with Cadet Wildman. I know it is not my business to get involved, but I knew your father, and I know your mother. She is an Army combat veteran who earned medals for her courage and bravery. I'm certain she is not happy with you being so closely associated with an individual such as Cadet Wildman."

"Sir, I have let it be known to my mother I am an adult and can make my own choices."

"I see, the rumors are true. You disappoint me, Cadet Westin. You could do so much better. A future with Cadet Wildman will not be a good thing for you. I'm also sure you could go on to do great things in the military. Your mother has confided in me about your desire to go to art school. That is a shame as you have so much potential and the right connections coming from a military family."

"Yes sir, but again, I am an adult and can make my own choices."

"You are correct. Cadet Westin, you are dismissed."

Jane turns around and walks in perfect military fashion to the door and leaves the Commandant's office. She is struggling to control her anger.

* * * * * * * *

Classes are over at the academy for the day. Jane and Paul had their evening meal together at the mess hall. They are sitting on a bench near a pond on the academy grounds enjoying the nice weather.

"I know everything is okay with the academy now, but I am really angry at how the Commandant feels he has the right to give me advice on my personal life. I didn't ask for his advice," says Jane.

Paul shrugs his shoulders and says, "He cares about you. In his mind, he is helping." says Paul.

"How can you take his side after what he said about you? Doesn't that make you angry?"

"Not really. I'm comfortable with people being angry at me and thinking I'm the worst. It means my image is intact."

"You can be really strange at times."

"I prefer the word complicated when discussing me. Strange is such a common term. I doubt it is proper to be used with anyone who owns a sports car."

Jane laughs and says, "I almost screamed when the Commandant talked about my mother getting medals and being a combat veteran. If he only knew."

"If he only knew what? There is no proof to the contrary."

"I guess you got rid of that paperwork?"

"Yes, and as far as I'm concerned there was no paperwork. You should not have seen any of those papers; it was a mistake. If you were to confront your mother or speak of this to anyone, I would not support you. I would claim I have no idea what you're talking about."

"Now, you are protecting my mother. A woman who is horrified at the thought of me dating you. Don't you think people should know the truth about her?"

"The truth is a double-edged sword. It can be used to do wonderful things. It can also be used to cause harm when no harm is necessary. Whatever your mother wants to leave in the past, it needs to stay there. She never did anything in the past to hurt you. I've heard your stories. She has been there for you all during your life. Whatever the woman's faults; she deserves your respect. She has been a good mother to you. If she wants to alter the truth from the past to help her self-esteem after losing her husband and raising children as a single mother; I don't see the problem."

"You really are quite the philosopher. What about your family? Why don't you see them as you see mine?"

"I know my father and grandfather better than anyone on this planet. They are greedy cowards who could rationalize selling off blood banks to ice cream factories if there was a profit in it. They have tried to control, manipulate, and use me and many other people for their personal gain for as long as I can remember. They've made enough mistakes that they can be kept in check. I know how to handle them."

"Don't you love your father and grandfather?"

"Let's just say I love them like a son and grandson. I am also aware of what they are and always will be in this world."

"It seems as if nothing in life is as you are taught to believe."

"I'm certain we aren't the first people to feel this way. Maybe it's just our turn to be disillusioned about how the real world works."

There is silence between Paul and Jane as they think about their lives at the academy and their families. After a short time, they both get up and head toward their individual barracks. Jane and Paul are falling deeply in love with one another. Neither one knows how to handle all the growing intense emotions that go with it.

# Chapter 30

## *Academy Graduation*

The most anticipated day of the year at Saint Michael's Military Academy is graduation day. Every cadet, as well as teacher and staff, is excited for this day to arrive. It is the moment when the school year officially ends. The graduating class is envied by all the other cadets. It is a time for those who are graduating to experience a sense of accomplishment they have worked for years to achieve. The graduating class is thought of as motivation for all current and future cadets at the academy.

The weather appears to be accommodating for the festivities taking place at Saint Michael's Military Academy. It will be a lovely day with only a slight chance of rain in the afternoon. It is a time when parents, family, and friends are arriving from all over the country. They are slowly filling the stands at the academy parade grounds. Many people can't hide their smiles and feelings of pride for the graduating cadet they know or are related to in some way. The graduation ceremony may be the first experience with the military for many of those attending. Others will have been in the military and many have attended previous graduation ceremonies at Saint Michael's Military Academy.

Paul is wearing his formal cadet uniform as are all the other cadets. He's walking toward the area where he will join his class to march in formation during the graduation ceremony. He looks up to see Dennis running toward him.

Dennis stops and is out of breath when he utters, "Paul, Paul, have you heard the good news?"

Paul says, "Does it involve money? Is the academy going to provide financial compensation for those of us who attend here?"

"No, don't be silly. Something happened and the academy is going to remain open. Isn't that great? The Commandant is going to announce it during the graduation ceremony. My little brother is going to be so happy."

"That is good news. I'm glad it will work out for you and your little brother. I'm happy for you guys."

"I have a feeling you aren't going to come back here after this year."

"Your feeling is correct."

"Hey, I got to go, but I'll talk to you after the ceremony, okay?"

"I'm looking forward to it."

Paul takes a few more steps and sees Jane coming toward him. When she gets to him, she corrects a few things on his uniform.

"Now you are a presentable cadet."

"Shouldn't you be getting to your graduating class?"

"Yes, but I am just feeling so happy today about everything."

"I say we celebrate in our own unique way when all of this graduation stuff is over."

"It's a deal."

Jane looks around and then quickly kisses Paul. He smiles and Jane hurries away. He eventually gets into formation with the other cadets in his class. Paul is happy this will be the last time he will have to march anywhere. Paul thought about suggesting to the Commandant that he and some people he knows have an organization that could provide a few interesting floats for the graduation ceremony. He then realized the Commandant might not be open to such an innovative idea. It could result in a great financial benefit to the academy by selling advertising on the floats. Paul knows the Commandant is probably not someone who would be interested in such a good money-making idea.

* * * * * * *

Eventually, the stands are filled and everything is in place. Peter Barnett marches up to the podium located on a stand in the center of the parade grounds. He welcomes everyone to the graduation ceremony. It is his job, as the top-ranking cadet, to announce the names of all the cadets who have earned honors during the school year. There are honors for academic achievement as well as excellence in certain military classes and more. Janes Westin is given an award for the best academic achievement of the graduating class. The honor of Saint Michael's Military Academy's best overall cadet goes to Dennis Martinez.

The ceremony begins with the academy color guard marching in front of the stands and is followed by the academy's band. The next group is the academy's rifle drill team. They stop in front of the stands and do a routine. Over the loudspeaker, the formation consisting of the members of the graduating class is announced as they march past the stands. The cheering from the stands is quite loud. Cadets in the lower classes then march in formation past the stands behind them.

All the cadets and the graduating class make their way to seats in front of the podium. Once everyone is seated, the Commandant comes to the podium and congratulates the graduating class. This is when each graduating cadet goes onto a platform where the Commandant is standing. They are given a diploma as their name is announced. People from the stands cheer for each name. Many people are struggling to not become too emotional.

Once all the members of the graduating class get their diplomas, the Commandant goes to the microphone and says, "It is with a great deal of happiness that I have the honor of informing all of you here today that Saint Michael's Military Academy is no longer being forced to close. We are now able to remain open. I hope we will be open for many more years. With that said, I would like to officially say the graduating class of Saint Michael's Military Academy is formally dismissed. Congratulations cadets on a job well done."

There are clapping and loud cheers from many people in the stands. Members of the graduating class are screaming with joy. Some people are coming out of the stands and running toward their loved ones who are part of the graduating class. There are many hugs and tears. All around the parade ground pictures are being taken.

Paul looks at everything going on and decides it's time to go back to the barracks, get out of his uniform, and finish packing his suitcase. He hears a familiar voice behind him.

"Paul, where are you going?"

When he turns around, Paul sees his mother coming toward him. He is quite surprised to see her. She never told him she was coming to the academy's graduation.

"I didn't expect to see you here," says Paul.

Paul's mother hugs Paul, looks at him, and smiles.

She says, "I would never miss my son's graduation."

"I'm not graduating."

"I know, but you did it. You finished the year here. I am so proud of you. I know it wasn't easy. The main point is you didn't quit or get kicked out. This may be the closest I ever get to seeing a college graduation ceremony involving my son in some way."

"Good point."

"I'm surprised your father and grandfather aren't here. I guess they didn't like being proven wrong about you. My son showing them how he can do amazing things when he sets his mind to it."

"Trust me, you have no idea how much they have learned that about me."

"What are you talking about?"

"It's not important. Hey, I'm glad you're here. Thank you for coming."

Paul's mother hugs him again and says, "I am so proud of you. I can't put it into words."

Paul fights tears trying to escape his eyes. He turns away for a moment and composes himself. After some more conversation, Paul agrees to meet his mother at her car after he changes out of his uniform. He wants to find Jane and talk with her for a minute.

As he walks toward the barracks, he sees Dennis Martinez standing with a group of people. Dennis motions for Paul to come over to them. When he gets there, Dennis introduces Paul to his mother and father as well as his older brother and sister. Dennis then introduces Paul to his little brother.

"This is my little brother Armando. He is now going to be able to be a cadet at the academy starting next year," says Dennis.

Paul looks at Armando and says, "You have some big shoes to fill with your brother being the best cadet. Do you think you can do it?"

"He's good, but I've always been better at everything," says Armando.

Everyone laughs. After some pleasant conversation, Paul sees Jane in the distance. He excuses himself and goes over to her.

Paul says to Jane, "I am going to be going out to dinner with my mother. Would you like to join us? I know you two already know one another."

"I can't because my mother and family are taking me to dinner. I will be so glad when this is over and I can get away from them. I'm being lectured about a career in the military, how it's ridiculous to go to art school, how you are not a good guy to date, and some other stuff."

"I say only give them your name, rank, and serial number. Demand to be treated in accordance with the rules set forth by the Geneva Convention."

Jane laughs and then gives Paul a hug and a long kiss.

"Cadet Westin, we can't do this in public in uniform. It is against school regulations."

"Oh, I don't care. I just graduated and you are done being a cadet. That makes it okay in my book. I am now former Cadet Westin."

"I like your attitude."

"I will be so glad to see you when today is over," says Jane.

"I am not going to make a joke or sarcastic comment. Former Cadet Westin, I think you are having a profound effect on me. I think we need to discuss this in a more intimate setting."

"I agree former Cadet Wildman. I think it's time I teach you some things I didn't learn from the academy."

"I promise to be such a good student."

"Oh, I'm sure you'll do just fine."

Paul and Jane laugh and then go to find their families.

* * * * * * * *

Paul is in his room placing things in a suitcase and whistling a happy tune.

Dennis walks into the room and says, "The Commandant wants to see you immediately."

"Why?"

"I don't know, but it seems like something pretty important."

"I'm no longer a cadet at this school. I don't have to go to see him if I don't want to go."

"What could it hurt? You'll have one last time to insult this academy to Commandant before you leave."

"You make a great point. I'm going."

On his way to the Commandant's office, a car goes past Paul and heads toward the front gate. The driver looks like Ruby. The girl has different colored hair and is wearing sunglasses, but the similarities can't be dismissed. He doesn't know why she would be at the academy on graduation day. There are so many people at the academy, he could be making a mistake. Paul stands outside the Commandant's office in uniform. He made certain everything on his uniform meets academy standards before he left his room. This will be the last time he wears it.

After knocking loudly on the door Paul says, "Commandant, former Cadet Wildman here to see you as requested."

From behind the door, Paul hears the Commandant's voice say, "Enter."

Paul walks into the office in proper military fashion. He then stands at attention in front of the Commandant's desk. He simply stares straight ahead.

The Commandant looks up from his desk and says, "I'm sure you will be surprised to know, I am now aware of what you have done on behalf of this academy."

Paul is stunned. He refuses to let the Commandant see what he is feeling. Paul struggles to control his shock. The Commandant is looking past the image he works so hard to project. It makes him feel vulnerable. Paul remains standing at attention and looking straight ahead.

"I assure you sir; I have no idea what you are talking about. Could you please share with me who provided you with false information of me doing anything for this academy? There may be legal consequences involved."

Thomas Loren gets up and walks toward Paul with his hands behind his back. He starts walking around Paul Wildman.

"Cadet Wildman, I remember your first day here. I thought of you as a poster child for misbehaving spoiled rich kids. I've seen them many times in my time. It is possible I may have even been one myself at one time. I was wrong about you. I believe many people may be wrong about you. What you have done for this academy under these circumstances shows a depth of character and the kind of courage that is a rare find in this world. You know, there have been many cadets who have graduated from here and gone on to become high-ranking individuals in business as well as the military. I don't know if any of them could have done what you accomplished. You may never be awarded the title of Best Cadet by this academy, but I assure you, that you will always be remembered as one of the best people we've ever had at this school. On behalf of the past and future cadets of Saint Michael's Military Academy, as well as all those associated with this school, I would like to thank you for what you have done for all of us."

The emotions Paul is feeling are overwhelming him. He is forcing himself to not cry. He still doesn't move and remains standing at attention and looking forward.

In a voice filled with emotion Paul says, "Sir, I still have no idea what you are talking about."

"Yes, you do, I know that you do, but I admire your desire to not seek out any recognition or benefit from what you've done. That is the stuff of real heroes.

After a moment of silence, Paul says, "Sir, my grades are average. I have struggled with every aspect of academy life. Do you really think a person, such as myself, would be able to do anything for this academy? Please don't believe everything you are told about me. If we are done here sir, I would like to be dismissed."

"I think we are done here. You are dismissed former Cadet Wildman."

"Thank you, sir."

Paul does a proper about face move and walks in perfect military fashion toward the door and leaves. He quickly finds a bathroom. Nobody is inside. Paul goes into a stall, closes the door, sits down, and lets the tears slide down his face. The intense emotions he is feeling are overwhelming him. This may be the first time anyone in a position of authority has ever acknowledged him doing something right. It feels good. After a few minutes, he leaves the stall and wipes his face with water from the sink. Paul looks in the mirror and makes certain his face doesn't reveal he's been crying.

Another cadet walks in and notices Paul.

He says, "Wildman, isn't it great the academy will be remaining open?"

Paul shrugs his shoulders and says, "Good for who? The sick and sadistic members of society who will still have a place to meet and be together? Yeah, sounds great."

"You never have anything good to say about the academy, do you?"

"Nonsense, it would be a great place for people to attend who I wish to be miserable. Maybe the academy could be permitted to conscript certain individuals from my neighborhood I don't like. If that happened, I'd love this place."

"There is no hope for you."

"Talk to me when you drive a sports car."

The other cadet is angry at Paul and doesn't respond to him. Paul leaves the bathroom feeling pretty good.

* * * * * * *

It's getting late on the day of the academy's graduation. A time when Cadets are loading their things into vehicles and leaving. Paul and Jane are in civilian clothes and walking hand in hand down a street in the local town. Both of them want to say something but are too emotional to speak. Paul decides to break the silence.

"So, any updates on your future art school?"

"Oh, it appears I've got an option to go to a couple of them. They all start in a few months."

"Any plans for the summer?"

"I haven't really thought about it. Do you have any suggestions?"

"How about I show you my latest vehicle? I'm sure you'll be impressed."

"Did you go out and purchase a new expensive sports car?"

"I think I'm over that phase of my life for now. They are good for getting women, but I don't think that's too important to me at the moment. I didn't need it to get you. So, that did significantly decrease the value of sports cars for me."

Jane laughs as the two of them walk down a residential street, Paul stops in front of a very high-end conversion van. He opens up the side door and inside is a bed, refrigerator, stove as well as quite a few things to make art. There are artist paints, paintbrushes, canvas panels, and an easel. There are sketchbooks, artist's charcoal, colored pencils, artist's pens, and more."

"What is all of this? You aren't thinking of taking up art are you?"

"I probably was better at being a cadet than I would be at being an artist. Look, the reason I did this is because I thought about you having nothing to do this summer. You have to wait until your art school begins. I may need you and your skills as an assistant, I mean partner, at some time in the near future. I figured we could spend some time driving around and the country seeing places. You can do your art thing, and I can get us into trouble. We would both be able to use our strong points. What do you say?"

Jane grabs Paul and holds him tightly as she kisses him. Her heart is racing. She feels loved and respected by Paul. He is a man who has taken the time to get to know all about her. Their relationship is special. She can't remember a time she has been with a person who made her this happy.

"Yes, I will go away with you for the summer. I think it would be the most wonderful thing that ever happened to me."

Paul clears his throat before he speaks. He is fighting his desire to say something funny or obnoxious. Paul knows he needs to be serious right now and it isn't easy for him.

"I don't know what to say right now other than to be honest. I have to say this or I will burst. Please be sensitive to my willingness to be vulnerable. I think there is a strong possibility I am in love with you former Cadet Jane Westin. It's true. You may be the first female I've ever truly loved. It is a struggle for me to be so open. So, please be kind with your response. I'd hate to get my attorneys involved."

Jane laughs and looks into Paul's eyes and says, "I love you too, former Cadet Paul J. Wildman. I don't know where this will go but all I do know is that I want to be with you. You almost made that entire statement without trying to be funny."

"The attorney thing? You think that was funny? Oh, ah, yeah, it was a joke. I think you are now the first official member of my inner circle."

"What does that mean?"

"It's complicated and may take the summer of you trying to get the answer out of me in ways only you can."

Jane laughs as the two of them get into the van and start exploring it. They start making plans for places to go during the summer. Outside, a gentle rain begins to fall on the van. It is ignored by Jane and Paul as they are busy making travel plans.

Paul's father and grandfather hear about him completing the year at Saint Michael's Military Academy. They don't talk about Paul much. Both of them feel anger and frustration toward him. In some remote parts of their minds, they are also feeling a little pride. These two men ended up learning more about Paul J. Wildman than they ever thought possible. Many important lessons were learned at Saint Michael's Military Academy. The type of lessons neither Paul nor his family could not have ever learned at any other place.

### *The End*

# About The Author

Lucas Kinkaid is the pen name of J. Michael Krivyanski. His previous literary fiction book was "My Canvas Bag." J. Michael is a syndicated columnist with Continental News Service. He is the author of four Christian fiction novels. He has also published four books of his humor columns that previously appeared in various media. When not writing, he is busy biking, hiking, and enjoying the outdoors with his wife.

*Please take time to leave a review for "The Best Cadet."